Praise for The Wi

"Set against the backdrop of the Armenian genocide by the Turks in 1915, Matthew Hamilton's *The Wishing Tree* is a remarkable story about one family's struggle for survival. Told in minimalist, poetic language, the novel revolves around fourteen-year-old Valia Stepanyan and her family. This is at once a coming of age novel as well as a compelling history of one of the darkest chapters in the Twentieth Century. *The Wishing Tree* should be placed on the shelves right beside other teen-narrator stories on genocide such as Wiesel's *Night* and Frank's *The Diary of a Young Girl*."

—Michael White, author of *Soul Catcher* and *Resting Places*

"Matthew Hamilton's novel is a gripping account of one girl's journey through a nightmare of death and war. The Armenian genocide comes to life in these pages in the way only a novel can do. Valia, the novel's protagonist, is a sensitive, resourceful person who sees many terrible events yet holds on to her humanity and her hopes. This is a moving account of a terrible time."

—Baron Wormser, author of *Tom o' Vietnam* and *Songs from a Voice*

Other Work by Matthew A. Hamilton

The Land of the Four Rivers: My Experience as a US Peace Corps Volunteer in Armenia (2006-2008), Cervena Barva Press, 2012

Lips Open and Divine, Winter Goose Publishing, 2016

THE

WISHING TREE

Matthew A. Hamilton

Winter Goose Publishing
45 Lafayette Road #114
North Hampton, NH 03862

www.wintergoosepublishing.com
Contact Information: info@wintergoosepublishing.com

The Wishing Tree

First Edition, September 2020

Cover Design by Winter Goose Publishing

Cover Photo and Author Photo by: Rick Haithcox

ISBN: 978-1-952909-03-0

Published in the United States of America

For the 1.5 million Armenians killed by the Ottoman Empire between 1914-1923

"In the Armenian grief – on the black expanse.
My soul lives and mourns…"

—Hovhannes Toumanian

CHAPTER 1

Adana, Turkey - April 10, 1915

The announcement comes without warning.

"You must be ready to leave in two weeks," the town crier says.

The excuse is that we are too close to the battlefront and need to be temporarily relocated. What everyone is calling The Great War inches closer to us by the day, or so the government tells us. Mom and dad know differently. They have formulated another plan. We will leave as a family. We will not go where the government orders us to go.

I watch him through an open window. The harshness of his voice finds its way inside the house. I rub my arms as if to remove the intruding sounds, chew my bottom lip until I taste salt.

"Stand still and let me take a look at you," Mother says.

I keep looking out of the window. The town crier turns off the main road and disappears into the fading morning mist.

Mother gently cups my chin in her hand. "Don't worry about him." The skin around her eye's twist into a series of reassuring wrinkles. Her cheeks resemble well-defined dough. "Lori's wedding is tomorrow, so smile. You don't want your face to look like the dead." She smiles. "Look at those blue eyes. You'll be the prettiest bridesmaid there."

"It's happening all over again, isn't it?" I ask.

"What's happening?" Arsen asks. My little brother turns another page in his picture book.

"The Turks have never been kind to us," Mother says. "No matter. We'll be leaving for Paris next week."

"Why can't we stay here, like before?" I ask.

Arsen looks up from his book. "What is Paris?"

"Read your book," I say, tugging on the sleeves of the dress.

"Valia," Mother says, narrowing her eyes. "It's a city, sweetie, in France, a country far from here."

Arsen's eyes widen with light. "Are we going on a boat?" He holds up the book. A large ship puffs smoke in the middle of the ocean. "Like this one?"

"Yes, something like that," Mother says.

"I don't want to go," I say, glaring at the picture.

"Your father and I don't think it's a good idea to stay, not this time, especially with the war." She picks pieces of lint off my shoulder. "It's not safe. Police soldiers grow in number by the day."

"To protect the city?" I ask.

"Yes, to protect the city."

I look in the mirror, give a weak smile, and brush off the remaining pieces of lint.

"Get changed," Mother says. "I need you to go with me to the market." She kisses me on the forehead. "Everything will be fine, Valia. I promise."

The sun warms my face. The cool air causes my eyes to itch, but it feels good against my sweaty face. I close my eyes, take a deep breath, and listen to the street traffic of people going to market. Mother waits for me in the covered carriage.

I rub my eyes red by the time we reach the market. Mother hands me a handkerchief. "Go clean the dust out of your eyes," she says, pointing to a water pump across the street, then gestures toward a line of fruit vendors. "I'll be over there."

I climb out of the covered carriage. Crossing the street, I dodge wagons, women with baskets of bread on their heads, and children darting around like wild dogs. When I finally reach the pump, I pull the lever five times before the water gushes out. I soak the handkerchief, wring it out, wipe my face and eyes, and breathe in the coolness, a wet cotton smell. Fresh, clean, and comforting.

I feel a tug on my skirt. Timur Hasim is standing next to me when I turn around. He is nicely dressed in a three-piece suit. "Hello," I say. "You look very handsome today. What's the occasion?"

"It's my birthday." Timur smiles. "I'm ten years old today!"

"The same age as Arsen," I say, rubbing his head. "Happy birthday." I scan the crowd. "Where are your parents?"

"Yasmin is with me." He points. "There she is."

Yasmin saunters over. "Pestering my brother?"

I narrow my eyes. "Why do you hate us so much?"

Yasmin crosses her arms, rolls her tongue across her bottom lip. "The soldiers will come for you soon."

"You can come live with us," Timur says.

Yasmin smacks her brother in the head. "Ouch! What ya do that for?"

"Shut your mouth," Yasmin says. "She's a Christian. You remember what Papa said. We are not to be their friends."

"He didn't say that," Timur says, then frowns.

Yasmin looks at me, her eyes dark and foreboding. "He's too young to understand."

Timur smiles at me. "Arsen is my friend."

"I said hush," Yasmin commands. She tries once more to smack Timur in the head, but he's ready this time, and dodges his sister's spiteful hand. "Ha! You missed." He steps toward me.

"Get over here," Yasmin says, grabbing him.

"My father will keep me safe," I say.

"And my father said you'll be gone in a few days," Yasmin says, pride flying out of her mouth like an evil spirit.

I plant my hands on my hips. "The town crier said two weeks."

Yasmin covers Timur's ears. "The police soldiers will bury you in the desert."

"You're a liar," I say, clenching my fist.

"Go ahead, hit me," Yasmin says. She gestures toward a nearby police soldier, who seems to be watching us with devoted curiosity. "See what happens."

"Stop fighting," Timur says. "It's not nice."

Yasmin widens her eyes in a sinister gesture of accomplishment. "Let's go."

"Okay," Timur says, "but first say you're sorry to Valia."

Yasmin jerks her little brother by the arm, but he manages to pull loose. "Get off me." Free, he digs in his pocket, then hands me a piece of candy.

I kiss him on the cheek. "Thank you."

Timur giggles. "Say 'hi' to Arsen. Sorry he can't come to my party."

"I'm sorry, too. Perhaps next year."

Yasmin grabs Timur's hand in disgust.

I unwrap the candy, pop it in my mouth, and watch them go, thinking about Yasmin's words. My face tightens with anger and fear, but I soon relax. *Father will take care of us*, I think. *He always does.*

"It looks like you have an admirer," a voice says.

It is the police soldier that had been watching us. He's wearing a crisp khaki police uniform, his boots licorice black.

"Children are always giving me candy," I say.

The police soldier licks his lips like a snake sniffing its prey. "Especially boys I bet. I must say, you are a very beautiful girl." He smiles. "But still, you are not to speak to Muslim boys. Understand?"

I lower my head. "Sorry."

"I'll overlook it this time, since it's a new law."

"Sir, is it true you are to take us into the desert?"

"Of course not, why do you ask?"

"We're leaving to go somewhere," I say. "The town crier said so. I want to know where."

"A safe place, I assure you."

The unnatural tone in his voice forces me to take a step back. "Excuse me, sir, but I must be going." I look around for Mother, finally spotting her negotiating with a fruit vendor. I hustle across the street.

"Maybe I'll see you later," he calls. His voice slithers in my ear. A sharp chill shoots up my back. I fear he may follow me, but when I look over my shoulder, he is in the same spot I had left him. I breathe a sigh of relief.

"What's wrong?" Mother asks.

"I'm fine," I say, catching my breath. "Here's your handkerchief."

"Keep it." Mother hands the vendor a few lira. She places a half dozen or so of apples and persimmons in a basket.

I look across the street. The police soldier continues to stare at me.

"What is it?" Mother asks.

"Nothing," I say, still clutching the handkerchief. "Here."

Mother gives me an irritated look. "What's gotten into you? I said you can keep it."

"It's nothing." I give Mother an uneasy look, wipe my face and eyes again, and then slip the handkerchief into my pocket.

"I'm sorry," Mother says. "I didn't mean to snap at you. It's just.... I can't.... I'll feel much better when we're in Paris."

"We'll be okay, won't we?" I ask, grabbing Mother's hand.

Mother gives a frail smile. "We can tie the handkerchief to the olive tree later. Would you like that?"

"Do you think it'll work?"

"Yes, if we pray hard enough." Mother takes a deep breath. "If we believe."

"I'll tie it to the tree tonight," I say. I peek inside the basket. "May I have a persimmon?"

"Yes, take the small one there."

I take a bite. A shiny drop of juice escapes from my mouth, and slides halfway down my chin. I catch the unruly liquid with my thumb and suck it at the tip.

"Not very ladylike," Mother says. She smiles.

"Sorry," I say, giggling nervously. My thoughts focus on the police soldier. I retrieve the handkerchief and wipe my hands and mouth with it. As I stuff the handkerchief back in my pocket, I look across the street again and notice the police soldier cheering a group of teenaged boys playing Korebe. He seems like a nice person from a distance, watching those boys, laughing with them, cheering them on. Maybe the world would be a far better place to live if all conflicts could be resolved with sports.

"What's wrong, Valia?" Mother says, patiently this time. "I can always tell when something's troubling you."

I take a deep breath and hold it for a moment as I timidly pick at my dress. "Yasmin said the soldiers are going to bury us in the desert."

"Yasmin," Mother says, infuriated. "That girl is nothing but trouble."

"Is it true?"

"Of course not."

"Then why can't we stay here?"

"Does this have something to do with you talking to that soldier over there?" Mother asks, pointing.

"You saw us?"

Mother rubs her fingers together nervously. "What did he say to you?

"That we're safe."

Mother hands me a basket of bread. "Take this back to the carriage and wait for me. I won't be long."

"Okay." I sense she doesn't wish to talk about it anymore. I pick up the basket and sniff the bread. The warm and nutty aroma is relaxing.

As I wait for Mother, I notice two police soldiers approach one of the vendors, an old man with a wrinkled and tanned face, his hands dirty, looking as though he had lived his whole life in the desert. I imagine I'm buried up to my neck in the desert like a common thief. My body shivers with apprehension.

"Remember me?" one of the soldiers asks the old man. The shorter one sports a scruffy beard with bits of food stuck in it. The fez atop his head is in tatters, and a tassel is flopped to one side like a withered snail. The other soldier wears a sheepskin cap with a star in the center of it. A clean-shaven face gives him far more dignity than a beard, but his eyes are coal black and suspicious. Both men carry rifles across their shoulders.

The old man frowns. "Captain Saabir."

"Good memory." He gestures toward his friend. "This is Mehmet, the man I was telling you about."

"I see."

"Have you thought about his offer?"

"Yes," the old man says.

Saabir rubs his hands together. "Well, are you going to tell us?"

The old man turns to the soldier named Mehmet. "You need the captain to do your bidding?"

Quickly, the one named Saabir slaps the old man hard across the face.

I cover my mouth. It's as if my body holds all the power and torture they fix on the old man. I don't know how I, a fourteen-year-old girl, might help him, but I sense I need to.

"You will not speak to us this way," Saabir says.

The old man rubs his jaw. "You should respect your elders."

Saabir pushes the old man into a basket of apples. Losing his balance, the old man falls to the ground. "You Armenians are all the same," Saabir continues. "No respect for the law." He cocks his leg, and kicks dirt in the old man's face.

The old man spits dirt from his mouth and brushes his eyes with his shirtsleeve.

I step from the carriage. My heart races with fear. My head throbs as if trampled by a stampede of wild horses. I pick up an apple and place it in the overturned basket. Then I pick up two more, and so on, until I hear, "Stop that!" It is the one named Mehmet.

I ignore him.

People walking by stop to point and whisper.

Mehmet jerks me up by the hair. "I said stop!"

"Get off me!" I say, kicking and screaming, but the strength of his arms easily overpowers me. He presses a hand against my throat. "Stop."

I bite my tongue hard. An Armenian woman's outburst to a Turkish man has had severe consequences.

"Look at her eyes," Mehmet says. "Blue and cold as lake water. The most stunning I've seen." His eyes flash lust. "How old are you, girl?"

I'm so rattled I cannot meet his gaze.

A small crowd begins to gather.

"Let the girl be," a Turkish man says.

"Mind your business," Mehmet says, "or we'll toss you in the jailhouse."

"She's just a girl," says another.

"There's no need to make trouble," says a third man.

"I know this girl," a woman says. You are Vartouhi Stepanyan's daughter, right?"

"Yes, ma'am, that's right," I say.

"Your father owns a watch shop."

"Yes."

"Who are you?" Saabir asks the woman.

"Elen Vartanian, a friend of the girl's mother." She looks at me. "Where's your mother, sweetheart?"

"Somewhere over there," I say, pointing with my head.

"Enough," Saabir says. "You say her husband owns a watch shop?"

"Yes," Mrs. Vartanian says.

"Go fetch him," Saabir orders.

Mehmet sniffs my hair. His tongue, cold and slimy, slides into my ear like a wet snake. I raise my shoulder and brush him away.

"Leave her be until her father arrives," says the third man.

Mehmet draws his pistol and points it at the small crowd. "One more word out of you and everyone here will go to the jailhouse."

"There is nothing to see here," Saabir says. He takes a step toward the crowd. "Get out of here."

Slowly, one by one, witnesses depart.

Mehmet puts the gun to my head. I stiffen in resistance, clinch my fists. I hear whispering close by. A woman gasps. My eyes blur from the tears.

"Your age," Mehmet repeats.

"Fourteen," I say, sniffing, my voice shallow and angry.

"A perfect age," Mehmet says.

"What do you mean?" I ask.

He laughs, then puts the gun away, and pulls me close. He kisses me on the mouth. His stale breath is strong with garlic and vodka. "To be my wife."

"No!" I cry. I stomp on his foot, and squirm from his grasp. He yelps like a spoiled child.

"She's too much for you," Saabir says. He playfully pushes his friend away, and then grabs me by the arm with the strength of a bear.

"Leave me be!" I scream again, slapping him hard in the face. "My father will be here any minute. He'll show you who's boss." My breathing is fast, like a train, my body warm with sweat and fear. Unfazed, Saabir grabs my wrist, twists my arm behind my back, places his other arm around my neck, and squeezes my body against his chest. "You're a feisty one, aren't you?" He touches my breast with his cold and sticky hand. "You will bear healthy children."

"Let her go," the old man whimpers.

"Shut up!" Mehmet shouts, as he kicks him in the leg.

I break away, tearing my blouse in the process. I fall to the ground in a swirl of panicked anger, landing next to a crate of persimmons. I pick up one of the pieces of orange-colored fruit and throw it hard and deliberately at Saabir's chest. Wet, sticky pulp splashes on his uniform.

For a brief moment, there is awkward silence. Then Saabir removes a gun from his side in a quick, smooth motion, and pulls the hammer back.

"Hold on there, please, sir!" It's Father, frantically waving his hands in the air. He places himself between the gun and me. "Please, she's a foolish girl," he says, panting.

I realize my nakedness, fold my arms across my chest, and stand behind Father, trembling. "Be careful, Papa."

"There child, it's okay," Father says.

The old man remains on the ground rubbing his leg, moaning.

Saabir lowers the gun.

"Where's your mother?" Father asks.

"Direct your attention at me," Saabir says.

"I don't know," I say. I tug at my blouse. "She told me to wait in the carriage."

Saabir presses the gun barrel against Father's shoulder. "What's your name?"

Father takes a step back and again holds up his hands. "Aram Stepanyan. I'm the girl's father. I'll pay whatever you like. Perhaps you're in the market for a new watch. I have a shop just up the street." He grabs my hand, motions for Saabir to follow us.

Saabir spits in disgust. He glances over at Mehmet and smiles. He returns his gaze toward Father. "Rich spoiled brats, every one of you. You think you can buy your way out of everything."

"Isn't that what you want, sir, a watch in exchange for my daughter?"

"You are a wealthy man," Saabir says. "I want more than that."

"No, sir, I am not," Father says, "but I'll do anything for my family. Perhaps two watches, or a piece of jewelry for your wife."

"I'm not married."

"Then what can I offer you?"

"Valia! Valia!" Mother yells, as she runs toward us. She clutches Father's arm. "Valia, what happened?" she asks. Fear governs her eyes. "How did you tear your blouse?"

I wrap my arms around Mother's waist, cry into her dress.

"Your wife, I presume," Saabir says.

"Yes sir. Vartouhi."

Mother hugs me tight, rubs my back. "Don't worry," she says. "Papa will straighten this out."

I look up at Father. He gives me a faint smile. "Everything will be fine."

"Yes, Papa," I say, wiping a tear.

Saabir knocks the pistol against his leg. "Tell me about this shop of yours," he says. "What's the name of it?"

"Stepanyan's: Watch Maker and Repairs," Father says. "As I mentioned, it's just around the corner from here." He points the way.

"I suppose I could use a new watch," Saabir says, scratching his head. What about you, Mehmet?"

Mehmet smiles. "Yes, sir."

"Good," Father says, bowing his head.

"Don't let your daughter roam the streets like a common whore," Saabir says. He smiles. "You never know what might happen to her. Don't forget, we are at war."

"Yes, sir. I'll have a watch waiting for you."

Saabir shoves Father aside, then kicks the old man one last time, and spits on him. "Armenian pigs." He looks at Mehmet. "Let's go."

When the two police soldiers leave, Father helps the old man to his feet. Mother and I finish picking up the apples and place them in the basket.

"Thank you," the old man says, flinching.

"Are you hurt?" Father asks.

"Yes, my ankle."

"Can you walk?"

"Help me to my chair. I'll be fine."

Father helps the old man to his chair and brushes the dust off him. "What was that about?"

The old man lets out a deep, frustrated sigh. "The short one wants to marry my granddaughter. I reckon a watch is more appealing than a wife at the moment."

"I suppose," Father says.

"But keep an eye on your daughter."

"He is not interested in her."

"They are all interested," the old man says, and frowns. "It's only a matter of time before they come and take my granddaughter away." He looks at his old, dry hands. "What can I do to stop them?"

"I'll pray for your health and safety," Father says.

"You better do more than that," the old man says. "You better learn to fight."

Chapter 2

Father removes his muddy shoes and puts on his slippers. His breathing is deep and strong.

"Hi Papa," Arsen says, glancing up from his book for only a second.

Father steps over Arsen, sits beside me on the sofa, and pats me on the knee. "What are you knitting?"

"A pair of socks," I say. "They're for you."

Father rubs the wool against his fingers. "Nice. They'll keep me warm this winter."

I tuck the knitting needles inside the ball of yarn on my lap.

"Sweetheart, don't worry about what happened earlier. We'll be leaving soon." He sniffs the air, and smiles. "What are we having for dinner?"

"Lamb," I say, as I fiddle with the ball of yarn.

Father gently places his hand on mine. He has the strength of two men. "How are you feeling?"

"I'm fine."

"You don't sound fine."

I adjust my blouse. My eyes water, but I hold on to my tears. "Moving to Paris sounds like a good idea after all."

He leans down and gives me a kiss on the forehead.

"Look Papa," Arsen says.

"What have you got there?" Father says.

"A book on Egypt," Arsen says, holding it up. "See?"

The picture is an artist's imagination of what the Pyramids of Gaza might have looked like three thousand years ago. Smooth limestone covers all four sides, their tips made of solid gold.

"I'm going to be an explorer," Arsen says.

"A fine one at that," Father replies.

Arsen's eyes dance to life. "Kings were buried there a million years ago. I'm going to dig them up."

"Thousands of years ago," Father corrects him. "And there were many kings. They were called Pharaohs."

Arsen scratches his head. His little face scrunches in confusion. "Phaaaraohs," he repeats.

"That's right, son. Pharaohs."

Arsen closes the book. "Mama said we're moving to France. How far away is it?"

Father smiles, gets up from the sofa and, pulling an atlas from the bookshelf, he turns to the page illustrating Europe. He places his finger on France. "Here, far from Egypt, but maybe we'll visit one day." He closes the book, and places it back on the shelf. "France has plenty of treasures of its own. Go wash up for supper. I want to talk to your sister for a minute."

Arsen's feet happily scamper across the room.

When we hear the bathroom door shut, Father says, "Let's go outside."

We walk into the kitchen. Mother is standing over a steaming pot, stirring it gently. Small pellets of hot water pop softly against her apron. Father gives her a soft kiss on the cheek, leans over the pot, and sniffs. "Smells delicious."

She gives him a cold look. "What happened today with that police soldier at the market…." she pauses, stops stirring, steps away from the pot, picks up a knife, and begins slicing a yellow onion— "we need to do something."

Father scratches behind his ear. "Have you forgotten what happened six years ago?"

Mother narrows her eyes. "Of course not. Have *you* forgotten that a lot of our friends were killed by that dreadful group—" she paused— "the Young Turks." Mother looks at me. Then she returns her cold gaze at Father. "Now they're harassing our daughter. What's next? Will they take her away from us? That evil little girl, Yasmin, told Valia soldiers were coming for us, said they'd bury us in the desert. We know how she is, a little Muslim brat…"

"Honey…please," Father says.

"We need to do something—and quickly," Mother says, holding the knife as if preparing to stab someone.

I lick my lips, Mother's words leaving a bad taste in my mouth.

Father gently takes the knife out of Mother's hand and sets it on the counter. He pulls her close and wraps his arms around her waist. "Enver Pasha is not as lenient as Hamid was. They'll put me in jail, or worse, if I dispute what happened. Besides, we'll be leaving soon." He gives her another kiss on the cheek. "Let it go, sweetheart. There's nothing to worry about."

Over 300,000 Armenians and Assyrians were murdered between 1894 and 1896 during the reign of Sultan Abdul Hamid II. It is now known as the Hamidian Massacres.

Mother gently pulls away from him, places the lid on the pot, and wipes her hands on the apron. "I thought everything would be all right for us, like last time, but now—I'm worried."

Father snatches a piece of raw carrot on the cutting board and pops it into his mouth. "I'll talk to Gagik tomorrow at the wedding, ask if we can leave earlier."

"See that you do," Mother says, retrieving the knife.

Father glances at me, smiles, then returns his attention to Mother. "Valia and I are going outside for a bit."

"Don't be long," Mother says, her voice squeaky like a rusty door. She coughs. "Supper's almost ready."

The late afternoon air wrestles with the leaves. The sun burns up the sky with a pinkish red color as it creeps behind the Taurus Mountains. Father and I sit under a gnarled olive tree.

"You were five when we planted this tree," Father says.

"I remember," I say, looking up at the red sky. "You told me the story of Saint Blaise." I study my hands. I remember watching Father digging the hole, my fingers smoothing warm soil over tiny roots. I remember Father's words as if he had spoken them yesterday.

Saint Blaise was a martyr, Father begins.

What's a martyr? I ask.

Someone that dies for their faith.

Like Jesus, I say.

Yes, like Jesus.

Papa, why are people so mean?

I don't know, sweetie.

Artush says the Muslims killed Jesus.'

No, sweetheart, the Muslims were not around during the time of Jesus. But their forefathers killed Saint Blaise, hung him on an olive tree, like this one. They have killed many Christians.

I hate Muslims, I say.

My father sighs. Do not hate, Valia. We must forgive those that harm us. That is why we plant olive trees, to remember the dead, pray for them, even pray for our enemies. And when the trees grow big and strong, we tie handkerchiefs to them, call them Wishing Trees.

I awake from my daydream thinking about the old man at the market. Men like him have made their home in the Caucasus region of Eurasia for over 3,000 years. We have been independent for most of our history. At the beginning of the 4th century, Armenia became the first nation to officially make Christianity its official religion. But Armenia was conquered by the Ottoman Turks in the 15th century, and we have been under their ruthless, anti-Christian government ever since.

I wonder if the old man and his granddaughter are safe. I can still smell the vodka and garlic on the police soldiers' breath.

Father gently shakes my arm. "Valia, are you alright?"

"Yes, Papa. I was just thinking."

"About?"

I try to speak, but the words die in my mouth. I cannot hold back the tears any longer. I bury my face in Father's chest, muffling my cries. I shake uncontrollably from the thought of the police soldiers coming to take me away as a replacement for the old man's granddaughter.

Father gently lifts my chin and looks directly into my eyes. "We'll soon be far away. I hear Paris is a spectacular city."

"I don't want the police soldiers to take me away," I say, sniffling. I pull out the handkerchief Mother had given me at the market and wipe my eyes and nose with it.

"Don't worry, sweetie," Father says. "We will be in Paris before the police soldiers come knocking on our door."

"But I am worried."

Father glances at the olive tree. "Would you like me to tie your handkerchief to the tree?"

"Mother says it'll help." I sniff. Do you think so?"

"Yes, I think so. Let's see." Father takes the handkerchief from my hand and inspects the tree. "There," he says, finding a low branch. "This one." He smiles. "It's good?"

"Yes, pretty," I say.

Father ties the handkerchief tight and gives it a tug. "Now, what shall we pray for?"

"The protection of Saint Blaise," I say.

"And a safe voyage," Father says.

After we pray, Father asks, "Feel better?"

"I'll feel better once we're on the ship," I say.

Mother pops her head out, wiping her hands on a rag. "Supper's getting cold."

"Coming," Father says. He kisses me on the forehead. "And Valia, remember, not a word about us leaving to anyone."

"Yes, Papa."

"Promise me."

"I promise."

After Father says grace, he places a shish kebab on his plate, and spoons a few tomatoes and pickled beets as if it's a typical evening supper. "Should be a nice wedding tomorrow," he says, fingering a few shallots out of a small bowl.

"Did that dreadful man visit your shop?" Mother asks.

"No," Father says. "Let's try and forget about that, shall we?"

Mother takes a sip of wine. "Did you hear what the old man said?"

"What?" Arsen asks.

"Nothing," Father says. "Did you and Valia find a wedding gift for Lori?"

"Nothing?" Mother raises her voice. "That man threatened to take our daughter away from us! You need to tell Gagik."

"No he didn't," Father says.

"Not in so many words," Mother says, "but I could tell. He wanted to take her."

Arsen gently kicked me under the table, smiling. "Are you getting married?"

"No," I say. "Nothing like that."

Father cuts a piece of lamb. The knife and plate merge violently. The scraping sounds tingle my ears. "I told you I'll talk to him at the wedding," he says, lifting his glass with gusto. "We'll be fine."

The noise of silverware scraping against dishes renders me jittery. "May I be excused?" I ask, picking at my food. "I'm not feeling well."

"Go ahead," Father says. He grabs my arm as I walk by him. "Remember what we discussed, Valia."

"Yes, Papa."

I hear laughter coming from the dining room as I head up the stairs. "Is that so, son?" I hear Father say. His laughter calms my worries. I trust him with my life, but even so the police soldier from the market does not leave my thoughts for long. There is something about him that makes me feel uneasy. Christian Armenians have very few political and legal rights under Turkish rule. We pay higher taxes. Muslims and Christians of the opposite sex are not permitted to speak to one another. There seems to be a new rule added every day. But despite the many challenges we face, we are typically better educated and wealthier than our Turkish neighbors. This has me worried. The Turks have always looked at us with disdain, but it seems to be getting worse. I don't want to believe it, but I fear something terrible is about to happen.

Chapter 3

Saint Mariam Church stands in the center of the Armenian District of Adana. Its large pointy dome reminds me of Mount Ararat, a great symbol for the Armenian People. It is where the Ark settled, where Noah experienced his first rainbow, and where God promised He'd never flood the earth again.

Narrow stained-glass windows, 30 feet high, grip the dome's sides with depictions of various saints holding up their hands like weapons of mercy. A long center aisle leads to an altar adorned in candles, and a tabernacle made out of gold that Father says was mined in Jerusalem.

Lori Hasan and I have been best friends since primary school, but our fathers knew each other long before our births. Mr. Gagik Badalian, a banker, approved Father's loan for his watch repair business. Father is Lori's godfather. Mr. Badalian is my godfather.

The fire-red dress Lori wears flashes with gold trim. An ornate headband, with white beads dangling off its edges, adorns her head. Looking at her softens my worry and helps me forget about the town crier. The knots in my stomach relax.

"Such a pretty dress," Lori says.

"It matches your eyes," Milena says, one of the bridesmaids.

The other bridesmaids, Azaduhi and Nazani, agree.

"Where did you find it?" Nazani asks. "I looked in all the shops and could only find this." She models the dress as if it's a hand-me-down from a homeless woman.

"Mother made it for me," I say, holding my head high like a proud queen.

"Your mother can do anything," Nazani says.

"She could have made yours had you asked," I say. "But your dress is pretty. Blue is a suitable color for you."

"When I marry, I'll have your mother make all the dresses," Azaduhi says."

"She'll be happy to," I say.

I feel a hand on my shoulder. "How are you feeling, Valia?" It's Mrs. Vartanian, the lady at the market that went to fetch Father.

"I'm fine, Mrs. Vartanian, I say."

"Have you been ill?" Lori asks.

"Did you not hear?" Mrs. Vartanian asks. "Valia was attacked at the market the other day by one of those nasty police soldiers." She shivers in disgust. "They're nothing more than wild animals I tell you."

"Valia," Lori gasps, "you didn't tell me that."

"Nor me," Azaduhi says.

"Yea," Milena adds.

"Why didn't you tell us?" Nazani asks.

"I don't know," I say.

The wrinkles around Mrs. Vartanian's eyes bunch together like ancient sediment. "I don't care what the government leads us to believe. They're not here to protect us."

Mother approaches. "What are you girls talking about?" She looks at Mrs. Vartanian and smiles. "How are you Elen?" They embrace, share a kiss on the cheek.

"I'm fine," Mrs. Vartanian says. "I'm happy to see Valia recovering well from her ordeal. Those police soldiers are dreadful, just dreadful human beings."

Mother's smile grows solemn and distant.

"We were just telling Valia how beautiful her dress is Mrs. Stepanyan," Lori says, deftly changing the topic.

"Why thank you," Mother says. "All you girls look so pretty, the prettiest bridesmaids and bride I've ever seen.

"Thank you," they say in unison.

"Mother latches on Mrs. Vartanian's arm. "Let's have no more talk about police soldiers. I have friends I want you to meet."

When they leave, Lori says, "Tell us what happened?"

"I don't want to talk about it," I say.

"Did ya'll hear the town crier the other day?" Azaduhi asks. "He frightened me."

"I heard my father talking to some of his friends last night," Nazani says. "He said something about a revolt."

"No," Lori says. "The Russians have invaded. They're killing women and children and poisoning the water." She twists her lips as if to spit. "Such savages."

"What do you know about war?" Nazani asks.

"Father says they're far away," Lori counters. "In Van, I think. And Hakob tells me we're safe here."

"My father says the Russians are here to protect us from the Turks," Nazani says.

"You're saying my father is wrong?" Lori asks.

Nazani narrows her eyes and says nothing.

"I hear many families are fleeing to Europe to escape the war," Azaduhi adds

"Father told me that's where the war began," Milena says. "Why would anyone go there?"

"There are a few safe places," I say.

"How do you know that?" Nazani asks.

"I just do," I say, remembering my promise to Father, to never tell anyone, even my best friends, that we're leaving, but I fear I have said too much already.

"That's not an answer," Milena says.

"Oh, leave her be," Lori scolds. "Hakob is very handsome," I say, changing the subject. My eyes sinfully trace his tall, muscular frame. I imagine running my fingers through his ink black hair.

"He's a good man," Lori says. "And mine," she adds, giggling.

My face flushes with embarrassment. "No…. I mean…."

"It's alright," Lori says, playfully tugging my arm. "He is handsome. And he recently graduated from the university. He'll soon be working at the bank."

I smile. "I'm happy for…."

A trumpet sounds. Guests rush to take their seats.

The door to the nave opens. Mr. Badalian steps forward and takes Lori's hand. "Time to line up," he directs, standing tall and confident beside his daughter. His broad shoulders stretch the wrinkles out of his suit. The ascot flowing from his neck resembles a presumptuous lion's mane. He takes a deep, confident breath. "Ready sweetheart?"

"Yes, Papa," Lori says.

"Ready girls?" he asks the bridesmaids.

"Ready," we say, holding tight to our flower arrangements.

"Wait!" someone shouts. We turn to see Lori's brother, Dikran, standing there, panting.

"For heaven's sake, son, what is it?" Mr. Badalian asks.

"Take off one of your shoes, Lori," Dikran says, kneeling. He holds out a hand, revealing two small coins. "For good luck."

Lori wipes her eyes and leans over and kisses her brother on the cheek. "My sweet brother."

Dikran places the coins inside her empty shoe, and then places the shoe back on her foot. "Feels comfortable?"

"Yes, its fine," Lori says.

Mr. Badalian smiles. "Okay, are we ready now?"

"Yes," Lori says.

Mr. Badalian proudly escorts Lori down the aisle. The four bridesmaids follow. Five hundred pairs of eyes meet ours.

"I feel like a princess," Milena whispers.

"Sush!" Azaduhi hisses. "This is Lori's day."

Nazani rolls her eyes.

I hold my breath, trying not to giggle.

Duduk and guitar melodies bounce off walls. When we reach the foot of the altar, Mr. Badalian kisses Lori on the cheek, handing her off to her husband to be, Hakob Torosyan.

"Here you are young man," Mr. Badalian says.

"Thank you, sir," Hakob says, bows, and takes Lori's hand in his. Mr. Badalian returns the bow, and then stands by his wife. Mrs. Badalian is wearing a long blue dress with gold buttons. Her high cheekbones and smooth complexion give the impression that she is of noble birth, possibly a descendant of Tigran the Great himself, a once powerful Armenian king.

Father Bagradian plays with his neatly trimmed beard as if he's pulling burrs out of an Angora goat. "Do you have the rings?"

"Yes, Father, Hakob says.

An altar server opens a large bejeweled book and transforms into a human podium.

Father Bagradian scans the pages, looks up at the crowd. Making the sign of the cross over the couple, he says, "Let us begin in the name of the Father, and of the Son, and of the Holy Ghost."

"Amen," the crowd says.

A happy tear escapes down Lori's blushing cheek as she and Hakob exchange rings, simple gold bands that shine like an angel's halo.

Father Bagradian slides a piece of blue cloth off a second altar boy's arm, and then joins Lori's and Hakob's hands together with it. "A symbol of your unity," he says. "With God's protection, may nothing or no one separate you. And…"

Father Bagradian's voice fades as my thoughts consume me. I look up. Jesus hangs on a cross above the altar, his eyes closed in death, forsaken. I want to feel happy, but Saabir's stale breath, his powerful hands and snakelike eyes, jab my memory. My mind swells with panic. A sharp pain shoots up my chest. I close my eyes, take a deep breath, and convince myself I'm safe. When I open them, Nazani is staring at me. "Are you okay?"

"Yes," I say. A smile reassures her.

The clock tower chimes 10 o'clock.

"…these crowns symbolize the kingdom of God present in your home," Father Bagradian continues. Standing next to him is a third altar boy holding two gold crowns resting on a burgundy pillow in his angled arms.

Lori and Hakob turn to face each other. A man dressed in a dark blue suit stands between them, holding a cross over them as Father Bagradian places the crowns on their heads. "May God's protection and grace follow you all the days of your lives," he says.

"Amen," Lori and Hakob answer.

Father Bagradian motions for a fourth altar boy.

"How much longer?" Melena whispers.

"Shush!" interrupts Azadhuhi.

Father Bagradian looks up, and we quickly bow our heads.

After a minute, I look up, and see the fourth altar boy marching over like a soldier on parade. There is a gold cup and a small carafe of wine in his hands.

Father Bagradian slowly pours the wine until the carafe is empty. He makes the sign of the cross over the cup. "Take and drink from it in remembrance of the wedding feast at Cana, where our Lord performed his first miracle." He hands the cup to Lori, who takes a small sip, and then hands the cup to Hakob, who empties the cup in one healthy swallow.

"Turn and face the crowd," Father Bagradian instructs Lori and Hakob. When they do so, Father Bagradian proclaims, "I present to you and to almighty God Mr. and Mrs. Hakob Piranian."

Melana breathes a sigh of relief. Azaduhi elbows her side. "Behave."

"Stop it, the both of you," I say, then hold a finger to my mouth. "Everyone is watching." Melana and Azaduhi nervously look around the room.

"No one is watching," Azaduhi says.

"Yeah," Melana agrees.

Happy applause interrupts our little spat. The cheerful noise sounds like the voice of God dancing inside the dome. I look up at the crucifix for the second time. I'm reminded of the resurrection as a glimmer of hope tiptoes into the cracks of my heart.

The reception room, ten blocks away at the Bahi Hotel on Abadin Pasha Street, thickens with thirty or so guests. "Here they come!" someone shouts.

"The bridesmaids, where are the bridesmaids?" a woman barks.

"We're here," I say, waving my bouquet of flowers above my head.

"Get over here, girls," the woman says, frantically motioning with her hand. "Let them through," the woman continues. "Those with flowers stand here, those without flowers move out of the way." The woman elbows a path to the door and we dutifully follow her. Empty-handed guests make their way to the center of the room.

"Hold up your flowers, like this," the woman instructs the small crowd of flower bearers, angling her arm. "Okay, this is it," she says.

Lori and Hakob enter the reception room through a manmade tunnel of blossoms. Everyone, in happy and hopeful unison, cheers and claps to the rhythm of drumbeats, duduks, and classical guitars. Cognac and wine bottles pop open.

"Now!" a man's voice rings out.

A flock of doves burst out of a small steel cage. A man claps his hands twice. Six doves fly out a window. The seventh dove dives toward one of the ten dining tables, lands on a wedge of cheese, and pecks at its editable perch.

"Get that crazed bird out of here before it messes on everything!" a man yaps.

"Mind your tongue, Hagop," a woman hisses.

Whispers and silent giggles haunt the room.

"I'll get him," Dikran says.

"Yes, good boy," Father Bagradian says.

"I'll help," Arsen says.

"No," Mother says. "Dikran can manage on his own."

Arsen's lips quiver as he lowers his head. "He needs salt," he mumbles.

"What did you say?" Mother asks.

"Salt," Arsen says. "Dikran needs to put it on the dove's tail."

"That's not true," someone says, encouraging playful laughter amongst the guests.

"Is so," Arsen says.

"It's okay, Arsen," Mother says. "Look."

We all watch as Dikran tiptoes toward the dove as quiet as a kitchen mouse, and gently scoops the hoary creature in his strong, adolescent hands.

"Whatcha gonna do with it?" Arsen asks.

"His friends are waiting for him," Dikran says. He quickly opens his hands, and the dove disappears out the window in a dozen wing flaps.

"Okay, fun's over," Father Bagradian says, ringing a small brass hand bell. "Everyone to their places." He smiles. "Mr. Badalian and Mr. Torosyan please, have your family join my table. And you, Mr. Stepanyan, you and your lovely family join me as well. All the bridesmaid's families, please, come join us."

We all gather around our respected tables and join hands. Perfumed candles and flowers mix with the steamy smell of dolma and baked chicken, bean salad, basterma, cheeses, pickled beets and cucumbers. My mouth waters. My tongue wiggles free, catching the salt along the edge of my lips, wondering if what Arsen had said is true. Can you catch a bird by putting salt on its tail? I ask.

"Of course not," Mother says, laughing.

"Dear Heavenly Father," Father Bagradian begins. I tune out his words and focus on the window, envious of the dove's freedom. I pray to God to give me wings. *Is the war as far away as people say, or will it knock on our doorstep at any moment?*

"Amen," Father Bagradian ends the blessing.

Father holds up a glass of cognac.

Arsen snatches a small square honey cake and crams it in his mouth.

"Wait," Mother demands, blushing.

"I'm hungry," Arsen complains.

Mother leans into Arsen's ear, whispers something I cannot decipher.

"Okay," Arsen says, red-faced.

"To your daughter," Father says, standing next to Mr. Badalian on the far end of the table. Everyone clinks their glasses together and empties them in one methodical gulp. Guests toss coins in the air and cheer. Mr. and Mrs. Badalian acknowledge them by placing a hand on their chest and nodding their head.

"Well, Gagik, its good you decided not to cancel the wedding," Father Bagradian says. He glances at the other guests, now focusing on their food and drink. "It would have drawn suspicion."

"Indeed," Mr. Torosyan says. "It's a good turnout."

Father Bagradian turns to Father. "How are you doing?"

"Fine, thank you."

"I'm sorry, but I'm a bit restless," Mother says.

"Oh, whatever for," Father Bagradian says.

"We'll talk later," Father says.

"I think now is a good time," Mrs. Vartanian says, sitting at the table adjacent to us, "so we can all hear."

Mother narrows her eyes." "She's right. They have a right to know."

"Know what?" Hakob asks.

The chatter among guests grows more intense. Their words are in a jumble, like a chain of broken syllables.

Father pours another glass of cognac, fuller this time, and takes a sip. "There was an incident at the market yesterday." He takes another sip. "There's nothing to worry about—really."

"Nothing to worry about?" Mrs. Vartanian asks, narrowing her eyes, and breathing heavily. "I'll say there's something to worry about."

Mr. Vartanian reaches for his wife's arm. "Please, honey, sit down. We can discuss this later."

Mrs. Vartanian catches her breath, and jerks away from her husband. "No, they need to hear this."

"We understand the circumstances," Mrs. Vartanian," Father says.

"Do you?" she counters. "The Turks resent us, always have. They think we're more loyal to other Christian governments, such as Russia."

"What does that have to do with anything?" Hakob asks.

"You're too young," Hakob, you wouldn't understand," Mrs. Vartanian says.

Hakob stands, arms clinched by his side. "What don't I understand?" "Elen, please," Mother says.

Mrs. Vartanian narrows her eyes. "We've been under Muslim rule for too long. "It's about time we fight for our rights."

Mrs. Torosyan grasps her chest. "What happened to Valia?" she asks.

"One of the police soldiers harassed Valia, shook her up a bit," Father says.

"Oh, dear," Mrs. Badalian says.

"Let's not jump to conclusions, Satenig," Mr. Badalian says, placing a hand on his wife's back.

"Indeed," Father says. "Thank God he didn't harm her."

"Thank God," Father Bagradian agrees.

I take a sip of water. My heart thumps like a drum against my chest. "Yes, Father. I'm fine," I lie.

"You don't look fine," Nazani says.

"Pale as a ghost," Azaduhi says.

Mother puts her cheek to my forehead. "Do you need to lie down, sweetheart?"

"Shall we summon a doctor?" Mr. Torosyan asks.

"No," I say. "I'm fine, really."

Lori takes my hand in hers, squeezes it gently. "Really, if you need to lie down, do so. Hakob doesn't mind fetching a doctor, do you honey?"

"Of course not," Hakob says, kindly hiding a frown.

"What can we do?" Mr. Badalian asks.

"Nothing to worry about," Father says. "You've done so much for us already.

"We want to leave tomorrow," Mother says. "Can you manage that?"

Father sighs. "I apologize for Vartouhi."

"Tomorrow's too soon," Mr. Badalian says, rubbing his beard.

"We leave in three days," Mr. Torosyan says. He turns to Mr. Badalian. "Might they leave with us? I'm sure we can rearrange something."

"A splendid idea," Mrs. Torosyan says.

"We cannot all leave at once," a man says, his voice tired and edgy. "The police soldiers will catch on to us. They're watching our homes like hawks."

Mrs. Vartanian blushes with surprise. "Who else knew about this and didn't tell me or my husband?"

About half the room shake their heads.

"I see," Mrs. Vartanian says. She turns to Mr. Badalian. "You'd rather flee in cowardice than to fight for what has been rightfully ours for thousands of years."

"It's not that," Mr. Badalian says.

"Then what is it?" someone I do not recognize shouts. "You were going to leave without telling us. How can we defend our home alone?"

"Spies," Mrs. Vartanian," Mr. Baladian says. "We didn't tell everyone because of spies."

"So only those that you trust, is that it," Mrs. Vartanian says. She curls her lips as if to spit.

Others nod in agreement.

"We are in a very delicate situation," Mr. Baladian says. "We're doing the best we can under the circumstances." He narrows his eyes. "But now that we all know you can certainly join us."

"I think it's a wise decision, sweetheart," Mr. Vartanian says, rubbing his wife's hand.

"We're being forced to leave, all of us," Father says. "You heard the town crier just like the rest of us." He pauses a moment, then says, "We just don't want the Turks to provide an escort." He turns to Mrs. Vartanian. You should know more than any of us what the Turks can do." Mrs. Vartanian lost her first husband during the reign of Sultan Abdul Hamid II. "It's not wise for us to go with them. We need to leave on our own."

Concerned whispers from other guests fill the room like a thick, ghostly fog.

I'm in agreement that escaping is the best solution," the man I do not recognize says.

Others mumble in agreement.

"We won't all leave at once," Mr. Badalian says. "One or two families at a time, and at night."

Lori squeezes my hand tighter. "Won't it be just lovely, you and I walking the streets of Paris."

I give her an uncertain smile. "Yes."

Mr. Badalian snaps open a lighter. The tip of his cigarette bursts orange. The smoke curls from his nose and fades as it rises higher in the air. He turns to Father. "Would you like one?"

"Yes, thank you," Father says. He inhales the smoke deeply, turns to me, and smiles.

"I'll see what I can do," Mr. Badalian says. He places the lighter in an inside pocket of his jacket. "Leaving with the Torosyans shouldn't be a problem."

"Any news from the other towns?" Mr. Torosyan asks. "What about Van?"

"What's happening in Van?" Father asks.

"We hear of Russian troops moving in," Mr. Torosyan says.

Mr. Badalian flicks ashes in a nearby tray. "Rumor is the Russians are proudly convincing the Turks that the Armenians in Van are conspiring with the Tsar to overthrow the Pasha."

"See, like I was saying," Mrs. Vartanian says. "We should join them."

Mr. Torosyan raises an eyebrow. "Sure, that has always worked out well for us," he says.

Many nod in agreement. No one is concerned with Mrs. Vartanian's opinions anymore. Many of the elders crunch their faces in horrid remembrance of years past. Our relationship with Russia has never turned out well for us. They have been battling off and on with the Turks ever since the Russo-Persian War began in 1826. We Armenians have been sandwiched between their disputes for decades. Some of us fought for the Turks out of fear, and some fought for the Russians out of desperation. At the end of these disputes, we have never gained our freedom. We have been tormented, persecuted, and tortured for much of our history. Sometimes it's best to admit defeat. Sometimes it's best not to fight over a piece of land no matter how sacred it is. Running away is often the better part of courage.

Father cocks his brow. "That explains the unusual number of police soldiers at the market yesterday, and why they're watching our homes."

Mr. Badalian looks at Mother. He glances at the rest of us, and smiles. He takes a reflective puff from his cigarette, slowly exhales the smoke. "Don't worry. I'll send a wire to Constantinople later today about our change of plans. If the war reaches this far, we'll be gone before it begins."

Music interrupts our conversation. Guests get up from their tables and proceed to the dance floor. Young women in flashy dresses crash against their husband's arms with happiness and assurance. Even the man with the edgy voice seems satisfied with Mr. Badalian's revised plan.

"They don't look worried the least bit," Mr. Badalian says. He turns to Hakob. "I think it wise to follow their lead."

"Yes, sir," Hakob says. He takes Lori by the hand and they join the dance party.

"Are you sure Paris is safe?" Mother asks.

"The Germans control everything up to the Somme River, but the British and French are slowly pushing them back," Mr. Badalian says. "I assure you, Paris is safe."

"What about the Americans?" Father asks.

"I think they'll join the war…"

The door to the reception room bursts open. Standing there in the open doorway is Saabir, the captain that had torn my blouse at the market. I cannot believe it. I tremble at the sight of him. He's alone this time. Battle ribbons hang from his uniform. He protrudes his chest like a satisfied rooster. His shoes shine like obsidian.

"What is it?" Mother asks.

"That's him," I say, "the one at the market. Remember?"

Mother's eyes widen. She whispers in Father's ear.

Father whispers in Mr. Badalian's ear. Mr. Badalian whispers in Mr. Torosyan's ear and so on, until the whispers reach all of the tables.

Mr. Badalian stands, offering his hand.

"I need you to come with me," Saabir says.

"It's my daughter's wedding. Can it wait?" The two men speak as if they know each other. Mr. Badalian pours a shot of vodka, offering it to Saabir, but he waves it away. "I'm afraid not," the captain says. "It's very important that you come with me now."

"Whatever it is, we can discuss the matter here," Mr. Badalian suggests. He sits down, points to an empty chair.

Saabir remains standing. "The mayor is waiting," he says. "He needs your advice."

"About the Russians?" Father asks. Mr. Badalian's tense look confirms Father's mistake.

Saabir raises his eyebrows. "You," he says arrogantly. "I almost didn't recognize you." He looks at Mother, and then at me. I rub my sweaty hands, refuse to look at him.

He lifts my chin. "How are you my dear? Valia, isn't it?" A sinister smile snakes across his face. I imagine his mouth houses a forked tongue.

"Yes, sir," Mother answers for me.

Saabir turns to Father. "So tell me, Mr. Stepanyan, what do you know about the Russians?"

"We hear stories."

"What stories?"

"What Mr. Stepanyan means is—" Mr. Badalian begins.

"Mr. Stepanyan can speak for himself," Saabir interrupts. "Go on."

"It's nothing," says Father. "Only rumors."

"Explain," says Saabir.

Father Bagradian stands, introduces himself. "Why are we being ordered out of the city? I see no reason to leave. We're perfectly safe where we are."

"Are you?" Saabir asks, a sarcastic tone to his voice. "The Russians captured Van a few days ago. They're advancing. If anyone has told you differently, they're lying." Saabir scans the room, addresses the crowd. "The mayor needs help recruiting. We need every able-bodied male to fight, twelve and older, to prove to the Pasha, to all of Turkey, you all are fighting for the Tsar are in the minority. Prove you are loyal to your native country and join in the fight." He pauses a moment. "We cannot win this war without your help."

Arsen points to Saabir's gun. "Is that real?"

"And who might you be?" Saabir asks.

"Arsen," Father says. "My son."

"How old are you, boy?"

"Ten," Arsen says, his eyes wide as walnuts.

"A fine boy you have there," Saabir says.

"Thank you," Father says nervously.

Saabir glances down at the weapon. "Yes, boy, it's real." He smirks. "Maybe you'll have your own one day," raising his voice so everyone can hear.

"Our son will be a watchmaker, like his father," Mother says, pulling Arsen close to her.

"Yes, of course," Saabir says. "A craftsman. Don't think I've forgotten about the shop. I'm sure I'll find something to my liking."

"Papa makes the best watches in the world," Arsen gleams.

"I'm sure he does, boy," Saabir says.

Father pours a shot of cognac and sets it in front of Saabir. "Please, join us for one drink."

Saabir shakes his head. "Like I was saying, we cannot win this war without your help. "Do you want your women and children butchered by the hands of the Tsarist hoard? We'll transport them to a safe place until the war is over. You have my word."

Silence turns to anxious whispers.

"What do you think, Aram?" Mr. Badalian asks.

"It doesn't matter what he thinks," Saabir says, impatiently rubbing the holstered pistol. "We must obey the mayor's orders."

"Yes, of course," Mr. Badalian says, standing. He pours one last drink. "For Turkey," he says, downs the drink in one fluid and uneasy swallow. "Please understand. Everyone is concerned about the war. We hear very little news coming from the front, and when we do, some of us jump to conclusions."

Saabir gives a satisfied grunt. He motions for Mr. Badalian to follow him. Whispers return to dead silence as the wedding guests watch the two men leave.

"What does this mean?" Mother whispers.

"He's lying," Father says. "We must leave immediately."

Chapter 4

I pack my clothes and a few of my favorite books. Sounds from the street below—dogs barking, children playing, neighbors chatting—sting my ears. The sun pours in from the window and splashes my face with sparkles of yellow light. I think about Paris. I know the city only from books. I picture the Eiffel Tower taller than the clouds. I imagine boating on the Seine River and visiting Notre Dame Cathedral.

My parents arguing interrupts my thoughts. Never have I heard them arguing before. It worries me.

"We should have convinced Gagik to cancel the wedding and left sooner!" Mother shouts. "Lori and Hakob could have just as easily married in Paris."

"Keep your wits," Father says calmly. "We'll leave soon enough."

"Everyone thinks poorly of us, not telling them of our plans."

"They didn't tell us, either, sweetheart. Everyone plans to leave."

"But the way they looked at me, at Valia, as if she caused all this."

"Don't be silly, Vartouhi. No one thinks that."

Arsen steps into my bedroom.

"What do you want?" I ask, irritated, shutting the suitcase lid. The argument downstairs grows louder.

Arsen's lower lip spasms like a dying worm. A tear travels down his cheek. "I'm sorry," I say. "I didn't mean to snap at you. Come here." I pull him close and hold him in my arms.

"Why are they angry?" Arsen asks.

"They're just trying to decide what's best for us." I give him a kiss on the cheek.

"Valia," Mother calls.

"Coming Mama," I say. Rubbing Arsen's back, I say, "Let's go help them."

We arrive downstairs and discover that the argument appears settled.

"I've been calling and calling," Mother says, rubbing an eye. "What have you been doing up there?"

"Sorry. I had the door closed."

"Very well, you're here now. Come help me organize these dishes."

"What are you and Papa arguing about?" I ask.

"Nothing important," Mother says. "It's settled." She folds a cup in paper and places it carefully in a box. "We're leaving tonight."

"What about Lori?" I ask.

"I'm sure the Badalian's will be along soon," Mother says. She gives a faint smile. "Remember what Mr. Badalian said, we all can't leave at once. We're going with Hakob's parents tonight. Papa will leave word with the Badalians."

"Lori can come with us," I protest. "One more won't matter, will it?"

"No," Father says wearily. He lifts a small trunk onto a larger one, and ties the two together with thick leather straps. "The Torosyan's are waiting for us. We cannot spare another minute. Now please, help your mother get ready to go." He pauses. "I'm sure Lori will be along in the next few days."

There is a knock at the door. We stand still as mice listening to a cat scratching at a wall. The knock grows louder and stronger. Father opens the door. A young lieutenant stands in front of us. He is handsome with eyes the color of a lion's mane. A thick head of black hair emerges when he removes his hat. His uniform is crisp and, despite the street dust, his boots shine ink black. Two other police soldiers stand behind him, both carrying rifles. They never speak.

"We leave now," the lieutenant says.

"We were told we had two weeks," Father says.

The lieutenant brushes Father aside, enters the house. The two quiet police soldiers follow. "But here you are packing already," the lieutenant says, gesturing toward the trunks. One of the soldiers opens a trunk, pulls out a dress, narrows his eyes.

Arsen watches the police soldier's every move, fascinated with the uniforms and weapons.

"What do you want, boy?" the lieutenant asks.

"I'm going to be an explorer like you when I grow up."

The police soldiers laugh.

"We're police soldiers," the lieutenant says, "not explorers." He kneels, still holding the dress, and removes his pistol, holds it out for Arsen to take. "Do you want to be a soldier?"

Arsen reaches for the weapon.

"No, son," Father says, "pistols are dangerous. We do not play with them."

"Yes, Papa," Arsen says, pulling his hand back.

The lieutenant smiles, stands leisurely, and holsters the pistol. "You have an obedient son," he says. "Were you planning on leaving without proper escort?"

"No, sir," Father says. "Of course not."

The lieutenant grunts, gestures at the dress. "Too fancy of a dress to be wearing at a liberation camp."

"It's my favorite dress," I say, so nervous I almost bite my tongue.

"Leave it," the lieutenant says, tossing it on the floor.

I pick up the dress, clinch it to my chest, suck in a nervous breath.

"We have a lot of valuable possessions," Father says. "We don't want to lose them."

"Take what you need only," the lieutenant says. "We'll make sure the rest is safe and secure." He picks up a vase, holds it in front of Father. "What do you need this for? You'll only be gone a short while."

"Where are you taking us? Father asks.

"Deir ez-Zor."

"Syria?" Father asks. "Why so far?"

"I have my orders," the lieutenant says.

"Why do we have to leave at all?" Mother asks, stepping closer with open arms, and reaching for the vase. "Please, it belonged to my mother."

The lieutenant hands her the vase. "Leave it, it'll be here when you return."

"But why must we leave?" Mother asks a second time.

The lieutenant turns to me, and smiles. I pull Arsen close. "You have a pretty daughter. You can trade her for the vase if you like."

Mother gently sets the vase back on the table, glares at the lieutenant.

The lieutenant glances around the house, his expression evidence of his growing impatience.

Father narrows his eyes. "May I ask why you're in such a hurry?"

"The Russians, of course," the lieutenant says.

"Yes, we know, but they've made it this far south?" Father asks. He chews on the inside of his cheek.

"Soon."

"What about my store? "I'm a watch maker. I need to pick up a few items from there, important tools."

"We'll keep your shop safe," the lieutenant says, nods at his two assistants.

"I'll show you where it is," Father says. "I'm supposed to meet another soldier there. He wants to look at some of the watches. His name is Captain Saabir. Maybe you know him."

"Yes, I know him," the lieutenant says.

Father relaxes his shoulders. "We can go together, then. Might you fetch him?"

"No time for that. You have fifteen minutes to pack up what you can, only essentials, and be ready to leave."

As the lieutenant and his men are about to depart, Father says, "Wait, please. There is one other matter."

"What?" the lieutenant asks crossly.

"A friend of mine, Gagik Badalian, he had a meeting with Captain Saabir and the mayor. Might I see him before we leave?"

"No," the lieutenant says. "Remember, fifteen minutes."

"Do you know his whereabouts?"

"No." The lieutenant slams the door behind him.

We find hundreds of families gathering in the streets. The wealthier families are piling two or three wagons high with boxes and crates. Poorer families have their belongings stuffed in makeshift bags and are carrying everything they own on their backs. The weight of the bags forces the carriers to walk crooked, their legs bent and resembling ancient tree branches.

Mother helps Arsen and I into the wagon. "We should have left earlier," she mumbles tearfully.

Father sighs. "There's nothing we can do about it now." He straps in a set of medium-sized trunks in the back of the wagon. "Look," he points, smiling proudly from one side of his mouth. "Here comes Satenig and Lori." Mrs. Badalian and Lori, carrying two large suitcases, dart across the street.

"They look frightened," Mother says. "And I don't see Gagik or Hakob anywhere."

"Thank God we found you," Mrs. Badalian says, out of breath.

I jump from the wagon, hug Lori as tight as I can. "Where's Hakob?"

"They took him," Lori says. Her bloodshot eyes hold small pools of tears.

"Took him where?" Mother asks.

"To dig trenches," Lori says.

"What about Gagik?" Father asks.

"He didn't return home," Mrs. Badalian says. "It's been hours. I think that police soldier from the wedding did something to him."

Father's smile moans a look of worry. He gestures toward the wagon. "Don't think such things," his voice besieging hope like a lonely vessel. "I'm sure he'll be along shortly." He gestures at the wagon. "Perhaps he's waiting for us at the camp. Come with us. I'm sure everything is fine."

"Thank you," Mrs. Badalian says. Father places their luggage in the wagon.

Mother's face flushes with worry. Grabbing Father's arm, she says, "What if the police soldiers come for you?"

"They won't," Father says.

"What if they force Gagik to tell your whereabouts?"

"Your worry has gotten you talking nonsense," Father says. "I'm no threat to the government." He places his index finger against his lips. "Now, not another word about it."

Lori, Mrs. Badalian, Arsen and I cluster in the back of the wagon while Father and Mother load the last of our bags. Arsen pulls out a bunch of grapes.

The sweet juice relaxes my nerves. I offer some to Mrs. Badalian and Lori. "Thank you," they say, each grabbing a sprig.

The streets fill with more families. Children cling to the backs of fathers, or tug on their mother's leg. An elderly woman stuffs gold coins in her mouth. A young girl packs clothes in a bag sewn into a makeshift backpack. The air smells of rotten eggs, sweat, and animals.

"Hey, Aram." A man approaches Father, waving his hand. "We have a plan," the man whispers. His open coat reveals a pistol.

Father shoots him a foul look. "Put that away. There's nothing we can do. Go back to your family before you get us in trouble."

"We're all going to die," the man says wanly. "Like what Sultan Hamid did to us twenty years ago." The man narrows his eyes. "Don't tell me you've forgotten."

Father's face twists into a bleak snarl. "Go."

The man reaches in his jacket once more. Father grabs the front of the man's shirt, pulls him close, whispers sternly, "Never say that again. Understand?" He pushes him away. "We survived 1909. We'll survive this."

"It's different now," the man says. He slips inside the crowd, gone. Father lets him go, then retreats into the house.

"That Muslim girl is waving at us," Arsen says, tugging my dress.

"Where?" I ask.

Arsen points. Two girls dressed in elaborate Muslim garb stand on the side of the street, their faces covered with only a horizontal slit in the fabric, revealing their eyes. The shorter one waves me over.

"Who's that?" Arsen asks.

"Not sure," I say. I climb down from the wagon.

"Where do you think you're going?" Mother calls.

"Just there," I say, pointing across the street.

"I'll go with her, Mrs. Stepanyan," Lori says.

"Oh no you won't," Mrs. Badalian says.

"I'll be fine," I say.

"Mother sucks in her lips. "Make sure I can see you. And don't be gone long. Your Father is almost ready to go."

"I will."

"I want to go," Arsen says, but Mother latches onto his arm. "You stay put."

I'm almost across the street when a horse gallops toward me. The girl that had waved at me grabs my arm and pulls me to safety. I turn to see Mother grasping her chest, relief saturating her eyes.

"Valia, it's me," the girl says. She lifts her veil. "Artush."

"Artush!" I cry, hugging her.

Artush and I are classmates. I met her when we were in the 3rd grade. Students often bring a stick of wood to school to help keep the furnace going during the winter. Students are assigned each day to make sure the fire never goes out. Students are assigned a partner. Artush and I were assigned to each other, and we have been best friends ever since. "Should have let her die," the girl standing beside her says.

My tone changes. "Yasmin, is that you?" I narrow my eyes. "Why am I not surprised."

"You're going to die out there anyway," Yasmin says.

"Yasmin, please," Artush says.

"Fine. But she should have married an officer. That way she'd be safe."

I notice the beginnings of a tattoo on Artush's hand. "Is that what you did, Artush, marry a Muslim officer?" I glare at Yasmin. "Did she talk you into this?"

Artush lowers her eyes. "It was the only way to keep my family safe."

"Look at me," I say, arms folding across my chest. "You could've come with us," I say, gesturing toward the wagon.

Artush grabs my hands, holds them as if she'd never see me again. "I'm afraid Yasmin might be right. You're in danger."

"Father will keep us safe."

"Marrying is a small price to pay to stay in Adana," Artush says. "You could still marry and stay here with us. Isn't that right Yasmin?"

"I suppose so," Yasmin says.

"I could never do that," I say.

"Suit yourself, Valia," Yasmin says. "Artush, my father is expecting us for dinner. We need to go."

"Sure you won't change your mind?" Artush asks.

I look back at the wagon and see Mother and Father waving. "Yes, I'm sure."

"I'll pray for you," Artush says.

"And I for you," I say. "Saint Blaise will protect us."

"Your saints can't help you," Yasmin says.

"What do you know about it?" I ask. "You're a Muslim."

"I…" Yasmin hesitates, looks around with spy like eyes.

"What is it?" I ask. "You have something more to say to me?"

"Take this," Yasmin says, "and hide it." A gold coin shines in her hand like a small sun.

"Why are you being nice all of a sudden?" I ask.

"Never mind that. Just hide it until its time. It's best you swallow it."

"Time for what? Artush asks.

"Yea, time for what?" I repeat.

A police soldier watches us closely.

"You'll know," Yasmin says. "Now go before we attract too much attention."

I take the coin, pop it in my mouth, hug Artush one last time, then scurry across the street.

"Who was that?" Mother asks as I climb into the wagon.

"Artush."

"Dressed like that?" Father asks. Where are her parents?"

"They're staying in Adana," I say. I take a deep, disappointing breath. "Artush married a Turk."

Mother sucks her teeth. "That so?"

"Yes," I say. "She said I should marry, perhaps an officer, so we wouldn't have to go."

"Blasphemy," Father says. "Our faith is much stronger than that." He inspects the wagon. "Aw, forgot something. I'll be right back."

I watch Father go, massaging my thumb anxiously. "That's what I told her," I say, my voice soft, faltering.

"You don't sound convinced," Mother says.

"I was thinking…well…maybe I should marry a Muslim. Maybe we'll be left alone."

"I want to stay, too, Valia, but you can never marry a Turk, that's sinful. I'd rather die in the desert than for you to marry a Turk."

"Mama, don't say such a thing," I say, tears stinging my eyes.

"We'll be fine," Mother corrects herself. She glances at Lori and Mrs. Badalian. "Don't worry. I shouldn't have said that. I'm sure Gagik is waiting for us. Hakob, too."

I turned to Arsen. "You ate all the grapes," I say, holding a strand of empty stems.

Arsen giggles. "There's more," he says, handing me another bunch. I break off half, offer again to Mrs. Badalian and Lori, but this time they shake their heads, their smiles distant.

"It'll be okay," I say, putting an arm around Lori. "Father will take care of us."

"What of Hakob and my father?"

"I'm sure they're fine," I say.

"How can you be sure?" Lori asks.

Father returns with two large suitcases. "That's everything," he says, placing the suitcases in the back of the wagon. Arsen helps him slide the bags in place.

"You left that blue handkerchief," Father says to me. "Want me to go back and get it?"

"No. Leave it," I say. "Saint Blaise will watch over our house until we return."

"That's my girl," Father says. He kisses me on the cheek. I wrap my arms around him, we share a smile, but a pain deep in my chest remains.

Father climbs into the wagon, grabs hold of the reins. "Hold on." He glances at our house one last time. Mother stares straight ahead. Father faces forward, snaps the reins, the wagon jerks, and we move. Our house slowly disappears from sight. "God, please bring us safely home," I silently pray, but knots remain in my stomach.

We pass Turkish civilians ransacking Armenian homes as we ride through town. Two men cart out furniture and rugs. A woman stuffs jewelry into her pockets. A cluster of police soldiers standing nearby do not interfere. A group of men shout at each other. Soon the verbal attacks switch to punches and kicks. Father shifts the wagon away from them, just missing overturned baskets of produce. A braying donkey struggles to free itself from a tree. Two horses buck each other for territory. Their owners quickly join forces, breaking them apart. In the midst of it, more people and animals fill the streets like a strong tide overpowering the banks of a river, shoving and elbowing each other as they battle their way forward. Mothers scoop children in their arms. Sheep bump into each other. When the chaos gets out of hand, the police soldiers yell for order and push people into line.

"I'm going by the shop," Father says.

Mother looks concerned. "Remember what the lieutenant said."

Father shrugs. "It'll be okay," he assures her. "I just want to take a quick look."

We skirt our way through the crowded marketplace. People dart around, looking last minute for food and clothes for the journey. When we arrive at the shop, we discover a police soldier standing at the entrance. "Wait here," Father says.

"You said a quick look," Mother says. "Let's go."

"I agree," Mrs. Badalian says. She squeezes both Lori's hand and mine.

"I want to see for myself," Father says. He hastily climbs down, attaches the horse to a tie rod.

"I want to go with Papa," Arsen says.

I grab hold of him. We struggle briefly, but I finally force him in my lap. "Papa will be fine." I, too, am uncertain of this, but hold my distress like my body holds the gold coin I swallowed.

"Not this time," Father says. He winks. "I just need to check on something. You keep an eye on things here."

Arsen smiles proudly and then settles in my lap without any more protest.

"Good boy," Father says.

I watch nervously as Father approaches the shop. The police soldier standing at the entrance holds up his hand, gestures for Father to halt.

"But this is my shop," Father says.

Two more police soldiers exit the shop with two small boxes.

Father blocks their way. "Why are you emptying my shop?"

They give him a confused, but condescending look. "Someone might break in," the taller one says. "We'll keep everything safe until you return. Certainly you were notified of this."

"Yes, I was."

"Then let us pass or we'll throw you in jail," the other one says.

"But—" Father begins.

"Enough!" The police soldier Father had spoken to first says. He steps closer and butts Father with his brawny chest. "Get back in the wagon and go." The corners of his mouth curve upward, the smile of a demon. "These women you're with are very beautiful," he adds. "I'd hate for anything to happen to them, especially the young one there," waving to me. I look away. The police solider laughs and says, "I know how to deal with her kind really well, make her moan and yelp like one of my goats."

"So you've been with a goat, have you?" Father asks. The expression on his face validates his foolish mistake. The police soldier slams his fist across Father's face. The strength of the blow knocks him backwards, but he catches himself on the wagon, keeping his balance.

Mother gasps. Mrs. Badalian and Lori lower their heads. I bite my tongue, feel a blaze of anger and fear rush through my body. My eyes water. I violently scratch at the wagon's floor, breaking a nail. "Ouch!" I say in a muffled voice, but no one hears me.

"Leave my Papa alone!" Arsen yells.

I ignore the pain in my finger and grab hold of him. "No, Arsen," I say. "Keep still."

"A boy as brave or as foolish as his father," the police soldier says.

"He's only ten," Father says, breathing heavily. "He doesn't understand." His breathing subsides, and he puts a finger to his lips. Arsen calms down, but he keeps holding on to a determined, wrathful look.

Father wipes a trickle of blood from his mouth. "It's okay, son. I'm alright."

The police soldier pulls a knife, grabs hold of Father's hair, yanks his head back. "One more remark about my goats and I'll gut you like a fish." The police soldier glares at Mother. "Is this your husband?"

"Yes, sir."

"Then come help him."

Mother wobbles off the wagon, helps Father back in his seat. Father grabs the reigns.

"Wait," the police soldier says abruptly.

I turn to see an elderly woman approaching us, balancing a basket of bread on her head, begging someone to buy a loaf.

The police soldier digs into his pocket, flips Father a few coins. "Buy some bread for the trip." He gives a haughty smile.

Creases form in the corner of Father's eyes. Shifting his body obediently, he steps off the wagon. He offers the woman two coins. She eagerly scoops them in her hand, drops them down her skirt at the waistline, her smile a mix of happiness and greed. "Pick any two you like," she says. Her tongue wiggles like a snake across charcoal-black teeth.

Father chooses the two smallest loaves, hands them to me. "Wrap them up and save for later," he says weakly.

"Now, get moving!" the police soldier shouts. He gestures toward a crowd of deportees, hundreds of them, heading out of town. Fifty or so police soldiers on horseback amble beside them, inflexible, with snarled grins identical to a pack of dogs prodding a herd of sheep. "Looks like the caravan is leaving," he adds. "Go!"

"May I ask a favor?" Father asks.

"What?"

"Inside my shop there is a gold watch dear to me. May I have it?"

"What for."

"It belonged to my father. All I ask for is the watch. Please."

"Very well. Go get it."

We pass the Municipal Garden, join another caravan, hundreds more, at the edge of town. Half dozen Turkish women with messy hair and dressed in rags are there to meet us. All of them stand motionless, except one, who throws her hands up to the sky. Then she beats her legs and shouts, "Curse the government for forcing these innocent people from their homes. You will one day suffer a similar fate." We lock eyes. "God be with you, my child," she says. I turn my head away and shiver.

"What does she mean, Papa?" I ask.

"Don't mind her," Father says. "She's a batty old woman."

The knots in my stomach worsen. I think of the gold coin swimming in my stomach. How will I know what it's for? What sign will there be? And why did Yasmin give it to me in the first place?

We cross the great stone bridge dating back to the Roman Empire. Ox and horse-drawn carts swell with furniture, crates, and boxes. Pots and pans clank to the rhythm of hoofs thumping the stone bottom. The Seyhan River runs beneath the bridge, stretching wide and long, dazzling my eyes with sparkles of sunlight. A kingfisher perches itself on a branch inches above the water's edge as it waits for a hapless fish to swim by. The bird's blue back reminds me of the handkerchief I left behind. I smile at the thought of it, its smooth fabric, the hope it brings. I bow my head and pray for safe travel, pray we'll soon be home.

Three days later we reach the valley below the Taurus Mountains. Limestone precipices mimic ancient pyramids. Scattered thickets of scratch pine grow at the base of the mountains. Red-footed falcons hover above. Knotted apple trees anticipate a bountiful harvest in May. The sun burns cruelly in the cloudless sky. Those without protection or water soon succumb to the heat. Not a single police soldier allows us any shade. A dozen or more of the elderly and children collapse from the heat.

"We should help them," Mrs. Badalian says.

"Not a good idea," Father says. "Look."

"Move away from there!" a police soldier shouts. "You can't help him anymore." He's yelling at a woman who's kneeling beside an elderly man, trying to shake him awake.

"But he's my father," the woman pleads. "Please help him. He needs water."

The soldier raises his rifle, the long bayonet at the end of it moving about like some kind of wild animal. "Get up," the police soldier demands, jabbing the thick air with the bayonet. The woman darts away screaming. The police soldier gives chase.

"You can at least try," Mother says.

Father takes a deep breath. "Very well." He maneuvers the wagon alongside one of the police soldiers and asks, "Sir, can we stop a while? Those having to walk are suffering greatly. They need water, rest."

"What are you offering?" the police soldier asks, his brusque voice imitating what I imagine as the sound of an avalanche.

Father rubs his leg, hesitates.

"Show him the watch, Aram," Mother says.

Father grunts, gives the police soldier a keen look. "I have to reach into my pocket."

The police soldier grips his pistol. "Easy does it."

Father slowly pulls out the gold watch he had taken from his shop. "It was my father's. Very valuable."

The police soldier snatches the watch out of Father's hand, holds it up to his ear. "Takes good time?"

"The best," Father says.

The police soldier promptly stuffs the watch in his pocket. "I'll see what I can do." He gallops away.

The police soldier returns a few minutes later. "We'll stop soon."

"Thank you," Father says.

An hour passes. We arrive at a large grassy field covered in bright red poppies. "We'll make camp here," a police soldier says.

The rich unpack their wagons. The poor and exhausted collapse where they stand. Arsen assists Father in attaching a large sheet to our wagon. Mother and I unload a few pots and pans, plates and cups. As we work, an old woman and two small boys appear. Drops of sweat crawl down their faces.

"May we share your tent?" the old woman asks.

"Certainly," Father says. He looks around cautiously. "Quickly though, before the police soldiers see you." He ties the last corner to a pole, forming a canopy, and we all duck inside the makeshift tent.

"Here you are," Father says, handing a cup of water to the old woman. She takes two large gulps. "Thank you," the old woman says wearily. She passes the cup to the two boys.

"Where is the rest of your family?" Mother asks.

"We don't know," the old woman says. She nods toward the two boys. "Their parents went to a birthday party the night before we left and never returned."

"Maybe they're here," Father says. ""I'll go look for them."

"We've looked everywhere," the old woman says. "It's no use."

"Have you heard of Gagik Badalian or Hakob Torosyan?" Mrs. Badalian asks, the tone of her voice forcing out the last bit of desperation.

"I'm afraid not," the old woman says. "Who are they?"

"Her husband and son-in-law," Father says, "and friends of ours."

"Perhaps they were taken to a different place," Mother says. "We did leave rather suddenly." She rubs the elderly woman's shoulder. "I'm sure they're fine wherever they are." She looks at Mrs. Badalian and Lori. "Gagik and Hakob, too."

"They brought us out here to die," the elderly woman says.

"Don't talk like that," Father says. "You don't know that."

"They have no use for the old, nor children, the poor especially."

"That doesn't make sense," Mother says.

"How else would you explain it?" the elderly woman asks. "They haven't taken any of your food. No, they have a use for you."

"Your safe with us," Father says. He turns to Mother. "Is the food ready?"

"Soon," Mother says. "Come on, Valia, let's go," and I follow her outside the tent.

"What is that woman talking about?" I ask.

"She's just tired. Doesn't know what she's saying," Mother says. She opens a bag, pulls out a large piece of flatbread and stretches it out on a table like a large snakeskin. "I'll cut this up, you get the potatoes ready. The water should be ready in a few minutes."

I brush the dirt off the potatoes, cut them up into tiny squares and toss them into the pot.

"Is everything alright?" Mother asks. "You look a little flushed."

"I wish we could share with everyone," I say, stoking the fire.

"If you're worried about someone stealing, don't be."

"You believe the old woman," I say.

"I don't know what to believe. All I know is that we're safe. Do you think Papa would risk our lives? We're safe, Valia."

I drop a few herbs in. "Doesn't seem fair."

"I know, sweetheart, but we can't help everyone. Your father is taking a big risk helping the old woman and her two grandchildren."

"I don't understand," I say.

"The police soldiers, perhaps they're testing us," Mother says, seeing who's the strongest. Wars are not won by the weak."

"They're going to make us fight?"

"Certainly not."

"What then?"

Mother tosses a bunch of bread slices into a basket. "Perhaps I'll cook for a general," she says, forcing a smile. "Mend his uniform."

"What about me?" I ask.

"I'm sure they'll find something for you to do."

"I'm not…" My hands tingle with shock. My eyes blink in disbelief.

"Valia, what's the matter?" Mother asks. She unfolds another bunch of flatbread. "You certainly do not look well. Go rest. I'll finish up here."

"That's him," I say, pointing. Saabir is walking toward our tent. A scruffy beard covers his face, unlike before, and his uniform is sporting new badges, but I know it's the same man. He has the same serpentine eyes, dark and unyielding; the same kind of eyes that convinced Eve to take a bite of Eden's forbidden fruit.

Mother looks deeper into the camp. "That's who?"

"Captian Saabir, the man that tore my blouse and took Mr. Badalian away."

"Are you sure? It doesn't look like the same man."

"Yes, I'm sure."

"Aram," Mother calls.

Father jumps from the tent in a nervous haste. "What's wrong? Are you hurt?"

"Look," Mother says, "isn't that the man that attacked Valia and took Gagik away? Go talk to him."

Mrs. Badalian pokes her head out from the tent. "You found Gagik?"

"No," Father says. "Go back inside."

I want to run, but have nowhere to go, so I stay put, plant my feet firmly on the ground, watch Saabir's black eyes grow larger and larger.

"Hello," Saabir says. "I didn't expect to see you again."

"Where is Mr. Badalian?" Father asks.

Mrs. Badalian and Lori crawl out of the tent. "Yes, where is my husband?" Mrs. Badalian asks.

"Where is mine?" Lori asks.

I let go of my stomach, breathe a little easier when the old woman and the two boys remain inside the tent.

Saabir looks at Lori and says, "You were the one getting married, I remember. Your husband is Hakob Torosyan, am I right?"

"Yes, sir."

"He's a fine worker."

"When can I see him?"

Saabir smiles as if he holds all the world's secrets. "Soon," he says.

"What of Mr. Badalian?" Father repeats.

"He is not with you?" Saabir asks.

Anger flares in Father's eyes. "You know that he's not."

Saabir places a hand on the gun strapped to his side. "Careful," Mr. Stepanyan."

"Aram," Mother says, gently squeezing Father's arm.

"I assure you," Saabir says, "I'm not aware of Mr. Badalian's whereabouts. He left for home after our talk with the mayor." He picks up a wooden spoon, gently stirs the soup pot. He leans over to catch the steam rising in aromatic twists and swirls. "Smells good."

"Tell us how they are getting along," Father says.

"I told you all I know," Saabir says. "I will hear no more about it." He takes a deep, frustrated breath, and says, "May I have a word with your daughter?" He pauses a moment. "Alone."

"No," Father says.

Saabir unlatches his gun holster. "You know I don't have to ask." He gestures at the tent. "Besides, I know you are protecting a worthless hag and two boys in there. I can make a lot of trouble for you."

"They cannot harm you," Father says. "How do they pose a risk to the war effort? And if the Russians are coming as you say, why not leave them behind and let the Tsar deal with them?"

"Enough," Saabir says. He pushes Father aside, gently grabs my arm and pulls me close, his breath the smell of garlic. I quickly turn my head away.

"Don't worry," Saabir says. "I won't hurt you."

"Let me go," I say, jerking free, running behind Mother.

"You know," Saabir says, "my mother gave me my name because I was a quiet child. It means patient." He turns to Father, pulls a gold watch from his pocket.

"It was you who allowed us rest?" Father asks.

"Easier to find your daughter that way," Saabir says. "When I saw this watch, I knew it was you." He turns to Lori. "Maybe this one would be of some use as well."

Mrs. Badalian pulls Lori close.

"But why?" Father asks. "How can they be of use to you?"

Saabir replies with a grin. He holds out Father's watch. "Keep it," he says, handing the watch to him.

"I don't understand," Father says.

Mystery crosses over Saabir's face like a shadow. "You may be a watch maker, but I have all the time in the world."

Father's body stiffens at the remark. His fingers, red with rebellion, rub the shine off the gold watch. "What do you mean?"

Saabir snickers, brushes dust off his shoulder, his eyes as patient as a tree. He turns and walks away, not uttering another word.

Fear splits the corners of my eyes. "You won't let him take us, will you Papa?"

Father hovers over us with peace, like a cool rain in the fall of the year. "Of course not."

Chapter 5

I wake up stiff the next morning. Cold air blows through Father's makeshift tent. Arsen, asleep next to me, snores softly, a tiny arm lying across my chest. I gently roll off the pallet, and tiptoe out of the tent. The morning sun shimmers like a large firefly. I rub my eyes, blink until they adjust to the light.

"Wake your brother," Father says. "We're leaving soon."

"What about breakfast?"

"They're not allowing us any."

"It's because you disrespected that man…Saabir," Mrs. Badalian says.

Father's eyes flash with anger. "He's not taking my daughter".

"I don't think she means it like that," Mother says, resting a hand on his forearm.

"No," Mrs. Badalian says. "I don't. But you were very forceful with him."

Father's head droops. "Nothing can be done about it now."

"Every male ten-years-old and up this way!" a police soldier, waving his hand, orders.

The crowd hums with nervous whispers.

"What for?" a man asks, palms out in front of him as if at prayer.

"Because I said so," the police soldier says, shoving the man forward. "Get moving."

"Let go of my son!" a woman demands, her words shaking with fear.

Another police soldier hooks a meaty hand around Father's elbow. He glances in the back of the wagon. When he returns his gaze at Father, he says, "You and your sons come with me." Arsen cowers behind me. Mrs. Badalian and Lori latch arms, stiff with fear.

"These boys belong to me," the old woman says, "and they're under ten."

The police soldier scrunches up his face, but before he can respond, Mother grabs hold of Father. "No," she says, pulling at his arm. She leans across his lap, points her finger at the police soldier like a teacher scolding a pupil. "No one is getting off this wagon until you tell us what's happening."

"I will…" the police soldier begins.

"Wait a minute," a man says, breaking from line. A pistol flashes in his hand. He fires the weapon before the police soldier can react. A spray of blood paints the air above the police soldier's head with large red dots.

"Let's go!" another man shouts, waving his arm forward. Dozens of men rip stitches from their coats, removing guns and knives hidden within. Our horse bolts across the field in a panic, following a trail of gun smoke stretching cruelly in the morning heat. Earsplitting metal flies in all directions.

"Woah!" Father yells, jerking the reins against his chest. The rest of us bounce around in the wagon—up and down, up and down—holding on to each other, an arm, a leg, anything to keep us from tumbling out. Then I see the horse's head explode in a pink mist. The wagon, unable to stop, crashes into the dead horse. The sound of wood and steel slamming into the animal's corpse muffles our screams.

I wake up underneath the wagon. My eyes blink with terror. The sound of footsteps grows closer. Gunshots mix with distant screams and shouts, and high-pitched cries of children. "Arsen!" I shout, my breath heavy with panic, my hands searching like a bird for seed in the warm grass. "Where is everyone!"

"Is that you, sweetheart?" Father asks, out of breath. He stretches his arm in after me. "Arsen is here. Mama, too. We're all here. Come on. We need to go."

I'm halfway out from under the wagon when I hear a police soldier shout, "Halt!" He rides up on his horse, pistol drawn, and shoots the old woman in the face. The blast is so near the sound of it knocks my shoulders against my jaws. He fires a second time. I feel Arsen's grip slip away. "Valia," he says, his eyes wide, color draining from his face, the center of his chest blooming red.

"Arsen! No!" I scream.

Mother falls to her knees, mouth open, hands and head up to the sky in violent lamentation. Lori and her mother prop themselves against the dead horse, frozen where they sit, foreheads pasty with sweat, eyes dull like vacant ovens. The two boys gently shake their grandmother's body as if trying to wake her.

"No!" Father yells. He drags the police soldier off his horse. His hammer-like fists slam into the man's face. "You killed my son! Why? He was just a boy!" Police soldiers gather around to cheer on their comrade. "Get him!" one yells. "Don't let that Armenian swine win!" shouts another. The police soldier's meaty hand finds an opening and slams Father hard in the jaw. Father staggers like a dead tree in the wind, falling hard, kicking up a cloud of dust. A string of red spit drips from his lips. The police soldier jumps to his feet with a sturdy grunt and pulls a knife.

"Yea!" his comrades shout. "Put an end to that Armenian trash!"

"Papa!" I cry. A surprise rush of courage burns through my legs. I kick the police soldier in the shin, but it does little good, his boots so thick it feels like kicking a snake's ruthless muscles. He grabs me by the hair, snarls, and draws his knife hand back.

"Let the girl be, Çetin!" a voice shouts. It's Saabir, riding up on a large, black horse. "Get the rest of these brutes under control!"

I look and listen all around me. The fighting is over. The smoke rolls up into the sky, revealing dozens of deportees soaking the grass with their blood; a suit of hearts scattered by the wind. Mother rocks back and forth, still holding Arsen's limp body in her unsteady arms. A short distance away, police soldiers group survivors into two large circles, separating the men from the women.

"She's a nuisance, Captain," the police soldier says, gripping my hair tighter.

Saabir slides off the large animal. "That one's mine," Saabir says, unlatching his holster. "Now let her go."

Çetin releases me and backs away. "Yes, sir."

"You can have her if you like," Saabir says, nodding toward Lori.

"Me, sir? B-b-b-but I'm a-a-a-already married."

Father presses his hands to the ground, shifts his feet to stand. Çetin kicks him hard in the ribs. Father topples over holding his stomach, curls up in a ball. "Stay put. Armenian scum."

"Leave him alone!" I demand. I swing at Çetin, but Saabir catches me by the arm, throws me to the ground, and presses his knee firm against my back.

"See what I mean," Cetin says.

Saabir smiles. "Actually, take the girl and her mother."

"And the two boys?"

Saabir smirks. "I have no use for them."

Pleasure escapes Çetin's face. He brushes the dust from his uniform. A wicked smiled stretch across his grimy face.

"Please, take me only," Mrs. Badalian says. She holds her hands up, and steps in front of Lori. "Let my daughter stay here."

Çetin stands over the two boys and fires his pistol into their heads. Their bodies fold across the old woman's body like two wet blankets. "Not another word." He forces Mrs. Badalian against the wagon and presses his knife against her chest. Buttons pop loose. He sheaths the knife. Starting at her shoulders, he rips the blouse from her body. Her breasts sag like two dried prunes. He cups one in his hand, presses his lips to her miserable neck. "Get moving, or it will be worse for your daughter."

Lori looks at me. She is shaking with icy terror.

I close my eyes. A sharp pain burns behind them. When I open them, Lori and her mother are gone.

"Bring them over here," Saabir orders. Two large hands pick Father up by his collar. Two more sets of hands pry Mother from Arsen's body. Saabir grips me behind the neck and pushes me forward.

We arrive at two circles. The women sit in the dirt with their legs crossed, their faces chewed up with grief as they watch the police soldiers search their husbands and sons down to their underwear and force them on their bellies.

Saabir hands me over to one of his men. He points his pistol at Father and Mother. "On your knees."

"Let them go!" I scream, trying to kick myself free, but thick arms squeeze the breath from me. My throat and lungs burn. Sharp cramps run down my legs. "Shut up!" the police soldier yells, smacking the back of my head. He places a dirty hand over my mouth.

"Leave her be!" Father yells.

Saabir arches his arrogant brow. "I told you that I'm a patient man." He smiles. "All the time in the world." Without hesitating, he shoots Father and Mother in the face. I feel a sharp pain in the back of my head.

The last thing I remember is Mother's surrendering eyes staring back at me.

It's evening when I awake. A large knot on the back of my head throbs. The moon shines an eerie light on the dead. Large pyres burn. Police soldiers toss corpses on the fire. No time to mourn. The wind twists the fire into threatening shapes. A restless gray light flickers above the trees until clouds blow in and cover the moon. A soft rain falls. My tongue crawls out of my mouth like an impatient worm. My thirst satisfied, I nibble on a stub of dry bread, listen to the burning wagons hiss and pop until the flames take their last fading breaths. My thoughts run wild with the fateful road ahead.

"Get up!" the police soldiers yell. They strip us of our clothes, force us to march naked. We are now only a few dozen women and teenaged girls marching in the rain. The air smells of death and wet rocks. Steam billows from piles of charred wood. Flies hover around smoldering corpses as they search for cool spots to lay their eggs. Frayed clothing and underwear lay scattered on the road, along with torn pieces of paper, and frayed Bibles. "Lori! Mrs. Badalian!" I cry, but they do not answer me.

"Shut up!" a familiar voice says. It's Saabir. "They're gone." He swats my head. His horse bumps against me, its stiff muscles unforgiving. Mucus shines from the animal's large black nose. I inhale a rush of stale breath, fall and cut my knee on a sharp rock. Strong hands jerk me up. We keep walking. Police soldiers toe fresh corpses. One of them removes a gold coin from a child's gaping mouth. It reminds me of the coin Yazmin gave me. 'Best you swallow it,' she said. But I cannot discern the advantage of possessing a gold coin, especially one lodged in my stomach. Just another trick from a heartless Muslim.

We reach Ceyhan on our third day on the road from Adana to Deir ez-Zor. Someone says the police soldiers are marching us in circles. What does it matter? I ask myself. My future is no longer attending university. I am in the desert. I am walking towards death. What keeps me marching towards such a future isn't acceptance, or even absurdity, but the gold coin inside my body. Its purpose continues to entertain my curiosity. What does it mean? Why did Yasmin give it to me? Is it a trick? Will the gold coin rest in my stomach forever as a sign of lost hope? Or is it perhaps only stored hope that will eventually buy my freedom? Will it bring me back home? Is it even safe to return home? Why would she, a Muslim, help me? I march to find answers, but for how long can I march. I face death ahead.

We loop around the city. The once rocky countryside turns flat with patches of shrubs and desert grass. This new road leads us to a poppy field nestled deep in a wide valley. The mountains, like a large set of crooked teeth, surround a small village. It feels as though we are marching inside a huge mouth. The deep breaths of the valley floor change the air considerably here, no longer dry and harsh, but sweet and cool.

An hour or so later, we meet a small troupe of mounted police soldiers on the other side of the city. One hundred or so deportees, tightly bound together with thick ropes, walk among them. The exception is a frail, bare chested woman, breasts like old wineskins, sitting in the middle of the road, and nursing a baby. Everyone ignores her, everyone but Saabir.

"Get off the road, stupid wench!" Saabir yells. The woman doesn't budge, not appearing to be obstinate or careless, but deeply attentive caring for her child.

"Stop!" Saabir orders us, throwing up an arm. He gallops ahead, waving and calling to the police soldiers from the opposite group. I'm glad for the break. I have never walked this far in my life. My legs tremble from exhaustion. A woman standing next to me looks at me with a dull gaze and collapses. A police soldier rushes up to her and jams a bayonet into her side. My heart feels like a heavy weight pounding in my chest. I slap my legs awake, rub my lower back, and try to stretch my pain away. I feel the police soldier standing behind me, waiting for me to fall.

Two police soldiers return with Saabir.

"She yours?" Saabir asks, pointing at the woman sitting in the middle of the road.

"You can have her if you want," the bigger one says. He's broad-shouldered and dressed in a potato-colored uniform with a dark green collar and single stripes on either arm. "Name's Yousef." He nods at the smaller one. "This here's Talik." He is slender and flat-nosed. He is sporting a wiry mountain man gaze, a tan wet weather cap, and a simple tunic to match.

"Saabir." He reins his horse. The animal stomps the ground. Dirt and mud spatter the woman's face and body. "Get up," he orders, but the woman doesn't budge. She pulls the child from her breast, and begins gently shaking it to sleep.

"Get up!" Talik yells. He climbs off his horse, and jerks the baby out of her arms, breaking the woman's state of motherly engagement. "No!" the woman screams. "Please give him back!"

"Catch," Talik says. He tosses the child to Yousef. The air bursts with the child's screams. The woman keeps shouting. Saabir pulls his gun, leans off his horse, and shoots the woman in the temple. My body jumps. I press my hands to my ears as I watch her frail body…I'll never forget it…bounce once, then quiver in a motion a headless snake makes a few seconds before dying. The three men look at her indifferently. Talik unshoulders his rifle, affixes bayonet. "Toss him back," he says, gesturing at the baby. Yousef flings the baby high in the air. Talik's bayonet silences the child's cries. My damp eyes burn from the sunlight. A tear escapes down my cheek. Despair blisters my aching chest. All I can think about is my parents, my little brother wrapped in Mother's shocked arms, Father's bleak eyes looking at me.

"Where are you headed?" Yousef asks, his tone casual, the way men talk about the weather or a new harvest.

"South," Saabir says.

"Taking the train from Osmaniye to Aleppo?"

"That's right."

"You can join us as far as Osmaniye," Talik says.

Saabir shifts in his seat. The leather saddle squeaks from his weight. He looks at us, then gazes at the mountains. A thin line of clouds hovers at the peaks. The smell of rain lingers in the air. "What are your orders?"

"To head farther south…Damascus," Talik says. "We are to assist building fortifications."

Saabir smiles. "These women couldn't build a sandpit in the desert."

"The prettier ones will be house servants to the officers," Yousef says, shoving a teasing elbow into Talik's side. "Why don't you come with us to Damascus?" He retrieves a canteen hanging from his waist and takes a sip. "Besides, we won't have to worry about the Kurds if we stay together. Strength in numbers as they say."

"We've had no problems with Kurds," Saabir says.

"You will," Yousef says, pointing at me. "I hear girls like this are in high demand." He laughs.

"I know," Saabir says. "They pay top price in Aleppo. Or perhaps I'll keep her for myself. Plenty of work for her to do in Deir ez-Zor."

"Deir ez-Zor, you say," Yousef says.

"Something the matter?" Saabir asks.

"We hear it's nothing but a death trap," Yousef says. "The Yeneze are everywhere down there. And even if you do make it, the accommodations are, shall we say, something to be desired."

"Our mission is Deir ez-Zor," Saabir says, an arrogant, skeptical tone to his voice. "I am not concerned with a bunch of bandits. Besides, why would Talaat Pasa send us on a pointless mission?"

"I don't know," Yousef says. "I'm only repeating what we've heard." He looks in the direction we are heading. "The Yeneze are a ruthless bunch. Don't underestimate them."

I lower my head and crack a hopeful smile. I can buy myself with the coin inside me. But it still doesn't explain why Yasmin helped me. Perhaps Artush persuaded her. That would make sense. Artush would have done anything to keep me in Adana. A Turk helping an Armenian is unheard of, and a Muslim helping a Christian. Or is it? My Father often spoke kindly of the Turkish executives visiting his shop. They sometimes ate dinner at our home. There are good and bad among all people. Where are the good Turks now? Where were they when Father needed them the most? I need to go home. Home will give me answers. Will Saabir accept the coin if I were to offer it to him? Can I trust he will let me go? What about the Yeneze? Is it true what Yousef says about them?

"That is *if* you make it to Aleppo," Talik says.

Saabir shrugs. "We'll be fine on our own." He swings his horse around and waves his men forward. "Let's go."

We walk for hours in the boiling sun. My leg muscles twitch with uncertainty and dread. We walk through a village with piles of dead people and animals, ghostly heaps of them hiding under the tall grass. I notice a young girl with a doll clutched in her hand. A few yards from the girl something blue lay across a sheepfold. I take a closer look and soon realize the blue figure is a woman, her body backwards, her open mouth packed with flies. Hundreds more bodies, lying on the ground in strange positions, have holes punched in their chests. We pass dead sheep, slain where they grazed. Dead mules and horses and villagers lay dead together. A brood of bloody and lifeless chickens lay in their torn feathers. There are homes with collapsed roofs, broken fences and gardens with hundreds of rotting potato plants. I yank a potato out of the ground and stuff it in my mouth. My lips pucker. I spit the potato out, then suck on my arm to get rid of the wet, sour taste. Where is God? What have we done to deserve His abandonment?

I beg for the villager's clothes.

"What will you give me in return?" Saabir asks.

The stubborn coin rests inside me. "I have nothing," I say. "Please, allow me, all of us, this comfort."

"Take them," Saabir says. He grins. "We'll settle this later."

The police soldiers laugh at us as we clumsily remove dresses from dead girls. Yousef allows his group to join us. Once we are fully clothed, we continue walking. We walk for hours. Thirsty, we suck the sweat off our clothes as we walk.

We reach the Ceyhan Nehri River late in the afternoon. The sun inches its way toward the back of the mountains. We are grateful for the cooler weather. A small stone bridge stretches across the water. Dozens of bloated bodies beneath the bridge float south where the current is strong. Sharp rocks and splinters from tree stumps snag a few corpses in the shallows. Bodies turn over on their stomachs. Large black crows scatter, screeching and squawking in the tops of oak trees. Some of the fearless birds ignore us. Beaks jam into rotten flesh. My stomach churns. I vomit what little food I have left in my fragile stomach.

"Kurds," Yousef says, shrugging.

Saabir clears his throat of phlegm, purses his lips and spits. "Let's cross."

I vomit again.

"Take some water." Saabir says, holding a water bag in front of me. When I reach for it, Saabir slaps my hand away. "Stupid girl, drink from the river." He yells to the others, "Drink from the river!"

We push the blood away and drink. The water has a salty and iron taste to it. The girl drinking beside me catches my attention. Her fingers are grubby like a potato farmer. Her feet are larger than any I have ever seen on a girl. No one, not even the police soldiers, seem to pay her much attention. It's as if she has some contagion swimming in her blood. When the girl sees me staring at her, she averts her eyes.

Chapter 6

We arrive at the Osmaniye train depot the following day. Ahead of us is a much larger group of deportees, around five hundred, coming from the north. I think it strange that none of them seem the least bit worried. Instead they appear tired, the way I remember mother looking after a day of washing clothes and sweeping floors. I soon realize distance was misleading, up close they look far worse than we do. Women, both young and old, walk hunched over holding their stomachs. Lice nest in their hair. Pain and misery cloud their eyes. They relieve themselves as they walk. Flies stick to their naked bodies. One woman looks at me with eyes that resemble flooded caverns: deep, dark, and empty. The left side of her face has swelled to the size of a small pomegranate. Deep scratches cover her neck. Her left hand is missing a finger. She opens her mouth to speak, but what comes out is nothing but a cough of stale, dusty air. The sour smell of defecation hovers in the air. I am nauseous from the stench of it. I know I will look like her soon enough. I look up to the sky with upraised hands. Where is God in all this madness? I ask myself again. I pick up a sharp rock, and press it to my wrist without thinking, desperate for a distraction.

"Get moving!" a police soldier shouts. He pushes me toward a cattle car. The force knocks the rock from my hand. A red dot of blood blooms from my wrist. The sight of it brings me to my senses. I remember the gold coin. I whisper to myself: Suicide is a sin. I must do everything I can to survive.

Each car has large wooden doors and two barred windows no bigger than my hand. A man in a business suit with a crumpled face holds a ledger in one hand and a pencil in the other, counts us off as we enter the car. Once everyone is in, he nods at a police soldier who then proceeds to shut the door behind us.

The car is smelly and crowded inside. The thick air makes it difficult to breathe. I cough, put my mouth against a hole in the door and sift small amounts of fresh air.

"Get off my foot," a voice whispers angrily.

I turn and recognize the masculine looking girl I had seen at the river.

"Sorry," I say. "I'm Valia. What's your name?"

Someone yells. Everyone shifts. The girl stumbles into me, and my hand brushes across her chest. "You're a boy," I whisper, my eyes wide.

"Quiet," he hisses. "Do you want me to be killed?"

"Of course not. Sorry."

"Name's Haik," the boy says. He looks around with cautious eyes, then hands me a piece of bread. I quickly shove it in my mouth.

"Is there more?" I ask.

"A little, but we should save it for later."

I wipe my brow. "Any water?"

"Afraid not."

"How do they expect us to stay in here?" I ask. "If they're going to kill us, then why not just go ahead and get it over with?"

"Who understands the logic of a Turk?"

"I suppose no one."

An hour or more passes. The heat becomes unbearable.

"We need water!" a man calls. He sticks his arms through the window, waves. I look through the hole in the door, see a police soldier dragging a hose toward us, laughing and waving as he does so.

"A cruel thing to do," one of his comrades says, "giving them hope."

The police soldier with the hose smiles. The water hits our car. The hot wood spits steam. I open my mouth and catch a few drops of warm water before the police soldier moves to the next car.

The screams and shouts for more water continue long after he finishes. We bang on the walls. "Let us out!" we shout. We do this for several minutes. Then there is a gunshot. The bullet pings against the metal bars of the small window, and slams into a girl's head, a hole now where an eye had been. A bloody tongue hangs out of her open mouth. The banging stops. We stand still in the blistering silence.

Another hour or so passes, then the people in the cattle car next to us begin screaming and banging on the walls. "Stop that," someone from our car says. "You're going to make them angry." The banging and the shouting persist. I hear boots thumping the ground, metal clanking, a cattle door opening. I peek through the hole and see a police soldier dragging a girl by the hair. She has short, scrawny arms and a large nose and eyes so far apart she looks like abnormal prey animal. The police soldier pushes the girl to her knees, aims a pistol at her head and fires. The sound of the gunshot ricochets off the train and thunders into my ears. The girl's body jerks about frantically before lying fixed to the ground. I clasp my shaking hands to my ears, open my mouth to scream, but nothing comes out. Then I realize Haik has a hand over my mouth and an arm around me. "I'm here," he says, "I'm here." He keeps repeating this until my breathing slows down and my hands stop shaking.

Evening comes. I watch the moon through the hole in the door. My shoulders shake with heavy sobs. The wind from the train pricks at my eyes. I squint from the pain. My stomach churns with hunger. The thick stale air forces a cough. I scratch out a piece of wood and put it in my mouth. "I'm so hungry," I say.

"We all are child," a woman jeers. "Be quiet, unless you want to suffer the same fate as the girl this morning.

"Don't mind her," Haik mutters. "She's just an old woman."

"I heard that."

"Hush," another woman snaps. "Someone's coming."

Cracks in the cattle car blink with moonlight as a police soldier passes by. He stops in front of the dead girl lying on the ground with a bullet in her head. He toes her shoulder. He lifts her skirt and digs around the filth with a knife. "Stupid whore," he says. He flips her over and inspects between her legs.

"He's looking for gold," Haik says. "Some of the girls are known to swallow it." He pauses. "Or hide it…. somewhere else."

I think of the coin again Yasmin gave me. "I know," I say. "But do you know why?"

"To buy their freedom, so I've heard."

My assumption had been correct. But why Yasmin would want me to buy my freedom makes no sense. She had said herself I'll die in the desert. I close my eyes. My memory swells with the blue handkerchief left hanging on the Wishing Tree at home. The hopeful handkerchief is all I have left to hold on to. I hold my aching stomach and pray that I will soon discharge the gold coin. How foolish of me wanting to kill myself. Now I'm determined to purchase my freedom more than ever.

The train moves forward. Wheels rub against the tracks. The train's whistle blows so loud it makes my head hurt.

We pass through the city of Osmaniye and its surrounding villages. The hole in the door continues to give me a clear perspective: smoldering houses and barns. Charred corpses scatter the potato fields in strange postures. Badly burned hands reach for the sky. Bodies jammed on fence posts. A dead mother and child stuck together against a tree as though they are resting.

I feel a tap on my shoulder. I jerk around to find Haik looking at me.

"Sorry," he says. "I didn't mean to startle you. "Here, this is the last of it." He jams a piece of bread in my hand.

"Thank you," I say.

The train dawdles down the tracks two more days before arriving in Aleppo. The pain in my side won't go away. I'll surely die if this coin does not leave my body. Perhaps that's what Yasmin had planned all along?

It is late in the afternoon. The train hisses and steams, screeching to a stop. The door opens. We push the dead aside and climb out. We gasp for air and beg for water. A large crowd of men are waiting on the platform, and waving slips of paper in their hands. The shouts mix with separate conversations. The noise is like energetic bees inside a hive.

"Move!" a police soldier shouts at us. We shamble toward a cluster of tents resting in an adjacent field. I look toward what I believe to be the city center. A mosque rises above the city like a large eye.

"It's beautiful," Haik says.

"How a magnificent building can represent such evil is baffling," I say.

Haik takes my hand. "Come on." Girls, children, and old women cry and sniff with exhaustion.

"Old women and children here, girls between twelve and eighteen here," a police soldier orders when we arrive at the tents. Two police soldiers grab Haik and me and toss us into an empty tent that smells of old cognac barrels and sweat. Screams from outside leak through thin, tent walls, but I dare not look.

"What's happening?" Haik asks.

"I'm not sure," I say.

"What do we do?"

"I don't know." I put my finger to my mouth. "Before they hear you," I whisper.

A police soldier brings Haik and me a small bucket of water, soap, and towels that evening. He sets an oil lamp by the bucket. The large rug beneath us shakes its red and blue colors out of tremoring shadows.

"Bathe!" the police soldier barks.

"May we have some privacy?" I ask.

The police soldier grunts. "Hurry up." He storms out of the tent.

"I can't remove my clothes," Haik says, his voice shaking with fear.

"I know," I say. "When they come back and check, I'll tell them you're sick. Now turn around."

Haik pokes his head outside. "Maybe I can make a run for it."

"Don't be foolish," I say. "How far do you think you'll get?"

The water feels good on my naked body. I am patting myself dry when the tent flap opens. Saabir steps inside.

"You!" I scream. I cover myself with the towel, backing away from him. "Don't touch me."

Saabir turns to Haik, sniffs. "Why haven't you bathed?"

"She's sick," I say.

"All the more reason." Saabir lifts Haik's chin. Suspicion conquers his eyes. "Can you not speak for yourself? Are you sick?"

Haik coughs, nods his head.

Saabir slaps Haik across the face, which draws a tear. "I said are you sick?"

"Sore throat," I say. "She can't talk."

"That so."

"Why have you brought us here?" I ask.

Saabir keeps his attention on Haik. "Take off your clothes." Girl's voices whimpering from neighboring tents echo in the dark. Haik and I look at each other, and quickly realize Saabir's intentions. Haik leaps to his feet and runs, making it just outside the tent before Saabir grabs him by a leg.

"Don't!" I yell, following them out.

Other police soldiers rush over. "What's happening?" one asks.

"We're about to find out," Saabir says. He nods toward me. "Keep her back." A police soldier grabs hold of me. My body hardens with panic. Cold water from my wet hair drips on my bare shoulders, giving me a chill.

Saabir pulls a knife, rips open Haik's dress, tosses the dress aside, grabs him by the neck, and lifts his naked body up for all to see. "Just as I thought, a boy!" he shouts. Then, without hesitation, he plunges the knife into Haik's neck. Haik's eyes go wide. His mouth gurgles with blood. His limp body falls with a dull thud on the sand. I try to scream, but nothing comes out of my mouth but warm, sour air. Saabir wipes the knife on his leg, returns it to its sheath, then pushes me inside the tent.

I fold my arms, shivering. Goose bumps tingle my skin. "You didn't have to kill him."

"Remove the towel," Saabir says.

I grip the towel. My breath is heavy and tight. "I'm having my period," I lie.

Saabir raises his hand high above me. I tilt my head away like an abused animal, prepare for a slap that never comes. He relaxes his hand, then lowers it to his side. "I've been more than patient," Saabir says, rubbing a hand along the knife. His eyes light up with lust. "If you will not have me willingly, then I have no choice." He rips my towel loose and tosses it to the side. I step backwards until I reach the tent wall. I press one arm to my chest and one hand between my legs.

Saabir smiles. "There is nowhere for you to go."

"Please," my voice quivers, "don't do this."

Saabir lunges at me, and grabs me by the shoulders, his grip strong and shameless. He forces me to the ground, his thick body on top of me, his hands tearing into me like a hungry lion. I scream. He covers my mouth. My lips mash against my teeth. I taste blood. He forces my legs apart and slips a finger inside me. My eyes bite down from the pain. I jerk my head back and forth. His hand is too strong. When he's done, he holds up his finger, its tip glistening with blood. Then he casually wipes it on his pants leg.

"See, I told you," I say.

"A sign of a virgin," Saabir says. "Nothing more."

"Please don't," I say. I cover my breasts with my arms. He pulls them away, buries his head in my neck, and pins my hands behind my head. He unlatches his belt with his other hand, slides his pants to his thighs, and straddles me. My eyes burn with tears. I struggle to free myself, but his weight crushes the breath out of me. "No!" I cry.

"It's my right!" he yells. He flips me on my stomach, pins my arms behind my back, and presses my face against the ground. As he enters me, I moan, choking on my own sweat and tears. Then, with a sudden jolt, he groans with relief, violently pumping his body against me. After several seconds, and panting loudly now, he arches his back in a long spasm, then collapses on top of me. The air is sticky with vinegary sweat. A few minutes pass before he peels his body from mine and walks out. He doesn't say a word. I lie there naked and helpless, my body slick with shame, blood, and hatred.

The following morning, I wake up on my stomach. I don't scream, although I want to. I feel my ribs groan under the strain. My legs quiver like an old woman walking up a staircase without a banister. I dip a rag in the water bucket, wring it like a chicken's neck, and wash the blood from my inner thighs. The cool water prickles my muscles as I gently brush the rag over the tender spots. I shake out my dirty dress. A bolt of pain shoots up my back as I lift the dress over my shoulders. I pick up a small mirror and stare into it. My face creases with frustration, fear, and defeat. I lift my skirt to my waist and squat on the tent floor, I listen to the sounds of the camp—clinking pots, crackling wood—and pray Saabir doesn't come back. When I finish, the gold coin I had swallowed days before shines like hope. I lift up my hands to Saint Blaise and to God. I clean off the coin, and stuff it in my pocket. The corner of my mouth cracks with renewed courage, but my heart also fills with regret. "Haik," I whimper.

Sometime later, I hear commotion coming from the train tracks. I poke my head outside and see dozens of mounted police soldiers a short distance away forcing hundreds of women of various ages and young girls out of camp. The women, naked, thin, and severely sunburned, wail and plead for mercy.

"Come on!" A police soldier jerks me out of the tent and shoves me into a group of girls. We pass the spot where Haik died. I press a hand against the dark patch of dry blood. My heart aches. All I can do is look up at the sky.

"No stopping!" A police soldier shoves me forward. I glare at him, keep moving. My feet stitch a crooked seam down the road. The dead cover the main road into the city. The air is warm, dusty, and stale. I tear off a piece of my dress, press the cloth to my face, and cover my mouth and nose. A dozen or so street cleaners load corpses into a wagon. The bodies are black and swollen with unimaginable proportions. Eyes bulge from sockets. Tongues slither out of open mouths. Another street cleaner further on is scooping up trash and filth and depositing it all in a large wooden wheelbarrow. He peels a dead dog from the warm street and tosses it into the wheelbarrow. The animal's guts are dry, almost ash-like. Its tongue hangs out of its partially eaten-away mouth like a piece of worn cloth. Its eyes glaze white, and one of its feet has been eaten away. I clinch the coin tight, thankful to be alive. Although misery tugs at my heart, I know I'll soon have my freedom.

We march deeper into the city. A small group of children beg in the middle of the street. The police soldiers yell and beat them with clubs. The children scurry out of the streets toward the gutters and sidewalks for protection. Nearby, four elderly women wearing rags and sitting on tattered blankets beg for bread. One of them grabs my arm. "Where are you going?" The woman is blind in one eye and has several missing teeth.

"Deir ez-Zor," I say.

"We hear no one returns from there," she says.

"How do you know this?"

"Accept Islam and repent. Don't make the same mistake we did."

"But yet you live."

"You call this living, child?" The old woman removes a portion of her clothing and reveals a thin, frail body that's not really a body at all, but more like a sack of bones. "Look at us," she says. "The end of our life is days away."

"Keep moving!" It's Saabir. He shoves me forward, smiles. "Thought I lost you."

I narrow my eyes, then return my glance to the old woman. "Repent," she repeats. "There is nothing but death for you in the desert."

"Shut up old hag!" Saabir shouts, arching his arm as if to strike her.

"Go ahead," the old woman says. "I'm already dead."

Saabir spits, wipes his lips with the back of his sleeve. "Move it," he says, shoving me forward, harder this time. We walk for hours in silence. He's so close to me I can smell his stale breath. I frown, trembling, fold my arms heart-shaped against my chest, and tuck my elbows in tight.

"What did that heifer say to you?" he asks.

"Nothing important," I say. I lower my head. Walking faster, I follow the caravan down a narrow alley. A putrid smell singes my nostrils, clings to my mangled clothes.

A boy, naked from the waist down, lies halfway out of a doorway, a skeleton protruding through a thin layer of skin. A rat tears loose small pieces of his shirt for nesting. "Shoo!" I say. I pick up a rock and heave it as fast as I can. The rat scurries away. Lent dangles from its covetous mouth.

"The boy's dead," Saabir says, picking at a thumb nail. "Get going," again he pushes me forward.

We turn down another street. A group of children, propped up against the wall of an abandoned building, look like ghosts. I search for any sign of life—coughs, a rising chest, a twitching leg—but hear and see nothing. Someone tosses out a bucket of rotten vegetables and fruit from a second-floor window. The children twitch alive from the smell, attacking the food, and lick it clean from the dirty street. I turn my head away. Tears burn my eyes. I see my brother in their weedy faces and hollow eyes. I ball my hand up into a mournful, heated fist.

We arrive at the market and find it teeming with all sorts vendors. It seems like a place of refuge compared to the rest of the city. The smell of coffee, fresh bread and meat replace the stink from the alleyways. "Stop here," Saabir orders. We congregate next to a large stucco building. Police soldiers stand guard with intimidating looks. Fingers never move far from their rifle's trigger.

Arabs and Turks move about as if it is an ordinary day, selling their wares, money quickly exchanging hands. An elderly Armenian man goes up to one of them and begs for bread. A police soldier shoves him backward, kicks him, and drags him away by the collar. The incident reminds me of the market in Adana, the old man hassled by Saabir and the man called Mehmet. I wonder about the old man's fate and the fate of my friends and neighbors. I ball my fists, spending my efforts and energy rooting firmly in my memory for all of the horrors I experienced. If by God's grace I manage to survive, I will one day make sure the world knows what happened here.

I watch the sky turn from pink to gold. A voice in a language I have never heard before echoes across the market. It's getting closer. Deportees gather around a train of wagons where four pale-skinned women dressed in long gowns are distributing bread, holding babies, laying hands on the elderly, now only feet away from me.

"Who are they?" I ask a Syrian woman passing by.

"Dominican nuns," the Syrian woman says. She is properly dressed, a woman of sophistication, maybe an educated woman, although her speech dare not give her away.

I study the nuns with fanatical interest. The thinly built one seems to be in charge. Her chiseled face and unwavering eyes exhibit a powerful demeanor. "What language do they speak?" I ask.

"English."

My eyes flash with hope. "Great Britain? America?"

The Syrian woman points to three women dressed in blue caftans. Their hands and forearms reveal dark tattoos. They move about with the reluctance of a drove of sheep walking in a dry field with no place to go. "What does it matter to you?" the Syrian woman asks. "Your fate is in the desert or a harem."

I look at the nuns, then glance at the concubines. Saabir, a good distance away, busies himself in deep conversation with some man in a suit. The crowd grows larger. The guards have lost interest in us. My eyes squint with faith. The nun in charge and I lock eyes. Holding up a piece of bread, she waves me over. I'm so hungry I don't care about the risk of getting caught. Although I know she will not understand me, I say, "Help me. Please Help me."

"It's okay, child," the nun says. "My name is Sister Gertrude. What is yours?"

My eyes widen. "You speak Turkish."

"Of course," Sister Gertrude says. She has the most beautiful and calming green eyes I have ever seen. "I'm an American." She nods toward the other nuns, they smile at me, but continue to pass out bread as they do so. "They are American as well, but they do not yet know your language. Are you Armenian?"

"Yes," I say. "Here, I can pay you." I hold out the gold coin.

"That is unnecessary, child. The bread is free."

"Take me with you."

"Certainly, child."

Saabir approaches with two other police soldiers. "I'll take that," he says, and snatches the coin from my hand. "You've been holding back on me."

"Give it back," I say, my voice brave as I stand next to the American.

"This one belongs to me," Saabir says. "You can have the whores, but the virgins are not to be touched." I manage to jump behind Sister Gertrude before he can grab me.

"It appears she doesn't want to go with you," Sister Gertrude says. She pulls me close to her. "I suggest giving back her coin." I keep silent.

Saabir slips the coin in a front pocket. "Property of the Turkish government. Now hand over the girl."

"No," Sister Gertrude says.

Saabir points his pistol at her. "Now," he says, "before I lose my patience."

A man approaches, broad-shouldered and distinguished looking, and sporting a gray three-piece suit and a trilby hat. Behind him stands a man wearing a crisp military uniform and, with the exception of his eyes, moving rapidly as they scan their surroundings; he's stiff and professional.

"Name's Jesse Davis," the man in the trilby hat says in Turkish. "I'm the American consul here in Aleppo. This is Corporal James Hamilton." The Corporal nods.

"Saabir." He grunts, lowers the pistol, but does not holster it. "I'm Captain in the Turkish police. I've been ordered to escort Armenian residents to Deir ez-Zor." He hands papers to Davis. "You're meddling in government business. "You'll all be arrested if you don't hand over the girl immediately."

Davis reads the papers, then returns them. "What is one girl to you?" Davis asks. "I'm sure the nuns here are more than capable of taking care of her." He says to me, "How old are you, child? Thirteen? Fourteen? No matter," he says before I can answer that I'm fourteen. "What business does the military have with such a girl? She's an orphan, no doubt. The nuns here have been granted permission by your government to take them in."

Saabir takes a step closer. Beads of sweat pop from his arrogant forehead. "I'm not in the habit of asking a second time."

Hamilton steps forward, his hand secured on a holstered pistol. The two police soldiers with Saabir mimic Hamilton's moves.

Davis quickly puts his hand up. "Everyone calm down. Please. We don't want any trouble."

"Then return the girl," Saabir says.

"We have an orphanage not far from here," Sister Gertrude says. "We can take very good care of her." She steps forward. "Do you have other girls? We can take them as well. They'll be safe and far from the war."

"You think you're making a difference, but you're not," Saabir says. "Return the girl or I'll arrest you."

"Can we not negotiate a deal?" Davis asks.

Saabir gestures toward his men. "We clearly outnumber you. It's foolish for you to defend this Armenian girl."

Davis is silent for a moment, then nods. "Do as he says, Sister."

Sister Gertrude pulls me close. "But sir."

"Sister Gertrude, please."

"Negotiating with a woman," Saabir scoffs. "No wonder your country is weak." He pushes Sister Gertrude aside and jerks me away. I shake my hands, hoping to stop them from trembling. "Go back home," Saabir says. "Don't concern yourself with our affairs."

Chapter 7

I stop counting the days. Someone says we are in Ar-Raqqah. The police soldiers tell us nothing. Our caravan has grown in the thousands. I think its September. The sun burns bright in the sky. My skin sticks to my bones. Shutters cover the windows on every house. Unattended clothes hang on the lines. Where is everyone? I know they're dead. Everyone is dead. I can smell them.

Saabir kicks in the front door of a house. It lies there, in shambles. Weeds smother the covered porch. A bird's nest, abandoned long ago, rests in a corner. Every window is broken. Bullet holes litter the outside walls. "Go in," he says.

The house is cool and smells of porridge. The sun no longer stings my face.

The walls and doors need fresh paint. The living room, empty of furniture, entertains empty beer bottles that are scattered on the floor like casualties of war. Bits of paper and moldy clothes cover the stairwell that leads to a dark hallway. In the kitchen, cabinet doors have been torn away. Broken dishes lie on the countertop and floor. A dead cat lies in the sink, giving off a raw musty smell.

"Are we staying here?" I ask.

Saabir steps inside the house, closes the door behind him, and smiles.

"Please, leave me be," I say, taking a step back.

"We are celebrating Ramadan now. Lying with a woman is forbidden."

"Why didn't you sell me to the American?"

"It's no matter now."

"But why?"

"I have the right to change my mind. Now shut up."

"May I have my coin?"

"No."

"May I have some water?"

Saabir strikes me hard in the face. My eyes water. My face burns. I shrink back. I'm afraid he might hit me again. My fear confers a look of malicious satisfaction across his face.

"No!" he says. He ties me to the stairwell, then steps over me, walking into the living room, he sits on the sofa. He places a large red cloth on the table in front of him, pulls out his pistol, and sets it on the cloth. From his bag, he takes out a small box. He removes a black brush from the box and rams it down the pistol barrel. After he finishes cleaning his weapon, he retrieves a bottle of vodka and a small glass.

He swallows multiple shots. "You want?" he asks, and gently shakes the bottle. He raises his and smiles like a crazy man.

I nod.

Saabir slits his eyes. "Stupid girl. Get some sleep. We leave tomorrow. Early."

I lie awake much of the night and listen to his immoral snores.

We arrive at the banks of the Euphrates River days later. Saabir rides beside me. I often catch him staring at me. This is not unusual behavior for him, but in no way is it any less unsettling to my wellbeing. I glare back at him and purse my lips. I want to spit in his face. But prudence encourages patience. I lower my head and keep walking forward. I imagine him raping me again when Ramadan ends. I imagine killing him in his sleep.

My body shakes with pain. My bare feet are rubbed raw. My head itches from the dirt and lice. Bleeding sores ooze from my arms and legs. The weather is cool and cloudy. The wind blows strong across the river. Stiff corpses litter the river and the water flows murky and unstable. Little pools form in the shallow parts where the dead have gathered against the rocks and large tree branches. We pull clothes off the dead and forage for seeds from rotten logs and animal dung. A crow pecks at a dead donkey's eye socket. I shoo the crow away, and then dig into the carcass to warm my hands with its blood. A woman sits next to a deep hole with her dead child tucked into a ball beside her. A police soldier hacks her to death with an ax. He tosses her and the child into the hole.

The moon rests high and bright in the sky, casting an eerie purplish light on the dead.

We reach a small village. Dozens of Turkish women approach us. They offer us bread and water. One of the women grabs hold of me. "The desert is filled with the Yeneze," she whispers. "Don't go any farther." Her grip is friendly. So are her eyes. I smile weakly, dip my finger in the bowl of water, massage my cracked lips. A slight burn. A taste of metal. I drink until I drain the bowl. I stuff a piece of bread in my mouth and chew it slowly.

"I don't understand," I say.

"They are the most despicable of men. You will not survive their wrath."

"The police soldiers will not protect us like they did from the Kurds?"

The woman scoffs. "Silly girl. Look at you. The police soldiers care for no one but themselves. She twists her lips and says, "Besides, the Yeneze are far worse. The soldiers are in danger, too."

"How do you know this?"

"We hear stories."

"I have nowhere to go."

"What is wrong with you?" a second Turkish woman asks.

"What do you mean?"

"You keep scratching yourself."

"Lice," I say.

"Vinegar helps," another says.

"Where am I to get vinegar?"

"Urine works, too," a third says. "Here, take some more water."

"Remember this place," the woman that had grabbed me says. "Meskene."

"Meskene," I repeat. "Why?"

"Our husbands can provide safe passage for you. To Europe." She clears her throat. "What is your name, child?"

"Valia. But I don't want to go to Europe. I want to go home."

"Mine is Belma," the woman says. "There's nothing left of your home."

"How do you know?"

"All Armenian neighborhoods have been destroyed. I'm telling you, child, there is nothing left to go back to."

Deep in my heart, I know what she says is true. It has been weeks since I have thought of home. I can smell roasted lamb in the kitchen. I can see the Wishing Tree with mom's handkerchief dangling courageously on one of its branches. I know now, more than before, it is unlikely I will see my home again. I nod toward the others. "What about them? You can take us all to Europe?"

"Bring as many as you can."

"How do I know you'll keep your promise?"

"You don't." She smiles. "I guess you'll just have to trust me. There is a whole network of us, from Deir el-zor to Aleppo, and farther south, from Jerusalem to Hama on the Orontes River. From there a boat takes you to Musa Dagh."

"I don't understand," I say, fiddling with the buttons on my blouse.

"Look, child. You don't have to understand. We are here to help you. And we have the means to do it, thanks to a few wealthy businessmen."

"You mean Turks."

Belma's eyes bear down harder. "Not all of us are evil. Certainly you know this. You wouldn't have made it this far otherwise."

I lower my head. "Yes, I know."

Belma's eyes light up with remembrance. "And the Americans. They have done wonders for us."

"Do you know a Mr. Davis or Sister Gertrude?"

"Can't say that I do. Who are they?"

"Americans in Aleppo. They tried to help me, but…"

"But what?"

"Saabir wouldn't allow it."

"He must be wanting to keep you for himself, to marry you." Belma narrows her eyes. "Or worse. Does this Saabir take interest in other girls?"

"I don't think so."

"You need to get away from this man as soon as you can," Belma says. "Kill him if you have to," slamming a fist into an open hand. Then she pulls out a pencil, scribbles something down on a small piece of paper. "Once you memorize the name, swallow the paper. If word gets out who this man is, we are all doomed."

"Okay," I say.

I begin to look at the paper, but Belma stops me. Panic attacks her eyes. "No, not now. Quickly, they're coming, put it in your pocket."

Saabir and five other police soldiers gallop up on their horses and dismount. "Get away from them!" Saabir shouts, motioning violently with his arms. One of the police soldiers jams a knife into a girl's neck, the blood spraying like a fountain, the blood warm on my face. Saabir smacks the bread from my hands, kicks me to the ground, and points his pistol at the women. "Go back to your homes!" he says. Then he fires his pistol into the air. Women scatter, disappearing into the darkness. Belma stands her ground. "You have no right to do this."

Saabir aims his pistol at Belma. "Disperse, old hag, before I put a bullet in your head."

Belma looks at me, then walks away, her stern face hiding secrets worth more than gold.

Saabir points the pistol to my head. "You fool." He cocks the hammer and presses the gun barrel to my forehead. I close my eyes and wait. Nothing happens. I open my eyes. Saabir holsters the pistol, smiles arrogantly. "On your knees." I do as he says. He unbuttons his pants and orders his men to do the same. With a loud grunt of relief, they urinate on me. Warm stench wets my hair and burns my eyes. Humiliation hangs over my head like a dark cloud. After they finish, Saabir kicks me in the ribs. Dust and air heave from my throat.

I stare at the ground, afraid to look at him. My side quivers in pain. "That woman you chased off, she said we're all in danger. Just like that man Yousef told you." I close my eyes and wait for another kick. Nothing. Saabir and the other police soldiers laugh. Then without saying another word, they mount their horses and ride away.

I rub my hands in the urine and scrub my head and it seems to provide some relief from the lice. I close my eyes, imagine home, Paris, anywhere but here. When I open my eyes, I look straight ahead toward the desert, toward the home of the Yeneze. My fate is clear if I continue on this path. Exile to Deir ez-Zor means death. I need a plan of escape, even more so now that I lost Yasmin's gold coin. How am I to escape Saabir's vigilant eyes? I pray the Yaneze will kill him. It is the only way I will survive.

Written on the paper is a name I'll never forget: Berkant Hasim. My hands shake as I stuff the paper in my mouth. Can it be true? Yasmin's father is a spy? But certainly, this is not the same man, the father of my old enemy.

The sun comes up bright and strong the next morning and illuminates the fog. Specks of sunlight bounce off the water, and reveals horrible stories of busted wagons, plundered luggage, and scorched bones. I expect to see the Yeneze at any moment, but there is no sign of them. By midafternoon, the sun and dust is my only concern. I suck my lips, try to gather spit, but my mouth is desert dry. The pungent smell of urine irritates my nose and burns my eyes. My lungs fill with dust. I pray for rain and, after a day or two, dark clouds blow over the mountains and the rain comes down in torrents and lasts for hours with no interruption. The road thickens with mud. The police soldiers cannot balance their horses. We stop until the rain blows away. The sun returns and dries the road.

The next day, screaming breaks the silence. Horse hooves slap against the cracked ground. Police soldiers cry, "Yeneze! Yeneze!" They fire their weapons, but the Yeneze are too many in number and we struggle to run. Those who cannot run meet a bayonet or sword.

"We have no quarrel with you!" Saabir yells.

The Yeneze ignore him. They yank girls from their crying mother's arms, sling them atop their horses, and dash away toward the mountains. Dozens more women run toward the river. I follow them, but they are too fast and I am too weak. I crawl to a rock. More shots ring out. I see Saabir. His horse bucks and stands on its hind legs. He falls off his horse, landing hard beside me, but the powerful black animal keeps its balance and runs toward the river.

Saabir grabs me, but lucky for me his grip is weak and I easily pull free. There is a hole the size of a fist in his chest. Blood pours from his mouth. He looks at me with dark eyes. I see nothing but death in them. "I pray you suffer for all eternity," I whisper. Saabir's hand creeps closer. I watch it as it quickly loses strength. Finally, it stops moving. His face rests against the sand. I cautiously put a finger to his nose. Nothing. The air is as still as the night sky. I dig in his front pocket and retrieve my coin in triumph.

My body is sore and heavy. I force myself to run to the river. I jump high and long. The sound of bullets and screams trail behind me. The current takes me under. The cold water clogs my ears, tickles my nose, and burns my eyes. Screams and gunshots reunite with my ears when I surface. Quickly, the water covers me again and the rush of it pushes me into a dead horse. The current takes us away far down the river and spits us out on a narrow beach isolated from the fighting, shouts, and chaos.

I lay there for hours, listening, until there is nothing left but the strange sucking sound of the dead clogging the beach. I fall asleep. A girl's whimpering wakes me. I jump to my feet, walk downstream to where the river forks and forms a small inlet. There I discover three girls soaking rags in a mud hole. Using the rags as teats, they suck out the water. The girls all look to be a year or two older than I, the oldest one perhaps fifteen or sixteen. I pick up a rock and throw it at a mangy dog lingering nearby. The dog yelps and runs off. The three girls jump up and run, too, but I stop them.

"Wait!" I whisper.

They stare at me in silence.

"Is there any more of you?"

"No," one of the girls says, "they're all dead." She points to where the inlet grows narrow A mud flat suffers in the heat beyond.

I adjust my eyes. Dark mounds I recognize as bodies. The stench overruns my nostrils. I hold my stomach and vomit. I will never adjust to the smell of death.

The girl that had spoken walks up to me. "Are you okay?" she asks as she puts her arm around my shoulders.

I embrace her and cry into her neck. She holds me tight until I finish. "We need to go before the Yeneze find us."

I wipe my eyes and point in the direction I had come. "Meskene. There is an elderly woman there, Belma. She can help us. All we have to do is follow the river."

"The Yeneze will be looking for us on the river," the girl says. "We need to go into the desert."

"But we'll die in the desert."

"We'll die for certain if we follow the river."

I pull the gold coin from my pocket. "Maybe we can bargain with this."

"The Yeneze don't bargain," the girl says. "They take."

I return the gold coin to my pocket. "Certainly, someone will help us." I look at the girl doing all the talking. "Where are you from?" I ask.

"Diyarbekir."

"The three of you?"

"Yes."

"Do you have family or friends there? Maybe it's safe to return."

"You speak foolishly," the girl says. She points at the dark bodies in the mudflat. "Everything beyond that point is dead. It's safer this way." She points in the opposite direction.

"It doesn't look safe to me," I say.

"Safer than here."

"What do you think?" I ask the other two girls.

"I agree with Narine," one of them says with a soft voice. Her shoulder-length hair is matted and dirty. The side of her face swollen, and a purplish color inks the skin below her left eye.

"Does it hurt?" I ask.

"What kind of stupid question is that?" Narine asks. "Of course, it does."

"What I mean is…never mind…"

"What?" Narine asks.

"There's no point in arguing," I say. "What's your name?" I ask the injured girl.

"Emma. It's not so bad now." She gestures toward the girl next to her. "This is Diana."

Diana is skinny and a foot shorter than Emma. Her light green eyes are set close to her nose, her hair ink black and frazzled with mud. Her faded dress, torn at the sleeve, appears one size too big. Bug bites scabbed over with a rusty hue cover her bony legs.

"I'm Valia. A pleasure to…"

"Shush!" Narine says. "Did you hear that?"

"Hear what?" I ask.

"Listen. Someone's coming." Narine puts a finger to her mouth. "There," she points. "Behind those shrubs."

But it's too late.

"I thought I heard someone over here," a man says in soft-spoken Arabic. He is thin and old with wide, brown eyes and a toothless grin. "I'm not one of them," he adds, nodding in the direction of where I fled from the Yeneze.

"Do you have any food or water?" Emma asks.

"I can pay you," I say, showing him the gold coin.

Narine glares at me. "Put that away," she says. "We cannot trust him."

He widens his smile. He takes a step closer. "Certainly you can," he says.

"Promise you'll help," I say, desperation piercing my voice.

"Of course."

I hand him the coin.

"Thank you," he says. He places the coin in a small bag hanging around his neck. "I have a wagon just there," he adds, cocking his head across his shoulder. "My village is not far from here."

"If you are not Yeneze, how is it that you're still alive?" Narine asks.

"How is it that you are?" He smiles. "The Yeneze and I are of similar blood, but I assure you I am a peaceful man." He studies us with his wide, brown eyes. "What are your names?"

"What tribe are you from?" I ask.

"I'm a Turkman."

I look for a rock, a stick, anything to defend myself. "But you speak Arabic," I say. I pull a stick from the mud and hold it in front of me. Narine grabs a rock, backs up toward the water. Emma and Diana follow close behind.

The Turkman holds up his hands and says, "No, I'm not one of them, either. A Turk, yes, but my family has lived here in Syria for hundreds of years. He stretches out his arms as if wanting a hug. "The desert has been kind to us."

Satisfied with his answers, we give him our names.

"All beautiful names," he says.

"What is your name?" Narine asks.

"Bashir. Come, there is food and water in the wagon."

When we arrive at the wagon, Bashir motions for us to sit down. "You're safe now. The Yeneze have gone." He gives us each a drink of water and a bit of bread. Then he allows the horse to drink. "An hour and you'll be sleeping in a warm bed," he tells us, rubbing the horse's neck, the animal's head bobbing in appreciation.

Diana scratches at a scab. A trickle of blood traces a thin line down her leg.

"Don't mess with them," Narine says, slapping Diana's hand.

"We'll take care of those bites when we get home," Bashir says. "Don't worry about a thing. My wife will take good care of you."

"What can you tell us about the war?" I ask. "Are the Americans coming to help?"

"What do you know about Americans?" Narine asks.

"I met an American in Adana, a nun," I say.

Narine rolls her eyes.

"Was she pretty?" Emma asks. "I hear Americans are pretty."

"Yes," I say, remembering Sister Gertrude's hopeful smile and green eyes.

Bashir narrows his eyes, points to the sky where a family of buzzards fly in a circle. "I've seen thousands of your people in the desert. Certainly, no Americans. I don't think they're coming to help."

I bite my lip. I want to tell him he's wrong. I want to tell him about Belma, that the Americans are helping. I want to tell him about Berkant Hasim, but something in his voice tells me to keep quiet. Instead, I ask, "Are we near Deir ez-Zor?"

"A day's journey that way," Bashir says, pointing down river. "Is that where you were headed?"

"Yes."

"It's a good thing I found you then. No one returns from there."

"How is it that you know my tongue?" Bashir asks.

Narine gestures toward her friends. "We speak many languages."

"I learned it in school," I say.

"Where are you from?" Bashir asks.

"Adana," I say.

"We're from Diyarbekir," Narine says.

"Your friends don't talk much," Bashir says.

"I'm still hungry," Diana says.

"Relax child," Bashir says. "Plenty of food at home."

"What is the name of your village?" Narine asks.

"Al-Kila," Bashir says.

"Is it nearby?" I ask.

"Yes," Bashir says. "I already told you that." He looks down river. "Let's get going."

We leave the river and travel down a desert road thick with corpses with their eyes gouged out, and their limbs cut off. Boys no older than ten hang from wooden crosses. Their naked bodies resemble burned strings of licorice. Horrid smells drift in the warm air. We wet a rag with water and cover our mouth and nose.

Farther on, we spot twenty or so survivors walking alone. Soggy clothing peels away from their backs. The sun burns high in the sky. The desert provides no protection. "For God's sake," one says, "take us with you. If you leave us here, the Yeneze will murder us."

"There's nothing I can do for you," Bashir says.

"Please help them," Narine says.

"Yes, please," Emma, Diana, and I agree.

"There's too many of them," Bashir says. "I cannot save them all. Who would I choose?"

"You chose us," I say.

"Because you have coin," Narine says. "They don't."

Bashir shrugs. "Then go with them if it makes you feel better," he says.

Narine grips the side of the wagon. She looks at me with an inflexible stare.

"There now, see," Bashir says. He turns his head back toward the road, smacks the horse with a whip, and the horse moves at a trot.

The refugees keep calling.

"What if they carry disease?" I whisper to Narine.

"We can at lease save some of them," Narine says.

"What are you whispering?" Bashir asks.

"Why can't we take in one or two of them?" I say. "Perhaps a child."

"No," Bashir says. "That's final."

My heart slumps with regret. What makes my life better than theirs? Only money?

Chapter 8

We arrive in Al-Kila late in the day. A mud-brick wall surrounds the small village. A tributary stretches its crooked arm from under the wall.

"I'm back," Bashir calls. A large wooden door opens and we ride in. I take a deep breath. Mud-brick homes hug the ground with hope and stability. Each house includes two windows with wooden frames. Curtains, fluttering in a light breeze, shield the windows from the desert sun.

"This is my home," Bashir says. He parks the wagon on the side of the house and pulls the brake. He steps off the wagon, and the wagon squeaks from less weight. "Come," he says, reaching out his hand. He helps us down one at a time.

A young man with hawk-like eyes and a thick neck runs over and says, "Why did you bring them here?"

Bashir shows the man the gold coin I had given him. "That's why. Now go home."

"And what if the Yeneze come?"

"They won't."

"You said we'd be safe here," Narine says.

"You are," Bashir says.

"The old man will say anything for money," the young man says.

"Money helps the whole village, but I'll make sure you don't partake if you feel that strongly about it."

"Money fills your own stomach with food, not ours."

"Away with you!" Bashir yells.

The young man holds up his right arm, revealing a stump. "The Yeneze are unpredictable. They especially do not like it when people steal from them."

"These girls are no one's property," Bashir argues.

"Did you not pass the dead on the way here? Every day the number grows. I go out and tend my goats and every day the Yeneze take one from me as they take girls like these." He looks at us with triviality. "And if you don't abide," the young man raises the stump higher, "this happens."

"I've had no encounters with them," Bashir says.

"You're putting us all at risk," the young man says. "You have their money. Send them away and that will be the end of it."

"Send who on their way?" a woman asks, popping her head out of a window.

"Nothing!" the young man shouts. "Mind your business."

The woman waves a hand in disgust, then disappears inside the house.

"Look who's talking," Bashir says.

More villagers appear from behind doors, wagons, every corner of the village it seems. "What's the shouting about?" a man asks, hobbling on a cane as crooked as his legs. "Who are they?" a woman asks, pointing. "Yes, what did you bring us this time, Bashir?" another woman asks.

"Nothing for you this time, Zora," Bashir confesses.

"My name's Valia," I say, extending my shaky hand. "This is Narine, Emma, and Diana."

"What will you do with four girls?" Zora asks. "Give one to me. I could use the help."

"They should go," the armless man announces.

"Maybe you should go, Onnig," Zora says.

"Bring them out back," a woman's voice says. Her glare settles the matter. Everyone returns to their homes, whispering as they go.

"My wife, Esra," Bashir says.

"Poor creatures," Esra says, motioning us around back. "From the looks of you, you're all covered in lice." She glares at Bashir. "Wait here. I'm sure you'll need a bath, too. If lice get in the house, we'll never get rid of them."

Bashir grunts and sits on the front stoop. Narine, Emma, Diana, and I follow Esra to the back of the house. "Strip off those filthy clothes and stand over there by the water pump," she says. She hands each of us a bar of soap, then pumps water into a bucket. Chickens move about freely and peck at the ground. A pot sitting on top of a fire pit bellows steam with a meaty smell to it. My stomach growls weak with hunger.

"Goat," Esra says.

"It smells delicious," I say.

"It'll be ready soon," Esra says, pumping water into a second bucket. "Where are you from?"

"Adana," I say.

"Diyarbekir," Narine says.

"A great distance. Do you have news of the war?"

"She met an American," Narine says, smirking.

"Really?" Esra asks. "I've heard of these Americans. They are unfriendly people."

"This one was kind," I say, "but…"

"What, child?"

"I don't think they can help us."

"How long have you been in the desert?"

"I don't know," I say. "What month is it?"

"October." Esra smiles. "I forget the day."

"Three months," I say.

"Us, too, maybe longer," Narine says.

"Poor girls," Esra says, wiping her eyes. "Okay, go ahead and wash up while I prepare supper."

"Thank you," we say.

Our bodies produce a humid smell of smoke and burning manure. The water is cold but satisfying. We scrub our faces, arms, and shoulders. By the time we finish, Esra pokes her head out. "Wait a second. I'll bring some towels."

After we dry off, we hang the towels on the screen, and grab our dirty dresses.

"Wait," Esra says. "Pitch those filthy rags in the fire. I have spare garments." She rushes into the house and returns with four sets of white caftans, four blue headscarves, and four pair of slippers.

"You come from a wealthy family," I say.

"Hardly, child. We make them. Your mother didn't teach you such things?"

"No time," I say. "I was studying to be a teacher."

"You can read and write, then. We don't have much use for that here." Esra smiles as if hiding something.

"Would you like me to teach you how to read?" I ask.

"Thank you, child, but…no matter. There are plenty of chores to keep us busy."

"Hurry up woman," Bashir yells.

"Wait your turn!" Esra shouts back. She hands us the caftans, headscarves, and slippers. "He's a good man, really, but not a lot of patience."

We dress quickly. Esra calls for her husband. She pours a fresh bucket of water for him, tosses a bar of soap in the bucket, and hangs a fresh towel on the screen.

"It's about time," Bashir says, growling like a hungry dog.

"Oh, be quiet before I knock you in the head with this pan," Esra says, raising the iron weapon parallel to her shoulder. "Let's go, children."

We remove our slippers and step into a large room. It smells of sweat and tobacco. A dark red carpet with a floral design bleeds across the floor. The center of the room discloses a low wooden table with large red pillows around the table for sitting. The same desert sand color as the outside walls hugs the interior walls as well.

"This way," Esra says.

We follow her across the bleeding carpet, then down a narrow hallway into a smaller room where we find another large carpet, pillows, and bare walls. The sun bursts through a small window. A square wooden table stands in the far corner of the room. On top of the table, a brass oil lamp casts alluring shadows. A clay pitcher of water and bowl rest on the table's lower shelf as if waiting for dirty hands.

"You'll sleep here," Esra says.

"We'll stay here until the war's end?" Narine asks.

"As long as you like," Esra says.

"I'm grateful to you and your husband," I say, "but I'd rather you help me find my way home."

"Perhaps after the war," Esra says. "Then we'll see."

Chapter 9

Eight weeks pass by with the year 1916 upon us. Still no sign of the Yeneze. We learn from passing travelers that the Arabs are growing in force, the Russians knocking at Turkey's border, the Turks retreating to the mountains.

"Perhaps the war will end soon," I say.

"Doubtful," Bashir says.

"Maybe we can return home," I say. Telling him about the secret journey to Europe remains static.

He looks at me with relaxed curiosity. "This is your home."

"I want to go home," Diana says. She sneezes.

"Bless you," I say. "Are you ill?"

"I'm okay."

I touch her forehead. "You have a fever."

"Perhaps a nap," Narine says.

"Finish your chores first," Bashir says. "Chickens can't collect their own eggs."

"I can do them," Narine interjects.

"I'll help," Emma says.

"We all will," I say.

"Bah," Bashir says.

"Where is Esra? She'll know what to do."

"About what?" Bashir asks.

"Diana."

"I'm fine," Diana says.

"Where is she?" I ask again.

"Onnig's," Bashir says. His voice is as quarrelsome as a set of dog's teeth. "She's helping his wife with something…don't know what. She'll be back soon."

Diana wobbles forward and collapses.

"Diana!" I scream. "Quick, go get Esra," I say to Narine. "Emma, help me carry her to the bedroom."

That evening Diana's fever matures with erratic breathing and violent shivers. "My back hurts," she says. We cool her down with wet rags and feed her cold soup. She gains strength after a few hours of this treatment, but the following morning she hacks and coughs to the point I think her guts will come up along with her breakfast. Her eyes roll back in her head, her skin as pale as a corpse.

"When will the doctor arrive?" I ask. "It's been hours since Bashir went to fetch him."

"Maybe something happened," Narine says. "You should have someone go look for him."

"He's been gone longer than this," Esra says, looking out the window. "We must be patient. "They'll be here."

Bashir and the doctor arrive the next morning. The doctor is beanpole tall and just as skinny. A lazy lower lip is slick with spit. He smells like apples.

"She's been this way since late last night," Esra says, patting Diana's forehead with a wet cloth. "Came on all of a sudden, isn't that right girls?"

"Yes," we say.

Diana slaps Esra on the side of her face. Esra loses her balance, crashes to the floor.

"Don't lie to me, Ekrem!" Diana yells. "He's standing right beside you!"

Narine and I help Esra to her feet. "Are you okay?" I ask.

"Yes, I think so," Esra says. She touches her cheek. She moves her jaw in a circle.

"Step back, please," the doctor says.

"Do as he says," Bashir orders.

Then the doctor turns to Bashir. "Hold her down while I take a look."

"Who is Ekrem?" I ask.

"I don't know," Narine says. "She's not making any sense."

"He was her brother," Emma says.

Diana continues talking nonsensically about animals and the forest. She speaks to invisible people. She comes in and out of consciousness several times.

The doctor lifts Diana's shirt. "See these red splotches on her chest. Typhus."

"How do we cure it?" I ask.

"No cure," the doctor says. "Allow her plenty of rest and keep applying cold compresses. Give her anything cold to drink and eat."

"Lice," Esra says.

"Yes," the doctor says, looking around the room.

"I keep a clean house, doctor," Esra says.

"I'm sure you do. These girls are refugees, are they not?"

"Yes," Esra says.

"It is dangerous to keep them here."

"What have you heard?" Esra asks.

"The war moves closer every day."

"Are we infected?" Bashir asks.

"I'd be more concerned about the Yeneze," the doctor says. He looks at Esra. "That is why we were late. They are growing in number. We had to be careful coming here. They are looking for girls like this."

"Are you sure you weren't followed?" Esra asks.

"Yes, I'm sure."

"But…"

"He said he's sure," Bashir says.

"Hush before I belt you one," Esra says with a clenched fist.

Bashir takes off his shirt. "Do I have any of those red marks?"

"No, you're fine," the doctor says.

"Will Diana get better? Narine asks.

"Hard to say," the doctor says.

"You must stay 'til dark," Esra says. "Safer that way."

"Thank you," the doctor says.

Diana's health improves after three weeks. The doctor comes to check on her every other day, depending on the Yeneze's movements. She walks with a limp. Her voice is as quiet as a fly's wings. Narine, Emma, and I continue her chores. Esra prepares a special drink for her every evening.

Onnig learns to accept us. He still keeps to himself, and rarely leaves the village alone. Bashir sometimes helps him tend his goats. Every time I see Onnig, he raises his stump and nods his head. It frightens me and I always avert my eyes.

One morning, as I throw breadcrumbs to the chickens, Esra sits on the back porch making a carpet. She weaves white yarn around a horizontal loom. She expertly hooks each strand together and forms several tight wraps. She tried to teach me once, but I could never master the skill. My fingers are meant for writing poetry, not making clothes. Everyone else is sleeping. The village is quiet. The sky burns a clear blue. A slight breeze grazes my cheeks. Tilting my face toward the morning sun, I close my eyes. The light covers me like a warm blanket.

"It's a beautiful day," Esra says.

"Yes," I say. "Shall I wake the others for breakfast?"

"I'll wake them. You go set the table. How is Diana doing? Is she sleeping well?"

"Yes, thanks to you. The drink is helping."

"Not me, child, the doctor taught me how to make it. Now, off with you," she says, smiles, "before the bread gets cold."

We eat quietly.

"Do not go outside the village for a few days," Bashir says, breaking the silence.

"What happened?" Esra asks.

"There have been reports of Yeneze and police soldiers fighting nearby," Bashir says, mopping up the rest of his yogurt with a piece of bread. "The Arab army is pushing from the south as well and refugees are multiplying." He stiffens, wipes his nose. "It seems the war is getting closer to us after all, as the doctor told us." He gently claws at the table with his left index finger. "But there's nothing to worry about."

I grow concerned. That's what Father had told us. "How can you be sure?" I ask.

"Don't let Onnig worry you," Bashir says. "I know what he's been doing, raising that ridiculous stump of his." He narrows his eyes. "I've seen him do it several times. Keep away from him," he adds, shaking his finger.

"I know what the Yeneze can do," I say. I tear off a piece of bread and dip it in the yogurt.

"As do I," Bashir says. "We're safe."

"What if we're not?" Narine asks.

Diana keeps quiet, focuses on her bowl of yogurt.

"You need to take us to Meskene," I say without thinking.

Curiosity dances across Bashir's wind-chapped face. "What's in Meskene?"

"Someone who can help us," I say.

Bashir shrugs. "Leave if you want. Take your chances in the desert."

Emma cringes. "You would force us into the desert?"

"You can come with us, both of you," I say, squeezing Esra's hand.

"No need for that," Esra says, her bright eyes blinking at me. "If Bashir says we're safe, then we're safe. Certainly the war won't last much longer."

"But…" I say.

"No harm will come to us," Bashir interrupts. "Enough talk about Meskene."

Chapter 10

At night, the open desert is an arena of noise. Gunshots in close proximity force me to imagine soldiers fighting outside my window. I wake up to the sun and the silence of the morning. Light inches its way across rooftops and slips behind corners.

Screams tear apart the silence as I uncover the fire pit. Dozens of Yeneze with broad-shoulders and thick beards wield their swords in the cool air. Horses, bearing white, fierce teeth, breath heavy as they run.

"We know you're hiding girls," a voice shouts. "Turn them over and no more harm will come to you."

I peep out the window. A Yeneze soldier, a gold coin in his hand, stands next to one of the refugees we had abandoned earlier.

I cover my mouth. They've found us.

"Even their own people betray them," he shouts at his men. Then he shoots the refugee in the head.

I jump away from the window. Tears race down my face. There is no time to mourn. I force myself up, and search every room in the house. "Esra! Narine! Emma! Diana!" I call.

"They're here!" Onnig's voice crashes through the front door. I jump behind a sofa. A Yeneze soldier pokes his head in, pivoting a rifle left and right. He looks behind the door.

Onnig follows behind him. "I know they're here," he says. "I heard one of them calling her friends."

I crawl outside and curl up behind a wagon.

Screams escalate from inside the house moments later.

"See, I told you," Onnig says.

"Get off me," Emma shouts, fear ingesting her words. I grab the ax that had been propped against the wagon. There is an explosion. Black smoke pours from the windows. Flames scratch at the door like angry cats. My hand fights the heat to my face as I look inside the house. The strength of the fire tosses me backward. The fire licks its way outside. Windows, like eyes, burst with urgency. A frightened goat with a burning back leaves behind a line of fire as it darts away.

I yank on the pump, lower my head into the cool water, and splash my face. My eyes steam with rage and fear.

"You!" Onnig says, smothering a small flame sizzling his stump, his face black with smoke.

"Stay where you are," I say, lifting the ax.

He lunges at me, and cracks a hard slap across my cheek. I feel the sudden sting. The ax stays firm in my hands as I tumble backward. When he whirls at me again, I swing the ax. The blade catches him on the collarbone. His screams follow me like a herd of panicky cows as I run toward the front gate. A burning wagon blocks my path. Bashir lies face down on the ground, his eyes wide open. Esra, lying beside him and barely alive, holds her stomach, the side of her body a dark red.

"Go child!" she moans, waving a limp hand. As I step closer, a Yeneze man appears, levels a pistol at her head, and fires. I scream. Having nowhere else to go, I disappear to the back of the house before his watchful eyes catch me. Onnig lays there. The ax quietly takes his final breaths. I have just killed a man. I reflect on the power it gives me, the freedom it gives me, but I do not feel any better for it. I feel relieved, despite the remorse burying itself deep in my heart. My chest aches with each breath I take. I step around him, careful not to look at his lifeless eyes. I check his pockets and find two silver coins. Then I stuff myself in a bulky laundry basket. Screams of war penetrate the basket's walls. I plug my ears with my fingers. The fighting grows more violent. Then, without warning, the guns fall silent. The Yeneze holler in guttural Arabic as they ride away. I remove the top of the basket, and peer outside. The back wall of our house is gone. Emma and Diana lie dead in what used to be our living room. Their caftans, pulled above their waists, reveal bare legs bloody and bruised. A man I do not recognize lies dead on top of them. "Narine!" I yell.

The fire turns everything black. How can anyone survive this? I have and I pray Narine has, too. I whisper her name. Dozens of men rummage the village, toeing fresh corpses and searching pockets. Dark skinned men. Stiff faces and thick hands. Not Yeneze, but Bedouins, recognizable by the white robes they wear and red-checkered Keffiyahs around their heads. I have only read about men like them in history books. I am both frightened and infatuated by their intimidating stature.

"Stop!" I hear one of the Bedouins shout. Narine rushes inside a house across the street. The Bedouins give chase. The one shouting is bigger than the rest of them, yet he moves quickly and easily, the way a cat runs after a mouse. He pulls her out of the house by her hair, speaks harshly to her. "Where are they going!" he yells. "Where is your camp?"

"No! Stop!" she screams, jerking and kicking.

"Stop! We're Armenians, not Yeneze women!" I yell. "Please! Have mercy!"

The large Bedouin looks up.

I remove my headscarf, scratch at my blonde hair.

The large Bedouin releases Narine. She runs over to me, and quickly grasps my hand.

"You are from the death camp," the large Bedouin says.

"We were heading to Deir ez-Zor before the Yeneze attacked our caravan months ago," I say. All around us, the sand soaks up the blood of the dead. A finger twitches, a foot. "The people from this village saved our life."

"I'm sorry for that," the large Bedouin says. "We thought the Yeneze had ridden into an abandoned village. We see many out here."

"What will you do with us?" Narine asks, wiping her eyes. Then she turns to me and says, "Where are Dianna and Emma?"

My head hangs heavy with grief. Narine falls on her knees and screams into her hands. I kneel down beside her, hold her close, but she continues to scream, this time into my shoulder. The Bedouins watch us the way men watch a fire burning out.

"It's my fault," I say.

"What do you mean?" Narine asks, sniffs.

"The refugees Bashir wouldn't help. Remember? They led the Yeneze right to us. I'm sorry. We should have never come here."

"No, Valia. You didn't do this," Narine says.

"But I did." My words fill with disbelief.

Narine frowns more to herself than to me. “We should have gone to Diyarbekir, the way you suggested. Perhaps it is safe there now. We should have listened to you."

“Nowhere is safe,” the large Bedouin says.

“We should take them with us,” someone suggests.

“Can you cook?” the large Bedouin asks.

“Yes,” I say. “We both can.”

“You will cook for me and my officers then,” the large Bedouin says. “My name is Kazim.”

"I am Valia and this is Narine," I say.

“Where will you take us?” Narine asks, wiping her eyes.

Kazim takes a sip of water, looks out into the desert. “The mountains,” he says, pointing with his long, muscular finger.

Chapter 11

It is snowing by the time we reach the mountains. The flakes catch on the pine trees and turn everything white. As we ride closer to the clouds, I stick out my tongue and catch a flake or two, taking the fresh taste in my mouth. The snow falls lightly at first and then, as the cold wind rushes down the mountain, flakes come thick, and in circles as they fall. We find a cave, and cover the hole with a large rug, which provides relief from the wind for only Narine, me, Kazim, and his officers. The tight space forces the rest of Kazim's men, two hundred or so, to pitch tents outside. We have been traveling for days with little rest and happy for a break.

Kazim begins breaking sticks for a fire. Once finished, the flame ignites, the officers huddle around the warm orange glow, and pass the time with conversation, and eat jerky. Narine and I prepare a pot of stew from a rabbit someone had caught earlier that day.

"What of the Yeneze?" I ask.

"It doesn't matter now," Kazim says. "We have another mission of greater importance."

"Kazim," the man sitting next to him says irritably. His mangled black hair has the appearance of a bird's nest. His beard, covered with twigs and bits of frozen sweat, reaches the middle of his chest. "We don't know if they're spies."

"They're harmless, Jarir," Kazim says. Kazim smiles at us. He pokes the fire with his bayonet. The wood pops, and sends sparks into the air.

Jarir repeatedly tightens his lips nervously or angrily, I cannot tell which. He makes me nervous. I keep a close eye on him.

"Are you fighting the Turks?" I ask.

"We're a small detachment working for the British Army."

"They're in the mountains?"

"A great distance away."

"Why are you so far from them?"

"See," Jarir says, "they even talk like spies."

"Scouting," Kazim says, ignoring his friend.

"Sir," Jarir pleads.

"Let them talk," Kazim says.

"You are to meet the British here?" Narine asks.

"Tell us about home," Jarir says. "You have told us little."

"I wish to go back there," Narine says.

"What about you?" he asks me.

"Are we going in the direction of Meskene?"

"Is that home?" Kazim asks.

"No. I met a woman there who said she could help us."

"We cannot take you to Meskene," Kazim says.

"Where is home?" Jarir asks.

"Adana," I say.

"Diyarbekir," Narine says.

"Your families are there?" Kazim asks.

We lower our heads and keep silent. Kazim and the others do not speak of it again. Certainly, they see the memory of death in our sullen faces.

"How will the woman from Meskene help you?" Jarir asks. "I hear it's burned to the ground. Everything north of here is gone, in fact."

I look at Narine. My fingers itch with tension. I have not told her about the boat to Europe. "She promised safe passage to Europe," I say. "She knows of a man from Adana, Berkant Hasim. She said he can help us."

"Trusting your fate to a Turk?" Jarir asks.

"No," I say. "But I must have hope in something. If I cannot go home, then I must go to Europe."

"Why didn't you tell me?" Narine asks, the grumble of betrayal in her words. "Were you planning to go on your own?"

"No, of course not. I know I should have told you. I'm sorry."

"We must win this war before you can go to Europe," another says, touching my shoulder. His crooked nose and tired eyes twitch. He smokes a pipe the way Father used to when contemplating.

"We'll win," Kazim says. He walks to the edge of the cave, watches the snow fall heavy and thick, and says, "Looks like we'll be here awhile. The war will have to wait."

"Where are we headed?" I ask.

Kazim squats by the fire and presses a cigarette against a hot coal. "Toward Damascus." He puffs on the cigarette. It burns red at the tip. Smoke filters from his mouth. "When the storm lets up."

The wind that night keeps me awake. It tears the rug off the cave's mouth and blows fear in along with the cold and snow. The fire hisses. Someone jumps up and reattaches the cover. It does little good against the mounting wind, which haunts the rest of the evening. Narine and I hold each other tight as the wind knocks persistently against the cave. It reminds me of the police soldiers knocking, and the Yeneze attacking. I feel as though they're coming after us.

"Don't worry. Try to get some sleep. I'm keeping watch," the man that had touched my shoulder says.

Narine leans up. "Is there any more stew?"

"A little."

"We'll keep watch with you," I say.

We carry our blankets closer to the fire. I pour each of us a bowl of stew. I stare at the fire as I eat and listen to the wind whistling outside. Everyone but the three of us is sleeping.

"It'll be gone by morning," the pipe smoker says.

"And if not?" I ask.

"Then I guess we're stuck here awhile, like Kazim said."

The warm stew settles my stomach. "You haven't told us your name," I say.

"Aram."

"That was my father's name." I picture Father's face and his dark gentle eyes. He is sitting by the wood stove, reading and smoking a pipe. "He smoked a pipe, too."

"You have good memories of him."

"This stew makes me think of Christmas."

"Tell me about…this Christmas."

"You've never heard of Christmas?" Narine asks.

"The desert keeps me from many things," Aram says. "Nor do I know how to read."

"It's a Christian holiday," I say, "when we celebrate the birth of Jesus."

"Yes, I know of this Jesus, a great prophet."

"We believe he is the son of God."

"Christmas, it's a great feast for you, like our Eid al-Fitr."

"We eat and tell stories from the Bible," Narine says.

"A priest blesses the house and prays for a fruitful new year," I add.

"I think I might like this Christmas of yours," Aram says. He smiles.

After we eat, I wash the bowls, Narine dries them, then we lie back down and sleep, easier now with the warm stew in our bellies.

That night I dream of Christmas. Father places a large comforter over the top of the tonir, and everyone sits around it, and pulls the comforter up to their waists to keep warm. The elderly tell stories, or read from the Bible as the children gobble down raisins, dried apricots, and nuts. I imagine baby Jesus asleep in his crib on a cold night two thousand years ago in the little town of Bethlehem. After the stories, we play cards for apples, and pomegranates. Our fathers talk politics over glasses of cognac. A priest blesses the house and prays for each family and for a prosperous new year. Then several of the older girls recite poetry. It keeps the literary tradition active. Islamic law forbids anyone to speak Armenian, so it helps us preserve our language. Christmas is the only time during the year that Armenians rebel against the rule. Speaking our native tongue is punishable by imprisonment or death.

When I wake from my dream, I pray Artush is still alive. I even pray for Yasmin. I know how unlikely it seems, but I pray her father is looking for me.

Chapter 12

The next morning, we prepare a quick breakfast of bread and coffee. We pack our things and saddle the horses. The sky burns clear now. Its reflection bounces aggressively off the snow. Open arms of an unforgiving landscape await us.

I give a hopeful smile to Narine. "Ready?"

"You should have told me about Europe," Narine says. A frown swells like a bruise on her face. "But I forgive you."

I give her a weak smile. "I'll never keep anything from you again. I promise."

She holds my waist tight. I nudge the horse. We follow behind Kazim, circle around the mountain, and ride down the other side. The hard snow crunches beneath the horse's hooves. I hold tight the reins. "Steady," I say. "Easy, boy." The ground levels out after a half hour or so, much easier now, and we continue travelling south.

I ride up along Kazim. His head is bowed. A book rests in his hand. He mumbles something, opens his eyes. He looks at me and says, "Yes?"

"What were you doing?"

"Praying."

"Is that a Bible? May I see it?"

"The Quran."

"You're Muslim."

"What did you expect?"

"I thought Muslims prayed on carpets."

"Is that what you learned in school?"

"It's what I remember."

Kazim laughs. "And that we're of the devil I bet."

"We learned many things in school."

"Yet it is your God that abandoned you."

"I'm still alive."

"You have good wit for a young girl." He smiles. "Better than most."

"Are the British in Damascus?"

"That is our hope."

"Have you ever met one?"

"Once."

"What are they like?"

"Pushy."

"I met an American. In Aleppo."

"I see."

"Sister Gertrude. A nun She was helping the orphans."

"And how come you didn't stay with her?"

"The man that took me wouldn't allow it."

"What happened to him?"

"The Yeneze killed him."

Kazim studies the sky. "Maybe your God has not abandoned you after all."

"Some days I'm not so sure."

"But you said yourself you're still alive."

"My family was murdered."

"Do you blame God for that?"

"No. Well, sometimes I do."

"What do you mean?"

"I don't know," I say, shrugging my shoulders. I sniff, wipe away a tear. "It's just.... I don't understand why all this is happening. What is the point of this war? Any war? Why has God allowed me to live and my parents and little brother to die? What about my friends?"

"Those are good questions," Kazim says. "I wish I had an answer for you."

We approach a small hill and begin our decent. Narine turns her head but remains asleep. I rub the horse's neck, then readjust myself in the saddle. The horse keeps his head forward and moves along at a slow walk.

"Do you have family?" I ask.

"A wife and son."

"Where are they?"

"Mosul. A city far north from here."

"You must miss them."

"Every day."

The sky begins turning an orange-yellow. "Time to make camp," Kazim says.

By the time we finish, the sun is hanging at the mountains edge. It hovers there a few moments before slipping behind the darkness, and turning the evening cool, but bearable. The warm fire ornaments a smile on my face.

"How much farther?" I ask.

Kazim pokes at the fire, thinking. "We must move cautiously and slowly and investigate all the country visible to us. Another week at least."

"Is Damascus a beautiful city?" Narine asks.

"I've never been," Kazim says. He pours coffee into a tin cup. "Want some?"

"Yes." We hold our cups out to him. I close my eyes and enjoy the warmth of the cup. My fingers begin to move with life.

It begins sleeting soon afterward. We cover the fire pit, and race to our tents. The sleet first comes in spurts, then hard. Narine and I cuddle together and listen to the sleet pattering on the tent walls.

"They are very kind to us," Narine says. "Gave us our own tent."

"Most of them," I say. "The man they call Jarir doesn't seem to trust us."

"He's harmless," Narine says. "One second." She gets up and lights a lamp, sets it within reach, then crawls back under the covers. "What do you think Damascus is like?"

"I'd rather think of home."

"I thought we were sailing to Europe."

"Turkey is still my home. I wonder…."

"What?"

"Will we ever see it again?"

Narine sits up. "I don't know."

"What was home like for you?"

"We raised goats and grew almond trees and wheat and had grapes as far as the eye could see."

"It sounds wonderful," I say.

"We were happy," Narine says. "What about your home?"

"A wonderful place," I say. My father was a watchmaker. My mother made clothes. We were not rich, but we had plenty." I snuggle closer to Narine. "I miss them very much."

"I hope I can visit one day," Narine says.

I smile. "Let's get some sleep." I blow out the lamp.

The sun comes up fast and burns away the water and ice, and leaves the ground wet in some parts and frozen in other parts, and makes the road difficult for travel. Yet we press on, pushing the horses hard through the cold mud.

Days pass. Warm weather revives the saffron layered meadow. Ankle high grass bends backward against horse hooves and wagon wheels.

Later that afternoon, we cross a set of empty railroad tracks. Unfamiliar footsteps scatter up ahead. "What is that?" I ask. I place a hand over my brow and look across the field. A line of heat hovers above the ground in the distance. In the center of the line wrapped in a whirl of dust is a horde of dark figures moving toward us.

"I don't know," Kazim says. "Perhaps more Armenians heading to Dier ez-Zor."

"Mounted soldiers," Jarir says.

"Their British!" someone whispers.

"No!" another protests. "They're Turks!"

"Lower your weapons," Kazim says. "Wait here."

He rides out to meet the soldiers coming toward us. One of the soldiers from the incoming group holds up a hand. He and Kazim meet in the middle of both armies, dismount from their horses and embrace, and kiss each other's cheeks and laugh.

"It's okay," Jarir says. "It's Mujab."

"Who is he?" I ask.

"A good friend."

"What do we have here?" Mujab asks. He rubs the scar across his forehead and ogles at Narine and me. A missing earlobe and his speech enhance his tough appearance.

"Valia and Narine," Kazim says, "captives of the Yeneze."

"What do they do for you?"

"Cook," Narine says.

"That so?"

Narine's face reddens. I adjust my dress, press my arms close to my chest, and clasp my hands together. "Nothing more," I say.

Mujab smiles. "Taking care of the wounded is far more useful than cooking these days. Do you know how to dress a wound?"

Narine and I look at each other. I relax my arms. Narine looks at Mujab, smiles and says, "I took care of my little brother when he fell and scraped his knee."

"That'll do. Most men just want someone to be with them before they die," Mujab says. Then he turns to Kazim and says, "It doesn't look good. Damascus remains in Turkish hands."

"What happened?" Kazim asks. "The British should have been there days ago."

Mujab takes a sip of water, and swishes it around in his mouth. Then he spits the water in the dirt, and wipes his mouth with the back of his hand. "Politics. Prince Feisal doesn't trust the British, so the British are stuck in Egypt waiting for Feisal's support."

"But you sound confident he'll give support," Kazim says.

"Something to do with this Lawrence fellow."

"Who?"

"He dresses and speaks like us. The prince likes him. That's all I know."

Chapter 13

March 10, 1916. It's my 15th birthday today. I tell no one but Narine. She wrinkles her nose at me. "We must celebrate."

"Don't put up a fuss about it," I say.

"My birthday was last month," Narine says. "I turned 17."

"Why didn't you tell me?"

"I don't know. I guess…."

"You don't have to tell me if you don't want."

"It makes me think of my parents and brothers," Narine says. Her voice is thick with grief. "We had such great parties. I don't want to remember what happened to them."

"Then don't," I say. I touch her arm. "Remember the happier times. Don't let their deaths invade those moments."

"I'll make you a cake," Narine says.

"Out of what?" I ask.

"I'm sure I can find something. Wait here."

"What do you have there?" I ask when she returns. I giggle. "It smells funny."

Frowning, she sets the object on the ground, and removes the towel. "Flatbread. I'm not as good a cook as you, I'm sorry."

I clasp my hands together. "It's okay, we can scrape off the burnt edges."

"You don't have to eat it if you don't want to."

"Nonsense. It'll be fine," I say. I bite off a small piece. "It tastes sweet."

"Jarir helped me," she says. "Really, he's not a bad person."

"I know. It's just…"

The tent flap opens and there stands Kazim. "Time to go."

"Okay," I say.

"What do you have there?" he asks.

"Flatbread," I say.

"It's her birthday," Narine says.

Kazim raises a brow as if birthdays are foreign to him. "We do not celebrate birthdays."

My lower lip curves downward. "How do you not celebrate birthdays?"

Seeing that he upset me, he smiles. "Pack your things. We leave within the hour."

A few hours later, we arrive at a village with beehive shaped houses dotting the landscape. The sun carpets a knot of hills in the distance with orange-purple light. An elderly woman looks up from her work, and smiles. "Hello," she says, as she laces various colors of wool string between her fingers.

"Where is he?" Mujab asks.

"There," the old woman says, pointing. "Ziyad," she calls. An old man wearing a long white beard and walking with a cane steps from a house that has a small fence around it. A goat sticks its head outside the gate, and sniffs the dusty air. "Get," the old man says. He pokes the animal with his cane, and it displays an irritated trot as it heads to the back of the house. "Come on," the old man says, and unlatches the gate.

"He'll have word on Damascus," Mujab tells him.

"Hello friend," Ziyad says.

"Hello Ziyad," Mujab says. He dismounts from his horse, then kneels in front of the old man. Ziyad places both hands on top of Mujab's head, and mumbles something. "What's he doing?" Narine whispers.

"I don't know," I say. "Hush."

"You don't have to be so mean about it," Narine says.

"I'm sorry," I say, my voice low. I gently squeeze her hand.

"I see your men are ready to move," Mujab says. He gestures toward a hundred or so men loading tents, tools, weapons, barrels, sacks of flour, cooking supplies, and fifty or so other things armies need.

"Your men can gather there," Ziyad says. He points at the village. "You and your officers follow me." He looks at me and Narine and smiles. "Bring your servants as well."

The men sit around a cooking fire. Narine and I, with two other women from the village, serve the men tea, cakes, and dried fruit.

"Much better than my flatbread," Narine says.

"It was fine," I say.

Jarir stares at his tea, occasionally sipping it. Aram looks about the village with his hand close to his pistol.

"What of Damascus?" Mujab asks.

"I sent a rider out a week ago," Ziyad says. "No word yet."

"What about the British?" Kazim says.

"Captured Gaza last I heard," Ziyad says.

"So they're getting closer," Aram says.

"Far from Damascus," Jarir says. He looks hard at Zayad. "Your rider isn't coming back."

"You speak a fool," the man sitting next to Ziyad says. His beard is thick and dark, and his unblinking eyes cold as sleet.

Ziyad places a hand on him. "That's enough, Shamil," but the man shrugs away.

"Damascus is a two day's hard ride from here," Jarir says. "Your man is dead."

"That man is my brother," Shamil says.

Jarir looks at him blankly. "My condolences."

Shamil stands. Ziyad latches on to his wrist and pulls him down. "The fight is out there." He tilts his teacup into the fire, dumps out the dregs, and lifts the cup. I refill it. Narine and the other two women provide more sweets and dried fruit.

"I think we should head toward Jerusalem," Kazim says, "with your men. I assume that is where they're heading."

"They're meeting Major Lawrence."

"You know this Lawrence fellow personally?" Mujab asks.

"Never met the man."

"But you trust him?"

"It's satisfactory that Prince Feisal trusts him."

"Where is he now?" Kazim asks.

"The Prince? I don't know," Ziyad says.

"No, this Lawrence fellow."

"Making preparations to lead the revolt," Ziyad says. "The prince believes he's the only one that can help us secure independence from the Turks."

The Turks have exercised autonomy over Arab lands since the early 16th century. However, the Turks have not been as harsh with them as they have been with us. Arabs have been allowed to speak their own language, pray to their own God, and travel freely throughout the empire. Things changed recently. There has been talk that the Turks have built a railway system connecting Medina to Damascus, which might mean an insurgence of tax collectors, customs agents, or Turkish soldiers. This could easily disrupt the Arab way of life.

"When do your men plan to leave?" Mujab asks.

"Two days."

A cool wind sneaks in during the night bringing a light rain that patters against the tent. The months continue to mash together into what seems like one long and horrible day. My thoughts of Father, Mother, and Arsen weigh heavily on me. They occur more often than they have before, and I want to cry as the sky cries above me. For some strange reason, I'm not sure why, I cannot cry, and I lie here like some silly girl listening to the rain. How I wish to leave this dreadful place.

Horse hoofs splash wet as the animal hurries into camp. "Turks!" the rider yells.

"Narine, wake up," I say, shaking her shoulder.

"What is it?" she asks, frightened.

"Turks. We need to hide."

She grabs my hand, and we dash out of the tent.

"Run to the village!" Kazim orders. He rides tall on his horse, his shoulders arched back, and his chest bulging with courage. "Ziyad's house. He'll help you." Large brown eyes dominate his determined face. He kicks his horse hard in the ribs, and dashes off with a trail of men hollering, horses sucking in lungs full of air as they charge close behind.

A gunshot booms in the distance, then another, then another, then hundreds of gunshots all at once. My ears buzz by the sound. The rain beats against my face as I reach for Narine's hand, but she's no longer beside me.

"Narine!" I scream. Men rush by me. Dark mud disguises their angry faces. Unable to tell friend from foe, I scramble through the mud toward a small rock.

"Narine!" I scream again.

A Turkish soldier dismounts from his horse and lunges at me. His hands pull me up fast and strong. The cool metal of a knife rests against my neck.

"Let her go!" Kazim's voice penetrates the wind and rain. He's sitting high on his horse and pointing a rifle at the soldier holding me. "The battle's over. You've lost. Let the girl go. Look." He points to a team of cavalry riding out of a thicket of woods and surrounding a company of Turks with empty hands held high in surrender. "The rest have retreated. Surrender yourself."

"I'll kill her!" the soldier shouts. He pulls me taut, and lifts the knife close to my chin. "Put the rifle—."

Kazim fires. A fountain of blood, warm and wet, splashes on my face. I scream. The soldier loosens his grip and falls over—dead. My hands shake.

"Are you hurt?" Kazim asks.

"No," I say. I wipe the blood from my face with a trembling hand. "They took Narine."

"I'll go—"

The sound of a bugle cuts his words short. Cavalrymen dressed in tan uniforms and slouch hats help secure captured Turks.

"The British?" I ask.

"Not sure," Kazim says. "Let's go see." He lifts me on his horse, and we ride down toward the men in the tan uniforms. We discover Mujab talking to one of them.

"You bring your wife into battle?" the man asks in Turkish. His nasally voice is curiously relaxing. His rich skin shines with the color and luster of the apples that grow at the base of the Taurus Mountains. When he removes his cap, he reveals a thick head of sweaty blonde hair the color of sunflowers. His large brown eyes are perfectly round and kind.

"This is Captain Wilson," Mujab says.

Kazim salutes. "No, sir. The girl is a refugee."

"One only," Captain Wilson says.

"Narine," I say. Dread stings my voice.

A soldier whispers something in Captain Wilson's ear. A frown breaks out across the Captain's face like darkness swallowing up the day. "We did find one other girl."

My eyes narrow with worry. "Where is she?"

Captain Wilson rubs his eyes. "I don't think it's a good idea for you to see her."

"I want to see her," I demand.

"There's nothing left of her, child. We know it to be a girl only by the blue scarf she was wearing, like the one you have on."

I collapse in the mud and cry into my dirty hands. A bile of grief bursts from my mouth.

"There now, child," Captain Wilson says. He hands me a handkerchief. "Let's get you cleaned up and out of this rain and into some dry clothes." He looks at Mujab. "Perhaps the village over there will have some."

"Yes," Mujab says. "Go see about some clothes for Valia," he orders one of his men.

"I'll go," Jarir says.

"It's not safe for them anymore," Kazim says.

Mujab looks back toward the village. "Ziyad doesn't want to come with us. They'll head to the caves in the morning."

"Ziyad can provide someone to take me to Meskene," I say. Sniffles choke my words. "Isn't that right?"

Wilson gives Kazim a curious look.

"Our camp is a two-day ride from here," Captain Wilson says. "You can join us if you want. Then we'll see about getting you home."

"No," I correct. "There is a woman in Meskene, Belma. She said her husband can get me to Europe."

Captain Wilson scratches his head. "Quite a distance from here."

I show him a silver coin. "I can pay you."

Captain Wilson smiles. “Now where does a little girl acquire such wealth?”

“It’s yours if you take me to Meskene.”

“Put your money away, child,” Captain Wilson says. “We’ll work on getting you where you want to be.” He sniffs. “But no promises. There’s a war going on, you know.”

“What about the dead?” Mujab asks.

“No time to bury them,” Captain Wilson says. The Turks that escaped will bring reinforcements soon. We need to go now.”

“A question for you, sir, if I may?” Kazim says to Captain Wilson.

“Certainly. What is it?”

"Our scouts told us just a couple of days ago that the British are still in Egypt. How is it you made this far in such a short time?"

Captain Wilson grabs his belly and laughs so hard I think he’ll choke on his tongue. “Goodness me, boy, do we look like a bunch of Brits?”

“I don’t know, sir. I’ve never met one.”

“We’re from Australia, the 3rd Light Horse Brigade at your service.”

Kazim’s face goes blank.

Mujab shrugs.

“It’s a.... oh, never....” Captain Wilson begins.

“An island country with kangaroos and men that carry spears like in ancient times,” I say.

“An educated girl,” Captain Wilson says. He gestures at his pistol, smiles. “But most of us have graduated from the spear.”

No one laughs at his joke.

Captain Wilson clears his throat. “Anyway, the Brits should be close to Jerusalem by now. We’re cleaning up small enemy positions farther north for an easier advance. Then we’ll march on Damascus and Aleppo together.” He spits and the spit flashes in the sun before the ground consumes a cavalcade of dark bubbles. “There’s a lot of us scattered all over this bloody place.” He wrinkles his nose at me. “Perhaps by then someone can escort you to Meskene.”

“Thank you,” I say.

Jarir arrives. “Happy birthday,” he whispers. “I’m sorry I accused you of being a spy.”

My face warms as I take fresh clothes from him. "It's okay, thank you." Captain Wilson turns to Kazim and Mujab. "We have a few other Arab detachments like you back at camp, courtesy of Captain Lawrence."

"We've heard of this Lawrence fellow," Mujab says. Who is he?"

"He's the reason why I can speak Turkish *and* Arabic," Captain Wilson says.

"We hear he's good friends with Prince Feisal."

"Yes, that's correct. Making friends in war is beneficial."

"And learning one's customs," Kazim says.

"It's been helpful, yes. I don't think we'd make it through this bloody country without the Arab people."

"I'm tired of hearing of war," I say. My words boil with frustration. "I don't care about this Lawrence person. All I want is to get as far away from here as possible."

"Relax, child," Captain Wilson says. "We'll take good care of you."

Chapter 14

We arrive at the Australian camp two days later. An orange sky welcomes us. A cool breeze blows over the mountains. It whistles as it comes through the valley, beats against the tents, and fills my lungs with the smell of lingering rain and mud. Australian and Arab soldiers dig ditches, clean weapons, move cannons, or transport lumber with horse drawn wagons everywhere I look. Canteens hang off the back of wagons, and clank against each other like church music.

"A lot to take in for a young girl," Captain Wilson says.

"So many men," I say. "You cannot spare at least one of them to take me to Meskene?"

Captain Wilson's warm eyes shift in the direction of the mountains. "In time. When it's safe."

I want to tuck his words into my pocket, hope against the fear that has ravaged me all year. Excitement catches my breath. "Soon?"

Wilson narrows his eyes. "I'm worried about a surprise attack. We can do nothing until the British arrive."

"I pray they arrive soon," I say.

"Get some rest," Captain Wilson says. "You'll have a busy day tomorrow."

The next morning, I prepare a pot of stewed elk Kazim had shot the day before, some bread, and a pot of coffee. I take the breakfast items to Captain Wilson's tent where a meeting is in progress. I place everything quietly on the table, ladling the stew into bowls for Kazim and his officers, and the three Australian officers sitting across from them. Captain Wilson, at the head of the table, hovers over a large map. Behind him stand neatly shelved books that smell of leather and old age.

"Do you like to read?" Captain Wilson asks, folding the map. Then he pours himself a coffee.

"I can do that for you," I say.

He waves my words away. "Nonsense. I'm very capable of pouring my own coffee. Continue tending to my guests." He smiles. "So, do you read?"

"Yes," I say.

"A very intelligent girl," Kazim says. "Wants to be a teacher."

"That so," Captain Wilson says. "I was a teacher before this bloody war started. I love books."

"What did you teach?" I ask. "And where?"

"Literature, of course," Captain Wilson says, "at the University of Sydney." He pulls one from the bottom shelf and sets it on the table. "Take a look."

I trace my hand across the leather as if I'm touching a sacred text.

"Open it," Captain Wilson says. "It's not going to bite."

I do as he says. "What language is this?"

"*Ingilizce*," Captain Wilson says. "English."

"I don't know your language."

"Maybe you'll learn one day."

"Maybe."

Captain Wilson places the book back on the shelf. He looks at me and says, "I'm sorry about your friend."

I feel my face wince. "She reminded me of a friend back home."

"This friend, she's alive?" Captain Wilson asks.

"Yes," I say.

"What's her name, this friend?"

"Artush."

"This is why you wanted to go home," Jarir says.

I turn and look at him. "I wanted to go home for many reasons," I say. "But now I think Europe is the best decision."

"What about your friend?" Jarir asks, "don't you wish to see her?"

"She's safe," I say.

"How can you be sure?"

"It's a feeling I have."

"Where is home?" Captain Wilson asks.

"Adana."

Gunshots boom in the distance. We all walk outside. Soldiers run about quickly. Several units move canons toward the noise.

"What do we do?" I ask, shaking as if a rush of cold air is biting my skin.

"A small detachment," Captain Wilson says. "No need for alarm. Let's go finish our breakfast."

We listen to the fighting in the distance as we finish breakfast. We wait for a larger attack that never arises. The skirmish lasts until rain quiets the morning. This calm doesn't last long.

"What's that sound?" I ask.

Kazim tilts his head. "What sound?"

"That buzzing sound coming from the sky."

"British airplanes!" Captain Wilson yells, waving his arm forward.

"Wait here," Kazim says. Then he, Captain Wilson, Jarir, and Aram follow in the direction of the airplanes.

I cover my ears. My lips tremble a bit, not exactly into a frown—I have gotten used to war—but at least a resemblance of hope that has been tugging at my heart. I blink away the fear and close my eyes. Nothing but the distant sounds of the battlefield keeps me company.

The next morning, I walk to the edge of a large hill that empties into a wide valley. A blanket of smoke and fog settles over hundreds of twisted and mangled bodies. Boots with feet left in them. Horses bent in unusual shapes. Despite the horror of it all, countless lilacs, tall and brilliant ones, roof the ground. Sparrows sing high above the ambulances that maneuver around jagged tree stumps and shell holes as deep as ten feet.

One ambulance gets stuck in the mud. The driver quickly hitches it to a team of horses. The horses jam their hind legs deep into the mushy ground, and grunt. Their muscles bulge, and the ambulance wheels move. After great effort, the wheels spring free.

Kazim rides up on his horse. His face is muddy and covered in blood. Exhaustion and great sadness glazes his eyes. An ambulance rides behind him.

"What is it?" I ask.

Kazim gestures to the ambulance. "Mujab is dead. And I told you to stay put."

"And the others?" I ask, ignoring his reprimand.

"Jarir and Aram are dead also. Captain Wilson...." He sighs. "He's fine, safe." He holds out an arm. "Get on."

We arrive back to camp exhausted.

"Get some sleep," Kazim says.

"I want to help," I say. "Besides, I can't sleep in all this noise."

"Head over to that tent," Kazim says, pointing. "I'm sure that could use an extra nurse."

"I'm no nurse."

"You said you wanted to help." He cracks a smile. "You'll learn quickly."

The artillery commences well into the evening and shakes the earth. It fells trees, collapses battlements, and buries men six feet deep in graves never found. Dozens of soldiers lie with shattered arms or broken legs. Their screams struggle to keep the saws away.

"Hold him down!" the surgeon orders. He's a very tall man with thick dark hair and intelligent, untiring eyes. As he works, a lantern hanging on a tent post rattles from artillery explosions. An Arab grabs the wounded soldier's ankles. Another Arab presses hard on the man's shoulders.

The surgeon picks up a saw, studies the wounded soldier as if negotiating the grains of a tree. Then the surgeon says something in a garbled voice, what I gather to be the British tongue. He looks at me. "Sorry," he says in Turkish. "Get me some more rags."

I return with the rags.

"Put them there," the surgeon tells me, gesturing to the soldier's leg. His command is patient. "Hold him steady," he orders the two Arabs. Then he cuts into the soldier's leg with rapid motion. The rags soak up a lot of blood, but not all of it and the table and floor turn red. The soldier screams, and swallows up the noise of the guns with his agony. Then he passes out. The surgeon hacks at the bone, then tosses the limb into a large bucket.

"Go and sit with that one," the surgeon says to me, fatigue curling his lips.

A large Arab man sits propped up on a nearby bed. His arm is black and resembles a rotten log eaten by beetles and worms. "Everything will be fine," I say, holding his hand tight as we wait for his turn for the knife. When I squeeze his hand tighter, he must sense something in me, because he says, "Don't leave me." His lips tremble when he says this. His hands turn cold. His face reminds me of the color of dough.

I know he's dying, but I bury my emotions, give him a soft smile, brush back his hair with my fingers, then kiss his forehead. "I won't," I say. Then the soldier closes his eyes, his hand relaxes, and he takes his last wheezy breath.

The surgeon wipes his bloody hands on a towel, walks over to where I'm sitting, the soldier's hand still in mine. "I don't even know his name," I say.

"He's gone, go on to the next one," the surgeon says, gently pulling me away.

The two Arab assistants scoop up the dead soldier and take him outside.

I tear a piece of the bed sheet, then tie it to the pole where the lantern hangs.

"What is that?" the surgeon asks.

"A prayer."

"I think God left this place long ago," he says.

"Then I'll ask Him to return." I'm surprised by the hope in my tone, weak, but present.

The soldier lying on the bed beside the one that just died, dies as well. I move on to the next soldier and then the next, until there is a string of soldiers outside the tent waiting for burial. The sour smell of death lingers like stale smoke. I cover my nose with a damp cloth. The surgeon continues hacking away limbs for hours, filling the buckets. I take the buckets out of the tent, and dump the limbs in a hole. "I'll be back in a bit, if I may," I say, wiping my sweaty brow. "I want to check the men in recovery." The surgeon nods his head.

I head to the recovery tent and find the wounded—many of them missing a leg or an arm—lying on bags stuffed with grass, the survivors from the agonizing blade of the saw. Most suffer from a minor gunshot or bayonet wound. One man shivers uncontrollably.

I fetch a bucket of water, dip in the ladle and bring it to his mouth. He sips slowly. His shivering diminishes. I move up the line of beds offering water to the soldiers. I bathe them and dress their wounds. I sit and talk with them until they close their eyes.

An explosion shakes the tent, and knocks me off balance.

"Whoa!" a nurse says, catching me by the arm. His bloody hand leaves an imprint on my sleeve.

"Sorry about that," he says, his voice weak with fatigue.

"It's okay," I say. "Needs washing anyway."

We both laugh, not out of happiness, but from the exhaustion and hysteria only war can bring.

"What are you two laughing about?" It's Kazim. He is sitting up in bed and holding his shoulder. His face crinkles with a mix of agony, anger, and humiliation. "Are you two alright?" he asks, and stands up.

"Better than you at the moment," the nurse says. "Now get back in bed."

"How are you feeling?" I ask.

"Dr. Smith said the bullet went straight through."

"He's going to be fine," the nurse says. "Just needs some rest."

"When can I go back to the front?" Kazim asks.

"You lost a lot of blood," the nurse says. "Not for several days, if at all."

At sunrise, I get up and poke the cooking fire. This day brings a cool and bright morning with a steady breeze. Captain Wilson is there sitting on a log by the fire with his arm in a sling. He's sipping coffee. A cigarette burns on the edge of the log. The fire pops as the breeze passes through it. The air smells like snow. "Fire," he says, nodding.

"What?"

"*Ates*. It means 'fire' in English."

"Fire," I say.

"Good. How about this one: wood."

"Wood," I say. "What does it mean?"

"*Ahsap*."

"Burns."

"Burns," I repeat.

"*Yaniklar*." Captain Wilson says. Then he says, "Fire burns wood."

"Fire burns wood," I repeat.

"*Yangin ashap yakar*," Captain Wilson says. "Fire burns wood."

"Fire burns wood," I say a second time.

"You're a bright girl," Captain Wilson says. "You'll learn English easily."

I smile and pour him more coffee. "Why must I learn English?"

"You want to move to Europe, don't you?"

"I suppose I don't have much choice."

He stares past me, toward the mountains, jagged silhouettes in the distance. "They say English will become the universal language one day. It might be good for you to learn it." He flicks his cigarette into the fire. "How do you like being a nurse?"

I stare into the fire. "I'd rather be a teacher."

"You saw Kazim?"

"Yes."

"I was sorry to hear about Mujab. An excellent soldier."

"Kazim lost many friends."

"I suspect we all have." He retrieves a pocketknife, and digs at the dirt from his nails with it. "Tell me about this friend of yours…Artush. What happened to her?"

"She married a Muslim. That's how she was able to remain in Adana."

"You did not have that option?"

My face turns to stone. "I will never marry a Muslim."

"You can't think they're all bad. After all, Kazim saved your life. And this woman…," his lips struggle to produce her name,"…what's the name? The one from Meskene."

"Belma," I remind him.

"Yes, of course. And Mr. Hasim, they are both helping you secure passage to Europe. All Muslim, are they not?"

"I don't want to discuss it further." My words come out sharp. I tell myself it must be the fatigue talking, because deep inside I know Captain Wilson is a kind man and would do nothing to harm me.

"I'm sorry I've upset you," he says.

"No, I'm sorry. It's just…I have mixed emotions about Turkish Muslims. I have seen their kindness. I've also seen their cruelty. More coffee?"

"Please."

He twirls the cup, watching the coffee settle. Then he presses his lips to the cup. "This bloody war," he mumbles. He looks at me as if he's intending to walk straight into a herd of mounted troops. "Tell you what, I'll help you find your friend and perhaps get you home, if that's really what you want."

Happiness thumps high with each rapid breath I take. "You will help me find Artush?"

"You have my word. Something good has got to come out of this war."

"Thank you so much, sir," I say. I kiss him on the cheek.

He smiles. "But I strongly encourage you to move to Great Britain after we find her. I think you'd do well there."

"Not France?"

"Not at all."

"Why not?"

He smiles. "Great Britain has better universities."

"Better than Australia?"

"Yes."

"Why don't you teach there?"

"Maybe one day."

I frown. "I don't think it's possible for Artush to come with me."

"What do you mean?"

"She's married to a Muslim, like I said, an officer in the Turkish army."

Captain Wilson takes a deep breath, rubs his cheek. "Let's just focus on finding your friend first, then we'll deal with the rest."

"Thank y…"

"Riders approaching!" someone shouts.

Captain Wilson and I jump to our feet. I put a hand over my eyes, shielding them from the sun, looking to see from where the riders are approaching.

"A good sign," Captain Wilson says. He nods toward the riders, a troupe of British cavalry escorting Turkish prisoners to a barbed wire enclosure. The prisoners wear pants that come down to their knees. Sores cover their legs. Their cheekbones stick out sharp and sickly. Eyes sink deep in their sockets.

As I walk toward them, Captain Wilson grabs my arm. "Not a good idea."

"I want a closer look."

He lets go. "Not too close."

I stand at a distance, behind a tree, and watch the British soldiers corral the prisoners inside the fenced enclosure. A priest, making the sign of the cross, walks with them, a large man wearing a black robe. Dark gray hair speckles his dapper beard. A silver crucifix dangles from his neck. He seems to have an unfriendly stubbornness about him. His whole person, from his diligently trimmed beard to his stiff cheeks, from the way he holds the reins of his horse and narrows his eyes, seems to follow his every decision. I watch him for a long time talking to the prisoners. Then I walk over and stand next to him. I touch one of the barbs with the tip of my index finger and stare blankly into the tiny enclosure. The prisoners lower their heads when they see me.

I grit my teeth. "Father, why do you talk to them?"

He turns toward me, smiles, not a look of surprise on his face. "I was wondering when you were going to unlatch yourself from that tree over there and come speak to me."

"I didn't….I was…."

"No need to be afraid of them," he says. "Look at that one," pointing with his head. "He's just a boy, probably not much older than you." The boy's gaunt eyes seem lost in a dream. A bony face, his clothes in tatters. A big toe protruding from a shoe that looks to be one size too small.

It begins to snow. The snow settles on the boy's shoulders. He shivers. I catch a few flakes in my hand. I slurp the water, a metallic taste. "They are horrible people," I say. "They do not deserve kindness."

"We are all to blame to some degree for the evil in the world," the priest says.

I consider the conversation I had with Captain Wilson minutes ago. A swirl of mixed emotions tangles my thoughts. "Yes, I know. I'm referring more towards the soldiers than civilians. I have found civilians to show kindness and sympathy. These soldiers murdered innocent people."

"Certainly," the priest says, rubbing his hands together. "But everyone deserves forgiveness."

"Even murderers?"

"Yes, even murderers." He cups his hands, and blows into them.

"How do I forgive someone that murdered my family?"

The priest scratches at his beard. "Have you ever been teased or accused of something you didn't do?"

"What does that have to do with anything?"

"Humor me, child."

Yasmin's baleful face invades my memory. "A classmate called me a cheat once."

"Did you forgive them?"

"I'm not sure. I mean, I prayed for her."

"But did you mean it?"

"I don't know. I guess so."

"You either did or you didn't."

"I'm not sure. She gave me a gold coin the last time I saw her. She said I'd know what to do with it when the time came."

The priest raises his brow. "To barter for your life, I suppose."

A tear slides down my cheek.

"It's okay, child. You don't need to speak of it."

"It's fine," I say, wiping the tear away. "I didn't realize the coin's significance when Yasmin gave it to me. I do now. Because of this coin, a couple from Al-Kila gave safe passage for me and some friends of mine."

"Now you're here. Perhaps I can meet your friends. And this couple, are they here as well?"

"They're all dead."

The priest lowers his head. "My condolences."

"I don't know why Yasmin wanted to help me. I don't think she expected I'd survive the desert, or that I'd be rescued by a group of Bedouins." I shake my head.

"What is it?"

"It's all just so confusing to me. I now see the significance of the gold coin, but how could she be mean to me one minute, then want to save my life the next? The mind of a Turk…it's so…" I think of what Haik had said… "irrational."

"We all think foolishly sometimes. "However, I suggest resolving little problems before tackling bigger ones."

"I don't understand."

"Forgive your classmate." The priest nods toward the prisoners. "Then maybe you'll understand the importance of forgiving these soldiers, especially this boy. Do you really think he knows the actual cause of the war? He's fighting for his life. Don't you think that's all he cares about?"

I kick at the ground, then glance inside the fence. Prisoners huddle together chicken-like. Snow covers their bare shoulders.

"This boy knows nothing of what he's done," the priest continues.

"I saw boys only a few years older than my brother murder women and children and old men. They knew what they were doing. They do not deserve forgiveness."

"Forgiving does not mean excusing," the priest says. Then he says, "What is your name, child?"

"Valia Stepanavan."

"I'm Father Eduard Ossian. Where are you from, Valia?"

"Adana."

"A very lovely city."

"You're from there?"

"I visited a few years ago. I live in Egypt now." Then he motions to a passing British soldier and says, "Can you spare some warm blankets and some soap for the prisoners?"

"I'll see what I can do, Father," and then the soldier rides away.

"You speak English," I say.

"Would you like to learn?"

"I don't know. Maybe. See that man over there sitting on the log? That's Captain Wilson. He taught me a few words." He's smoking a cigarette and starring into the fire.

"He looks troubled."

"He's a good man."

"What about the man sitting next to him with the sling around his arm? I don't often see a white man talking with an Arab."

"Kazim. He saved my life from the Yeneze after Bashir and Onnig were killed."

"The couple from Al-Kila?"

"Yes."

"You were near Deir ez-Zor."

"You have heard of it."

"Everyone has heard of it by now. There is this German photographer, Armin Wegner I believe his name to be, whom has been travelling all over Syria taking photos of the death marches."

"How will that help?" I ask.

"They say his photos have been in all the major newspapers, even The New York Times."

"What's that?"

"A famous paper in America."

"I'd rather see him pick up a gun and fight."

"But his photos are proof of what's happening. Even the American President has seen them and has sent aide, especially to the orphanages."

I think of Mr. Davis and Sister Gertrude, and decide not to mention them, but I'm not sure of my reason. Instead I ask, "Will this war ever end, Father?"

"War will only end the day we learn to love one another."

I glare at the prisoners. "I don't think I could ever love them."

Father Eduard stares up at the sky, scratches behind his ear. Some memory seems to strike him suddenly, an oppressive jolt. After a minute or two he says, "Years ago, when I was a young boy, a Turk killed my sister. She was about your age."

My eyes widen. "How horrible."

"There was nothing I could do."

"You saw it happen?"

Father Eduard blinks a tear away. "I remember his eyes mostly, his smell." He clears his throat. "We were walking home from school. He.... I hated him for a long time...."

"And now?"

Father Eduard's eyes attempt to suffocate my own feelings of hatred. "Hating him never made me feel any better." He studies the camp. "Do you have a chapel here?"

"I don't believe so."

Father Eduard unhooks his horse from the fence. "We'll have to change that, now won't we?" He cracks a sympathetic smile, then puts a hand on my shoulder. "I must go now, but we'll talk later."

Chapter 15

Warm April air blows in the rain and the rain turns leftover snow into brown slush. The sun appears after an hour or so and thaws the camp. The camp ripens. Sour air carries the clammy smell of horses and unwashed and sticky slept-in clothes. Father Eduard and I often stay in the recovery tent or the makeshift chapel he had built. Kazim and Captain Wilson sometimes join us for Mass, although Kazim's discomfort is clear. "I don't understand all this ritual," he once told me. "But I'm glad I come. It makes me forget about the war."

Afterward, Father Eduard often hosts some of the officers in his tent, treating them to coffee and canned pudding. Many of the discussions center on military matters with Captain Wilson informing his men that the brunt of the British force is battling their way to Jerusalem and we are to remain between them and Damascus. "But keep in mind, this rainy spell has quieted most military matters. Joining them may take longer than anticipated."

I do not understand most of what Captain Wilson says. I scribble the more complicated English words down on a sheet of paper to ask about later. If I can never return home and I move to Great Britain, I should learn as much as I can of the English language before I go.

Most of the time, after Mass, it's just me and Father Eduard taking our coffee alone in his tent and discussing personal matters. Our chats usually center on forgiveness. He's slowly convincing me to forgive the Turkish soldiers, because that is what's best, I know that, but it's difficult. It's a hard thing to forgive someone, especially an enemy. He mentions his sister from time to time, but only when I ask about her.

"A hardened heart is not good for the soul," he tells me during our last discussion.

"I know, Father."

"I don't think you do." He pauses, pulls at his beard. "I mean, you understand it intellectually, but I'm more concerned how you understand it here," he says, tapping a finger against his chest. "Every time we say an ill word to our neighbor, every time we refuse to help someone in need, every time we have an impure thought, all these things encourage hate." He touches my shoulder. "And it is hate that ignites wars."

"I keep thinking about that boy," I say.

"The prisoner of war?"

"Yes. He seems so..."

"Innocent?"

I curl my nose. "Remorseful."

Father Eduard rubs his beard. "Have you spoken to him yet?"

"No."

"Perhaps you should."

I awake to an unusually warm morning. The camp buzzes with flies. Soldiers occupy themselves with digging ditches, cleaning weapons, and writing, all of them comfortable with the daily chores of an army at war. There is not an expression of fear or anxiety among them. If not for their uniform, they would seem like ordinary men digging up a garden or shining their guns before a hunt in the woods. Father used to hunt boar with Mr. Badalian. I remember their bold expressions. "We'll have a feast tonight," Father had said. Mr. Badalian would pour them another shot of vodka and slap Father on the arm.

I feel my family's presence most days, but I miss Father the most, his strong hands and calm demeanor. I wish he were here to tell me not to worry, to be strong, as he was strong, not to give up or let go of my beliefs, even if it means death.

The warm weather encourages me to take a walk. After walking around camp for an hour or so and thinking about home, I take Father Eduard's advice and go talk to the Turkish soldier with the boney face and haggard eyes. I find him sitting on the ground near the fence with his legs straight out and poking at the dirt with a stick. A blanket lies over his shoulders like a dead lamb. His face looks thinner than it did before, but his eyes still have a weak look to them. He stands up and begins to leave when he sees me.

"Wait," I say.

The young soldier turns around, jams the stick in the ground, then leans against it.

"Come here."

"Why?"

I open my hand and reveal two pieces of candy. He narrows his eyes, steps closer, like a clever mouse that has seen its fair share of traps.

"I won't hurt you," I say. "Take one." I lean my hand inside the fence. "It's chocolate."

He snatches one of the candies out of my hand, takes a step back, then pops the candy in his mouth.

"Do you want the other one?" I lean my hand farther inside the fence, careful that a barb does not snag my sleeve.

His eyes flash hunger. Then he turns and looks toward the other prisoners. They are busy building a small shelter, slapping mud between stones and stacking the stones one on top of the other in an orderly manner.

"It's okay," I say. "Take it."

He snatches the last piece of chocolate and shoves it in his mouth.

"I'm Valia. What's your name?"

He licks his lips. "Zaki."

"What were you doing with that stick?"

"Something to pass the time is all."

I shrugged my shoulders and sat down. "How old are you?"

Zaki moves his fingers, remains standing. "16."

"I turned 15 last month."

"The candy was from your party?"

"No party. No friends to celebrate it with."

"Where are they?"

"Certainly you know the answer to that."

Zaki kicks at the dirt, studying it. "I assure you I don't."

"How many of us have you killed?" I ask. I grit my teeth, clench my fists, regretting that I gave Zaki the chocolate, talking to him even.

"What do you mean?"

"Armenians. How many Armenians have you killed?"

"I've killed no one."

"But you're a soldier."

"No." He answers so quickly it startles me. He tries to make his voice less harsh as he adds, "I don't want to be. The government is making us."

"Us?"

"Men from my village. I want to be a doctor, not a soldier."

"Why not run away?"

"They'd kill my parents if I did that."

"But you're a Turk, a Muslim like one of them. Why would they do such a thing?"

Zaki stares at me for a moment without saying a word. Then he looks across the camp. "Why are you here with all these soldiers?" he asks.

"You know why."

"If I knew I wouldn't have asked."

"You must have seen the marches."

"What marches?"

"We were all forced from our homes."

"Oh, you mean the evacuations…to avoid…"

"To avoid capture from the Russians. Yes, I know." I kick at the dirt. "It was a lie."

"I was not part of a lie." He sniffs.

"Silly boy."

"I'm a man." He touches his face, looks at his shaking hands. "I've lost a lot of weight," he continues, narrowing his eyes. "The men you're with, they are very cruel."

"I think they're kind."

"How can you say that?"

"You're alive, aren't you?"

He steps forward, as if wanting to lunge at me. "You didn't answer my question."

"Which is?" I ask, stepping backward. When I do, I trip, and my hand jams into a sharp rock. "Ouch!" I yelp.

"Here," Zaki says, holding out a handkerchief, "let me help you."

His touch is gentle, steady. "How's that? Not too tight I hope."

"It feels fine, thank you," I say, curiosity in my tone.

"Why are you here?" he asks a second time. "Are you married to one of the soldiers?"

"Your government. Police soldiers murdered my parents and brother. They're murdering many people."

"I'm an infantryman, not a police soldier. I've been fighting in the mountains."

"So you have killed people."

"Well… I don't know if I've killed anyone. I loaded my gun as I was taught, fired, took cover, fired again, took cover, and I kept doing this until I needed to reload and then I did it all over again. I never saw anything I hit." He sighs. "I hope I didn't hit anything. But I'm not a murderer, this I promise you. You must see that. Otherwise you wouldn't have shared your chocolate."

"Father Eduard said I needed to talk to you."

Zaki adjusts the blanket around his shoulders. "He's the only one that's been kind to us."

I look beyond Zaki's shoulders where the men are building the cabins. "Do you have friends inside the fence?"

Zaki shifts his eyes toward the hundred or so men behind him. "Three." He points. "They're helping with the cabins… over there."

Something about how he speaks of his friends compels me to look at him differently. I study him carefully, look into his eyes. They seem kind, trusting even.

"Where are you from?" I ask.

"Turkey, of course," Zaki says.

"I mean what part."

"Ankara."

"I'm from Adana."

"That's miles away."

My eyes widen. "You have been there?"

"No. I learned about it in school. I know all the cities of the empire."

A caring tear pops from my eye. "I think you'll make a fine doctor," I say, rubbing my hand.

Zaki tugs at his stomach.

"What is it?" I ask.

"Do you have any stew? Father Eduard said he might be able to bring us some."

I gesture at one of the guard towers. "Do they not feed you?"

"Very little."

"I'll have to ask Captain Wilson."

"Who's he?"

"I cook for him. He's a nice man. I'm sure he'll give me permission."

"That would be nice."

"I'll try and bring some tomorrow."

"For my friends, too?"

"I'll see what I can do."

Chapter 16

Day follows day. Before I know it, May arrives, and then June. The wounded trickle in steadily every morning from the front. I tend to them first, then I bring four tin cups of stew every afternoon for Zaki and his friends. I always look forward bringing the stew, even though it's for Turks. I bring the stew mainly for Zaki. Having gotten to know him, I now realize it's not his fault for what had happened to my parents and brother. He is just a boy trapped in a world he does not agree with. He is adamant about wanting to be a doctor. I do not trust him completely, he is a Turk after all, but helping him keeps my mind off the wounded soldiers, their faces walnut black and their uniforms frayed and dirty with blood all over them. The inside of the tents smell stale, sour, and wet with violence. It's good to escape such a tragic job as much as I can.

The fighting continues but does not advance in our direction. Prisoners come by the hundreds. The fence expands every day with more cabins constructed.

One afternoon I arrive late at the spot at the fence. The carriage wheel had busted and some of the stew had spilled, and it takes me twenty minutes to clean up and prepare more stew. It takes the driver longer to replace the wheel than it does for me to dress for church.

When we arrive, Father Eduard is standing by the entrance to the prison camp. Zaki and three of his friends walk out of the gate with their arms bound. British and Arab soldiers with rifles stand by a wagon.

"What's going on, Father?" I ask.

Father Eduard touches my shoulder. The weight of his hand feels cold and miserable. His watery eyes glisten with fear and anger. "They are to be executed," he says.

"What? Why?"

He gestures to one of the guards. "They say they tried to escape."

Zaki looks at me, shakes his head, his face weak with grief.

"Is it true?"

Zaki steps from the line. A British soldier grabs his arm, pulls him back.

"Let him speak to her," Father Eduard says. "Please. He's just a boy."

The British soldier grunts, then releases Zaki's arm.

"No," Zaki says. "I swear. There was this injured dog. We tried to help it."

"By escaping?"

"The dog was tangled in some wire. We asked the guard for help, but he wouldn't help us, so we jumped the fence and freed the dog ourselves."

I stare at Zaki a moment. His eyes twitch. His mouth quivers. Is he lying? Is this some kind of Turkish trick? I know it not to be true and it is at that moment I truly believe him. Though suffering in all this madness, I even begin to love him a little, or perhaps feel compassion toward him; it's difficult to know the difference sometimes. "You must do something, Father," I say.

"Can you spare the boy?" Father Eduard asks. "He's innocent of the charges."

"We have our orders," the British soldier says. He shoves Zaki forward.

"Then wait a few more moments, can you do that?" Father Eduard asks.

"One more minute," the soldier says.

"What is it, Father?" I ask.

"I'll go find Kazim. Maybe he can help."

"Oh thank you!" I say, hugging Father Eduard tight.

Father Eduard returns with Kazim a few minutes later.

"Kazim!" I shout. "Please! They were not trying to escape."

Kazim, his right arm still in a sling, pats his horse's neck with his good hand, then slides off the animal. "Since when do you care for Turks?"

"Zaki is innocent," I say. You must go tell Captain Wilson."

"What did she say about the Captain?" another British soldier asks.

"He can stop the execution," Father Eduard says.

The soldier smirks. "Tell her he's the one that gave the order."

"I don't believe him," I say.

"You're sure of this?" Kazim asks.

"I believe Zaki," I say.

"As do I," Father Eduard says.

"I'll be back," Kazim says. He swings himself up on his horse, yanks the reins, slumps forward, kicks the animal in the ribs, and speeds away.

"Coming Father?" It's the British soldier who had asked about Captain Wilson.

"We must wait for Kazim," Father Eduard says.

"Your friend is wasting his time. Now get in if you're coming."

"Okay," Father Eduard says, hesitation creeping from his voice. "Coming, child?"

"No," I say. I kick a wagon wheel. "We should wait for Captain Wilson."

A soldier, waving his arm impatiently, shouts something at me I do not understand.

"He wants you to move," Father Eduard says.

I step back and the wagon lurches forward.

I stand there in disbelief as I watch them go. Something comes over me. I run after the wagon, crying, "I want to come! Wait! Take me with you!"

The wagon stops. Father Eduard pulls me up. I squeeze his hand until mine falls asleep, but I never let go. The shattering violence I have come to know ruptures like a blister. I squeeze Father Eduard's hand tighter. The unpleasant sensation at the tips of my fingers reminds me of the pain my parents and brother must have felt right before they died. I imagine my face being the last image they saw before surrendering to the ruthless cruelty of a bullet. I feel guilty of not being able to save them. I do not want to experience that a second time. I want to believe the British are more charitable than the Turks. I hope my presence will rest the executioner's hands long enough before Captain Wilson arrives to stop them.

The wagon stops near a large hole. Flies buzz inside the hole. A sour smell leaks from dozens of corpses. We climb out of the wagon and walk with the prisoners to the hole. I hold Zaki's hand as we walk. I feel fear in his cold and oily hand. My head aches with worry. Will Kazim and Captain Wilson arrive in time?

Zaki and the other prisoners line up in front of the hole. A soldier places a sack on their heads. Ten Arab soldiers line up in front of them and prepare their rifles.

"Father, we must do something," I say.

"Might I say a prayer?" Father Eduard asks, looking around camp as if searching for a sign.

"Sure, Father," a soldier says. "But make it quick."

Father Eduard lowers his head.

The Arabs take aim after the prayer.

I turn back toward camp and see Kazim and Captain Wilson approaching. "Wait!" I say. "Here they come!"

"Hold up!" Kazim says. "Hold your fire!" The Arabs lower their weapons.

"Captain Wilson!" I cry. "I knew you would come. Please, they are innocent. Do not kill them. Please."

"Valia, I'm sorry, I cannot prevent this. I have my orders."

"But you're in charge. You can stop it."

Captain Wilson glances at Father Eduard. "There are men more powerful than me I'm afraid."

"Tell him, Kazim."

"I'm sorry, Valia."

I drop to my knees, pull up fists of dirt. My heart stings with fury. My whole-body shakes from the maddening sound of gunshots. I hate the sound of guns. I want the war to end. I want to find Artush and sail to Europe together, leaving her nasty and mean husband—as I've convinced myself he to be—behind.

But when I look up, Zaki's friends lay dead. Zaki remains standing.

"Zaki!" I cry, my eyes wide with shock. I pull the sack off his head, untie his arms, hug him.

"It's okay," he whispers in my ear. He gently rubs my shoulder. "Everything will be okay."

Chapter 17

Field guns roar in the distance the following morning as we eat our breakfast. My shoulders jerk. I cannot get used to the guns. I don't think anyone is numb to the guns.

"Thank you for sparing Zaki," I say.

"You're welcome," Captain Wilson says.

"What changed your mind?"

"You did."

"Me?"

"You've saved so many soldiers' lives."

"But won't you get in trouble for disobeying an order?"

"Don't you worry about that," Captain Wilson says, "everything's fine."

"Zaki's friends were innocent, too."

Captain Wilson picks at his teeth with a pocketknife. "They were men. They knew better."

"They were helping an injured dog."

Captain Wilson looks at Father Eduard. "You didn't tell her."

"Tell me what?"

Father Eduard sips his coffee. "They were trying to escape."

"No…Zaki said…they were helping him."

"That's what they led him to believe."

"I don't understand."

"We checked their bodies afterward," Captain Wilson says. "One of them had a map. The other two had homemade knives sewn in their shirts."

"But you didn't know that before you shot them."

Captain Wilson puts his utensils down across his plate, wipes his mouth. "We had our suspicions. We've been watching them a long time."

"They seemed sincere," I say. "They were always grateful for the stew I brought them."

"We must pray for them," Father Eduard says.

I pour more coffee. "Why must Zaki stay behind the fence?"

"He's still a prisoner," Captain Wilson says. "Besides, it's safer."

I narrow my eyes. "What will happen to him after the war?"

"I'm not sure."

I sigh. "How much longer are we to stay here?"

Captain Wilson jams a piece of bread in his mouth. "Until reinforcements arrive."

"May Zaki go with me to Adana?"

"Well, I don't know," Captain Wilson says. "I thought we decided Great Britain is your destination."

"I know, I'm sorry I keep changing my mind, but I'd rather go home."

"There is nothing left to go back to," Kazim says. "Reports come in everyday, you know this, all Armenian towns and villages have been decimated."

I ignore him, although I know what he says is true, and continue to focus my attention on Captain Wilson. "You already promised to find Artush," I say. "What's one more favor?"

"What Kazim says is right. It'll be a miracle to find your friend but, as promised, I will try." He leans back in his chair. "Besides, if you were able to return home, what then?"

I shrug. "I'm not sure."

"This nun you spoke of before," Kazim says, "maybe she can take the boy."

"A nun?" Captain Wilson asks.

Father Eduard's eyes perk up. "You've never mentioned a nun to me."

"Sister Gertrude," I say. "An American I met in Aleppo. But it's been almost two years. How would we find her?"

"An American, you say," Captain Wilson says. "The Americans have been in Aleppo for quite some time. But missionaries come and go, so I doubt you'll find her now. Nevertheless, we might be able to help the boy somehow."

My eyes brighten. "I would be most grateful."

We eat in silence for the remainder of breakfast. Afterward, Father Eduard helps me wash the dishes.

"I am proud of you Valia," Father Eduard says, picking up a dry towel.

"What for?"

"Saving that boy's life. Even I couldn't have done that. You are a special young woman."

"But it never would have happened had you not suggested I visit the prisoners." I rinse off a plate and hand it to him to dry. "Zaki owes his life to you, more so than he does to me."

Father Eduard nods. "Have you forgiven him?"

"He's innocent of all this," I say. "He didn't even want to be a soldier."

"But you wouldn't have known that had you not been willing to forgive."

I nod. "I suppose so."

"So perhaps the anger you feel now," he gestures toward the prison camp, "toward the others, maybe one day you'll forgive them as well."

"Maybe."

"Tell me about this Sister Gertrude. Why have you never mentioned her?"

"I don't know. Guess I forgot. And I only spoke with her briefly. Oh, and there was a man with her. Davis something. I can't remember."

"You don't mean Jesse Davis, do you?"

"Yes, that's it. Do you know him?"

"I'm happy to say that I do. I've been corresponding with him for quite some time."

I smile. "Looks like you've been keeping secrets as well."

"Truth be told, I wasn't so sure if he could help us. I didn't want to get your hopes up."

I pull a plate from the sudsy water, rinse it off, then hand it to him. "But now?"

"Now I think Mr. Davis has a little more power, especially with help from the American Ambassador, Henry Morgenthau. I hear he's a good man. A Jew, they say. They're taking thousands of refugees in, mostly orphans." He places the dry plate inside a small cupboard. "Tell me, you met them in Aleppo?"

"Yes."

"What happened? I mean, how did you meet?"

"I escaped. But the police soldiers caught me."

"Mr. Davis couldn't help…or Sister Gertrude?"

"Saabir threatened them."

"He was the police soldier in charge?"

"Yes, the one that murdered my parents."

"I think they can help you."

"Zaki, too?"

"Yes," Father Eduard says. "I'll write Mr. Davis a letter immediately. He's a very sharp man. I'm sure he'll remember you." He thought a moment. "Would you like to help me write the letter?"

"I wouldn't know what to say."

"I'll help you."

I place my shaky hands over my nose and mouth, forming a triangle. "I can't believe it," I say.

"Believe what?"

"It's been so long, the war. I'd do anything for it to end."

"You and me both, Valia."

We return to Father Eduard's tent. He reaches in the top drawer of his desk and pulls out a piece of stationery and an envelope. He puts on his spectacles. He picks up a fountain pen, dips it in an inkwell, and gently presses pen to paper. He scrawls the date 10 July 1917 in the right-hand corner. Dear Sir, the letter begins, but a voice from outside the tent interrupts his thoughts. He puts the pen down. "Come in."

A British soldier enters the tent. He's a young man with an unscathed face and clean uniform that has a newly enlisted look of high spirits and amity. "Good afternoon, sir. Captain Wilson ordered me to notify you that reinforcements are on the way. We shall be leaving in a matter of days. You are invited to accompany him when we leave."

"Tell the Captain thank you."

"Yes, sir," the young soldier says. He salutes and leaves.

Father Eduard returns his attention to the paper, picks up the pen, smiles. "Let's see." Then he begins writing. After he finishes with the letter, he shows it to me. "How does that sound?"

"I don't understand most of it," I say. "What's this word?"

"That's your name in English," Father Eduard says. "Here, sound it out: V-A-L-I-A."

"V-A-L-I-A," I say.

"Good."

"What else does the letter say?"

"That we're on our way to Aleppo." He slips the letter inside an envelope, seals it, then drops it in a small basket on his desk. "A courier will pick it up later." He looks at his watch. "Let's say a special Mass for the safe arrival of reinforcements and a safe journey home. Shall we?" He pulls out a small table and puts a cloth on top. Then he places two candles on the front corners of the table, lights them, pulls out a cup, a bottle of wine, a small chunk of bread, and a book from a drawer underneath the table. He yanks on a ribbon, opening the book, and places it on a wooden cradle. "In the name of the Father, Son, and Holy Ghost," he says. I make the sign of the cross and Mass begins. I squeeze my eyes shut and pray for the guns not to get any closer.

Chapter 18

I visit Zaki after Mass, but he's not in his usual place, sitting under a tree away from the other prisoners.

"Where is Zaki?" I ask.

A prisoner nods at one of the cabins. "Sick."

"What's wrong with him?"

"How should I know? I'm no doctor."

"I want to see him."

The prisoner smiles. "Then hop the fence." He's thin and bony with deep wrinkles under his unblinking eyes the size of 5-lira coins. His left hand is missing a finger, he keeps tightening his lips nervously, and his thin beard has the appearance of a smoldering forest fire. "Boy should have been shot, anyway, save us the hassle of taking care of him."

I narrow my eyes, then call to the soldier in the guard tower. "Will you help me?" He looks at me with an indescribable gaze. I realize he does not understand me. "Help," I say in English. He waves with the back of his hand and looks away.

I run to Father Eduard. "Come quickly! It's Zaki!"

"What's wrong?" Father Eduard asks.

"He's sick. They won't let me see him."

We arrive at the fence. Father Eduard orders the guard to open the gate and we enter. Two guards accompany us.

"Which cabin?" Father Eduard asks. A prisoner with the unblinking eyes points the way.

We find Zaki on the floor, his face pale and sweaty. He's mumbling and scratching at his legs and chest.

"What's wrong with him?" I ask.

Father Eduard pulls up Zaki's shirt. Red spots cover his chest.

"Typhus," I say.

"We are not certain of that," Father Eduard says. "But he does need a doctor."

"I've seen it before," I say. "It's Typhus. We can take him to Doctor Smith. He's a good person. He'll help him. But we need to hurry."

"Very well," Father Eduard says. He picks up Zaki and heads toward the door.

"He cannot leave," the guard says.

"The boy needs a doctor," Father Eduard says.

"I work with Doctor Smith," I say. "He'll help us."

"It's against orders to help the enemy," one of the guards says.

"Were you ordered to harass a priest and an orphan?" Father Eduard asks, fire in his eyes. "Move out of the way or, I assure you, Captain Wilson will hear of this."

The guard lowers his head, and steps aside.

We arrive at the recovery tent where I usually spend most mornings, and find Doctor Smith dressing a wound where a leg had once been. The wounded soldier is asleep. Sweat pours from his forehead. His color is good and I know he'll recover. Many of Doctor Smith's patients recover. He's an excellent doctor.

"We need your help," I say.

"Bring the boy here," Doctor Smith says, and gestures at an empty bed.

We place Zaki on the bed and Doctor Smith examines him. "Where did you…he's a Turk…."

"He's my friend," I say. "His name's Zaki."

Doctor Smith pulls at his ear, thinking. "I see. He came from the prison camp?"

"Yes," Father Eduard says.

"Can you help him?" I ask.

"See these red blotches," Doctor Smith says. "And his teeth…see how blue they are? The boy has scurvy."

"Not Typhus?" I ask.

"No."

"Is it as dangerous?"

"All he needs is a proper diet," Dr. Smith says. "There's a tent behind this one where we keep canned vegetables. Go find a can of pickled beets. A spoon, too. Be discreet about it. Don't think the men would take kindly in helping a Turk."

"Yes, I'll be careful. Thank you."

I return with the beets and hand them to Doctor Smith. He opens the can with a knife, then hands the can back to me. "Give him a little now, just a little though. Save the rest for later for soup."

I dip the spoon in the can. "Here, Zaki, eat this."

Zaki opens his mouth and sips at the dark juice. His lips tremble, which forces some of the juice to slide down the corner of his mouth. I catch the juice with the spoon. "Take all of it," I say.

"I'll fetch some water," Father Eduard says.

"Tea is better, Dr. Smith says." He points. "There in my box. There's a kettle outside by the fire."

Father Eduard nods. "Thank you."

Dr. Smith smiles. "Valia has been a big help to me. I think more men would have died if not for her comforting voice."

I blush.

"I have no doubt," Father Eduard says. He takes the tea outside, and returns a few minutes later with a steaming tin cup and hands the cup to me.

I dip the spoon in the cup, blow on the warm liquid, then tilt the spoon toward Zaki's lips. His eyes brighten from the warmth of the tea.

"You need to rest," I say after Zaki finishes the tea. "I'll bring more beets and tea later."

"Don't go," Zaki says, his voice weak and frightened.

"I have other chores," I say. "I won't be gone long, promise."

"Stay with me until I fall asleep."

"Very well." I take his hand in mine and sing an Armenian song Mother had taught me when I was a little girl:

The moon has appeared
its light descending on my house
for this day we must plow the fields
and from this there will be hope in my heart.

Zaki falls asleep after a few short minutes.

"A pretty song," Father Eduard says.

"Mother used to sing it to me when I was little." I let go of Zaki's hand, straighten his blanket, and brush the hair out of his face.

"What is it?" Father Eduard asks.

"He reminds me so much of Arsen."

"I'm afraid my Armenian is elementary," Doctor Smith says. "What does the song mean?"

"It's a song of hope," I say.

Dr. Smith sighs. "We can all use some of that."

Chapter 19

Zaki's condition improves after a week. His legs quiver when he walks, his voice frail, and the cane steady in his hand as it jams in the ground with each exhausting step. He keeps to himself unless I'm with him. We walk farther each day, not talking, just listening to the guns in the distance. The British and Australian soldiers keep a watchful eye on us, but never speak, I assume because of the threat of Captain Wilson.

"What will happen to me when the war is over?" Zaki asks.

"Father Eduard wrote to his American friend," I say. "They should be able to help you."

Zaki grasps my arm. "Wait. Can I not stay with you?"

"What do you mean?" I ask.

"I…well…Zaki stammers.

My lips part with joyous hesitation. "You wish to marry me?"

Zaki blushes. "Sure, why not?"

"You call this a proposal?"

"Marry me, Valia."

"So sudden. I don't think that's wise."

"Why not?"

"You have to ask? An Armenian and a Turk? We would be scorned, worse even."

"We wouldn't be the first," Zaki says.

"But I'm a Christian," I say. "I will never give up my faith, even if it would save my life."

"Then we'll move to Europe. Safer there."

"How can you be so sure? You have never been there, have you?"

He shifts his weight, leans heavily on the cane. "Surely any place is better than here. Listen."

The rumble of battle intensifies. "Let's go," I say, "before Father Eduard begins to worry." I grasp Zaki's arm. "And not a word about marriage to anyone, not yet."

We return in time to see Captain Wilson and Kazim leaving for the front lines, their backs to us some distance away. I'd recognize them anywhere. Kazim's broad shoulders. Captain Wilson's adept horsemanship. In front of them are fresh soldiers with rifles tucked under their arms moving forward out of camp with strict resolve.

"We were looking for you," Father Eduard says.

"We were out for a walk," Zaki says. He gestures at the cane. "It's my fault we were gone so long."

"Quite alright," Father Eduard says.

"When will they return?" I ask.

"Hard to say," Father Eduard says. "But Captain Wilson asked me to give you this. It's an Armenian/English dictionary."

"Where did he find this?" I ask, flipping through the pages.

"No idea. I haven't seen one since the war began, and even then they were hard to come by."

"Will you teach me?"

"Yes, of course."

"Me, too?" Zaki asks.

"I will teach you both."

Weeks pass and then months and the war continues and I wonder if life will ever be any different. October brings cool breezes. Clouds hang heavy with cold rain and the rain races down the sky for hours and turns the camp into one large mud heap. Loud claps of thunder shake me awake during the night. Cracks of lighting explode purple and pink across the dark sky. The storms have halted the fighting and Zaki and I spend our time learning English. Most of our conversations are in English now. We practice with the soldiers, especially the younger ones. Younger soldiers seem to not resent Zaki as much as the more hardened, older soldiers. Knowing their language brings them closer together. The more Zaki speaks with them, the more I grow to love him. Every word he utters is full of compassion and grace, every touch a helping hand in time of need. Morale grows stronger. The soldiers even joke with us. They teach us slang words like *bull dust, eating irons, deadset*, and *dinky-di*. Fun to say, but difficult to learn.

The storms grow stronger by November. The armies grow impatient. Fighting resumes despite the mud, rain, and wind. It's difficult to tell the difference between thunder and the sound of the guns. Ambulances bring the wounded in by the truckloads and those once carefree soldiers now have the face of unquiet despair and melancholy. Doctor Smith exhausts himself sawing off legs and arms and removing bullets from shoulders and legs. Zaki helps me change bandages and collect water. We hug our bodies close to each other and pray for the guns to stop. The guns and the rain do not stop. The thunder of the guns and the thunder in the sky collaborate in the turmoil.

The roar of the guns escalates on Christmas Eve. Dozens of British armored cars begin arriving from the south. British soldiers march confidently behind the rumbling machines singing like choirboys as they move forward to the smoky haze of the battlefield. Zaki works all morning chopping wood. I tend to the wounded.

"They're back," Father Eduard says. "Come."

Kazim is there to greet us when we step from the tent. He looks at me with inquisitive eyes. He climbs off his horse. "How is your friend? He has recovered well from his illness?

"He's fine. Chopping wood."

"Building another cabin inside the fence?" Kazim sighs with relief. "We're capturing many, then."

"No. He's just over there," I say, pointing.

Kazim looks at Dr. Smith. "Is that safe?"

"Won't you come inside the tent?" Dr. Smith asks.

"I'll make a pot of tea," I say.

"He's harmless," Dr. Smith says, once inside the tent. He takes a seat at a makeshift table in perfect view of the wounded. "I can't leave them for too long. The nurses are only capable of so much." He rubs his eyes. "We could use a few more doctors as well."

"He didn't want to be a soldier," I say. "The government forced him."

"What?" Kazim asks.

"Zaki," I say. "He was forced to be a soldier."

"You know this how?"

"He told me."

"I see. I guess that settles it, then."

"What does that mean?" I ask as I scoop tealeaves out of a tin can, placing them in a sifter.

"Will no one try to harm him?" Kazim asks. Sarcasm wets his tongue. "After all, he is a Turk."

"I thought you liked Zaki."

"I tolerate him…." He pauses. "For your sake."

"Captain Wilson ordered Zaki not to be harmed," I say.

Kazim raises his brow. "I see," he says. "Very well."

"Before you two left for the front," Father Eduard says.

"I don't wish to harm the boy," Kazim says. "But I do wonder what type of man he'll become."

"He's a good person," I say, my words gently prickling Kazim's ears.

"What she says is true," Father Eduard says.

"I have no doubt," Kazim says. "It's just…"

"You can trust him," I say.

Kazim empties his teacup in one gulp, then smiles. "I trust you."

"More?" I ask.

"Please," Kazim says, extending the cup.

"The boy has been a big help," Dr. Smith says.

"Good to hear," Kazim says. He takes a sip of tea, then leans back in his chair and lets out a satisfied breath.

Dr. Smith leans into the table. "Now tell us, what does the front look like?"

"We're pushing the Turks back," Kazim says. "Only a matter of time before their line breaks."

"What of Captain Wilson?" I ask.

"He's fine, exhausted, but fine. He seems in good spirits."

"He is here in camp, yes?" Father Eduard asks. "You did return with him."

"Yes, of course. Why do you ask?"

"I'm worried about the boy," Father Eduard says. "Some of the men look at him, I fear, with malicious intent."

"But you said Captain Wilson ordered no harm come to him."

Father Eduard nods. "It's just better if the Captain remains in camp, that's all."

"I'll keep an eye on the boy myself," Kazim says. "I assure you, no harm will come to him."

"I thought you didn't care for him," I say.

"But you care for him. I..."

Before Kazim can say more, a choir of voices distracts the hardened afternoon away from the arriving army. The wounded shift in their beds. Dr. Smith smiles. I smile.

"What is it?" Kazim asks.

"Christmas carols," Dr. Smith says.

Kazim's face turns blank.

"A song celebrating the birth of Jesus," I say. Then I open the tent flaps and tie them up. Captain Wilson and dozens of British and Australian soldiers are holding candles and encircling a tree that has been decorated with handkerchiefs and differing colors of string. My eyes flood with tears as they stare into the secrets of a Wishing Tree. It reminds me of the night before Lori's wedding. Father and I are in the back yard. The smell of supper drifts out an open window. Father has the handkerchief that Mother had given me in his hand. *Do not hate, Valia, Father says. We must forgive those that harm us.* I pray for an end to the violence, the hatred that has forced people out of the only homes they have known. No matter where I end up after the war, I hope that I can live in peace.

"What is it they're singing?" I ask.

"Silent Night," Doctor Smith says. He begins translating the carol as they sing.

"A perfect song for such a day like this."

Captain Wilson approaches me. "Good news from the north. It seems like Meskena is in rebel hands."

I stare at him blank faced.

"What?" he asks. "You thought I forgot?"

"No…I don't know. What are rebels?"

Captain looks at Father Eduard, smiles, then looks at me. "Look it up in the dictionary. You still have it I assume."

"Oh, yes. I keep it safely under my cot."

"Not a word that has come up in our lessons, either," Father Eduard says.

"So what does it mean?" I ask.

"In this case, Armenian soldiers," Captain Wilson says. "Somehow they escaped the Turkish barracks where they were assigned digging ditches and such, stole some guns and took to the woods."

"I can go home now," I say.

"I'm not sure. I still think your best bet is Europe, for you and Zaki both."

I scratch my throat. "But perhaps the Turks have been thrown out of Adana as well."

"And what of Zaki?" Kazim asks.

"What do you mean?"

"Certainly you don't expect him to live in Adana."

"And why not?" I know what he's thinking, but I want to avoid the harsh reality.

Kazim sniffs. "Isn't it obvious? He'd be killed."

I glance at Father Eduard, then back at Kazim. "The Armenians are a forgiving people," I say in a feeble defense, a trivial contradiction what I had told Zaki earlier. "If there is any chance for me to return home, then I'm going to do it. Zaki would be fine. He wouldn't have anything to fear."

"The Americans will not be here forever," Kazim says, "even this nun you spoke of."

"Enough talk of possible outcomes," Captain Wilson says. "Only this war can dictate to us what happens next." His stern face slowly relaxes, then he says, "What do you think of our tree? It's a fine one, yes?"

"A most splendid Wishing Tree," Father Eduard says.

"Thank you," Captain Wilson replies. "I thought it would bring some cheer to the place."

"Indeed it has," Dr. Smith says.

The decorations give the tree life. Even in the middle of hatred and greed, the tree stands as a symbol of genuine majesty.

"This is for you, Valia," Captain Wilson says. "Father Eduard said you lost one similar to it." He sniffs. "I hope you like this one."

"It's beautiful. Thank you." I glide my rough fingers across the blue silk. "But I did not lose the one before. I simply just—left it."

"I see," Captain Wilson says, disappointment straining his voice.

"It's beautiful," I say.

Captain Wilson smiles. "Aren't you going to hang it on the tree?"

"Yes, of course. But, why have you given me such a gift?"

"I saw things; things a man should never see. A young girl should especially never see them." A tear leaks from the corner of his eye. "It was something beyond what war should be."

"Nothing will erase the murder of my people from memory."

"Nor should it. It's just…the Turks…they are so…"

"Pitiful," I say.

"Evil," Captain Wilson says.

"That's not true of many of them, I realize that now. In fact, some of them saved my life. I thank God for that."

"God left this place long ago, I'm afraid," Captain Wilson says.

"My faith is what keeps me alive in all this madness," I say.

It begins to snow, like bits of paper dumped from a trash bin. Flakes melt in the palm of my hand.

"The frozen tears of God," Doctor Smith says. "That's what my mother used to tell me as a child."

The soldiers stop singing. They place a ring of candles around the Wishing Tree.

A soldier jogs over and hands Father Eduard an envelope, and Father Eduard puts on his spectacles and rips it open. "Good news," he says. "A letter from Mr. Davis. He remembers you. So does Sister Gertrude."

"They remain in Aleppo?" I ask.

"Yes." He opens the letter. "Says right here the orphanage is doing well and they've had little or no trouble with the government. Locals are helping them, too."

"That's great news," Dr. Smith says. "Great news indeed."

My eyes open wide. "When can I see them?"

Father Eduard continues reading. "It says here something about Meskene and…"

"What!" I say, almost jumping out of my shoes. "Meskene!" I rub my hands together like a child waiting for a coveted gift. "Then it hasn't burned to the ground."

"You know of this place," Father Eduard says.

"Ah, yes, I recall you telling me of this place," Captain Wilson says. He shakes his head. "We were told the locals were evacuated and many killed."

I clinch my fist. "Jarir said it had burned to the ground." Regretting my mistake, I turn to Kazim. "I'm sorry. I know he was a friend of yours."

"He would be happy to know he was mistaken," Kazim says.

"They can provide escorts to Aleppo," Father Eduard says. "It's the safest route."

"A lady there, Belma was her name, told me I can find safe passage there." I spit out a series of questions in rapid succession: "Does Mr. Davis mention Belma? When may I go? Will you take me? I need to…"

"Slow down child," Father Eduard says. "They don't mention a Belma." He scans the letter. "Someone named Berkant Hasim."

"What! Are you sure?"

"Yes, right here," Father Eduard says, pointing. "You know him?"

My body rocks with expressions of happiness and helpless anxiety. "His daughter, if it's the same man."

"Right," Father Eduard says. "Yasmin." He sucks in his teeth. "My goodness."

Looking at my hands, I shake my head. Underneath my nails is the dirt of camp. It makes me wonder if I will ever lie again under fresh sheets or will I be tossed in an unmarked grave, nothing more than a pale memory. "What will happen to me?"

Father Eduard pulls me close to him. His eyes are tired and gray, but still busy with hope. "There, child, do not be distressed. I will see no harm comes to you."

I hold on to him until I stop shaking from the cold—and fear.

Chapter 20

March 10, 1918. My 16th birthday. No birthday party this time, not even a private one. Although I am happy, I am not in a mood for a party. I miss Narine.

The army is packing. I poke at the cooking fire, and stare down the row of tents. I feel the morning rise with the unruly sun burning a reddish orange as it bends over the horizon. I lift my nose to the breeze, and take a deep breath. "It's getting warm."

"Yeah," Zaki says, as he washes his face. He scrutinizes the soldiers with a keen eye. The rumble of guns moves farther away. "Where are they going?" he asks. He dabs his face with a towel. Loneliness stains his words.

"Damascus," Father Eduard says.

Zaki looks at me with sodden eyes. "Let's go for a walk."

"Do you feel ill?" I ask.

"No. Just want to go for a walk."

"Let's go, then."

In the distance, swollen clouds collide with the chiseled mountains. Neither Zaki nor I speak until we are away from camp. We rest against a cedar tree stump. Soldiers chop firewood nearby.

Zaki pulls out a handkerchief and hands it to me.

"What's this?"

Zaki grins. "A handkerchief."

"I know that. Why are you giving it to me?"

Zaki drops his shoulders. "I saw the tree by the hospital tent. We can hang it on a branch. I know your people find such a tree special."

"It's beautiful, like the one Captain Wilson gave me."

Zaki's face wrinkles with disappointment. "You didn't tell me he gave you one."

"That was months ago. It's faded now." I smile. "Besides, this one is more beautiful, an excellent replacement." I sniff. "It's like the one…" I begin, but the words are swallowed by sobs.

Zaki grasps my hand. "It's like what?"

I give him a fragile smile. “The one at home.”

“Let’s hang it before I leave,” he says.

“What do you mean leave? Who said you were leaving?”

“I visited the prison camp yesterday. We’re being put on a ship.”

“Not you,” I say. “They—” I cock my eyes toward the prison camp—“might be moving, but not you. You will stay with us, with me. You want to marry me, don’t you?”

Zaki’s eyes flash with puzzlement. “You said that’ was a bad idea.”

“Not if we move to Great Britain.”

“You are a very complex woman,” Zaki says.

“What’s that supposed to mean?”

“One minute you say this, the next you say that.”

“This war, it’s got me all jumbled up. I’d rather go home, of course, but, I don’t know, I want to be with you, too.”

“No matter, Zaki says, “I’m on the list. A soldier inside the fence showed me the notice.”

“He’s lying,” I say, wiping away a tear. “There is no list.”

“I saw it with my own eyes.”

“I lost my family, friends, I’m not about to lose you, too.”

Zaki squeezes my hand. “Nothing can be done.”

“We’ll talk with Father Eduard,” I say. “He’ll straighten this out.”

“There’s nothing he can do.”

“He got you out of the prison camp. He can get you out of this.”

“I was sick then. I’m better now. I see how the soldiers watch me. They will come for me soon and take me away.”

I cover my mouth, and stare at Zaki with wide eyes. “Let’s see what Father Eduard has to say about this.”

We return to camp. We pass by soldiers carrying tent poles on their backs and, two by two, chests of ammunition.

One soldier holds up a piece of meat. “Want this, ol’ boy,” he says. A mangy dog with a moist tongue hanging from its mouth growls at us as we walk by. The soldier gives us a sinister look, then flips the dog the piece of meat. The dog snatches it with its greedy teeth and darts away.

“See what I mean?” Zaki says. “How they look at me.”

“It’ll be fine,” I say. “Wait and see.”

We reach the hospital tent and find Father Eduard burning used bandages. Two Arabs carry out a dead man, then load him on a wagon already covered with five or so corpses. Kazim is there, too, sitting on a log and drinking a coffee, his right arm still in a sling, and a cigarette between the fingers of his good hand.

"Where have you been?" Kazim asks. "They've been looking for the boy."

"We went for a walk," I say. I look at Father Eduard. "You'll make sure Zaki stays with us, right?"

Both men give me a sad look.

"See, I told you," Zaki says.

I narrow my eyes. "When were you going to tell me?" I ask.

"We just found out ourselves," Father Eduard says.

"But he can't go," I say. "There's Meskene. And what about Mr. Davis and Sister Gertrude? They can certainly help him."

"It's out of our hands, child," Father Eduard says.

"I'm not a child!" I shout. "I'm sixteen! You must do something. Where is Captain Wilson? We need to tell Captain Wilson."

"He's miles in the front," Kazim says.

"He was just here, earlier this morning," I say.

Kazim puts the cigarette to his lips, sucks in his cheeks, then tilts his head back before exhaling the smoke. "What can Captain Wilson do? The order came from high command."

"Having him executed came from high command, too, but Captain Wilson was still able to save his life. Why won't you help?"

"This is different," Kazim says.

"How is it different?" I ask, my breath thick with rage.

A few soldiers stop to watch us, whispering, pointing fingers.

"Away with you," Father Eduard says to them. "This does not concern you." The soldiers walk away, grumbling.

"It's okay," Zaki says.

"No! It's not okay," I say. "You helped me when he was sick." I point my finger at Kazim. "Maybe you don't like him because he's a Turk, you've said as much already."

"I've tolerated him," Kazim says, "this much is true. I don't much care for the boy. He's a prisoner. Like him or not, we must abide by the rules of war."

Zaki lowers his head but remains quiet.

"But you promised to keep him safe," I say.

"That I did, Valia." Kazim raises his hands, as if pleading for forgiveness. "For that, I am sorry."

I turn to Father Eduard. "You told me to forgive. I did what you asked. Now I'm asking you again. Help him."

"I'll talk with Captain Wilson when he returns," Father Eduard says. "He shouldn't be gone long, a few days."

"It'll be too late then," I say.

Father Eduard lowers his eyes. He returns his gaze toward me. His eyes somehow change. There is a sadness in them I have never seen before. It's like looking into the depths of a lifeless sea. "I'm sorry, Valia," he says.

"What is that in your hand?" Kazim asks.

"A handkerchief. Zaki gave it to me."

Zaki nods.

"You're tying it on the tree I suppose," Father Eduard says.

"Yes," I say.

Father Eduard nods his head, offers a feeble, but genuine smile. "Good. Most of them have blown away since Christmas."

I grab Zaki's hand. "Let's go."

"Mind if I come with you?" Father Eduard asks.

"Me as well," Kazim says.

"Sure," I say, with hesitancy.

"If you don't want us to join you, then…" Father Eduard begins.

"It's fine," I interrupt.

Father Eduard kneels by the Wishing Tree. Faded handkerchiefs hang on its branches like dead birds. I admire his patience and stamina, and his ministry to the soldiers. He prays with them, bandages and bathes the wounded. He speaks with the prisoners, gives them blankets, and makes sure they have warm food. If he can do all these things, then why can he not convince the soldiers to leave Zaki with us?

"There's a good spot," Father Eduard says. "Tie the handkerchief there."

"Father Eduard!" a gruff voice calls out. "We need to speak with a Father Eduard!"

"Get Zaki out of here—quickly," Father Eduard says. "I did not expect them so soon."

"I tried to tell you," I say.

"Go," Father Eduard says. "No time to argue about this now."

I take Zaki's hand and we rush inside a hospital tent. Zaki, breathing heavily, rests a hand on my shoulder.

"Relax," I say. "Father Eduard will keep you safe."

Zaki kicks at the dirt with the back of his shoe. "I'm not so sure. These British, they are a determined people."

"And so are the Armenians," I say. "I know what he said earlier, there is nothing he can do, but I believe he can, just you wait and see."

"And Kazim?"

"He didn't mean what he said, he likes you fine," I lie.

"It sounded like he meant it."

"He's just tired, that's all."

Father Eduard, seeing that we are safe, calls out, "I'm here! What may I do for you?"

Two British soldiers approach on horseback.

"They look mean," Zaki says.

I put a finger to my lips.

"Hand over the boy," one of the soldiers says. He is a tall figure of a man with thick legs, a broad chest, and a square face. A deep scar traces the right cheek of the other soldier.

"Under who's authority?" Father Eduard asks.

"General Allenby."

"Let me speak with him."

"He's not here," the one with the scar says.

"Tell him to dispatch a courier requesting the boy remain here, under my guidance," Kazim tells Father Eduard.

"What did he say?" the tall soldier asks.

"May we send someone to fetch General Allenby," Father Eduard translates.

"General Allenby has no time for such drivel," the tall soldier says. He spits. "Especially from an Arab."

Father Eduard looks at Kazim with heavy eyes. "He says no."

"Where is he?" the one with the scar asks. He grips his holster.

"Please," Father Eduard says. "He's just a boy. Let him be."

The tall soldier reads from a small note. "My papers say he's eighteen years of age, tall with dark hair."

"Even so, Father Eduard says, "might you make an exception?"

"All prisoners must be accounted for," the tall soldier says.

"I can't help you," Father Eduard says.

The soldier with the scar pulls his revolver, aims it at Kazim. "Either tell us, or we kill your friend."

Kazim places his index finger on his forehead, as if encouraging the soldier to shoot him.

"No, wait," Father Eduard says. "I'll fetch him." Then he turns to Kazim. "Don't antagonize them."

"They have disrespected me," Kazim says. "I have a mind to kill them."

"No," Father Eduard says.

"What's he telling you?" the tall soldier asks.

"He apologizes for any disrespect."

The tall soldier narrows his eyes. "Didn't sound that way to me, what about you?"

"Certainly not," the one with the scar says.

"Please, gentlemen," Father Eduard says. "I'll return with the boy in a moment. He's just in there," pointing at the hospital tent.

"Let's go!" I whisper.

Zaki wrests his hand away.

"What are you doing?" I ask. "Let's go-before they see us."

Zaki shakes his head. "Look around us. Where are we to go?"

"We'll dress you up like a girl," I say.

"Valia. Zaki," Father Eduard calls, his voice defeated.

"We'll go find Captain Wilson," I say.

Zaki points toward the front lines. "Out there?"

"Then hide. I'll tell them you ran away."

Zaki holds my hands in his. "They won't stop until they find me."

"But they won't find you. I'll help you. We'll go to Meskene, on our own if we have to. Sister Gertrude will help us, I'm sure of it."

"No. I will do as they say and go with them."

"Why are you so important to them?" I ask.

"I'm a Turk, nothing more."

"But…but…but I love you," I say.

"What?" Zaki asks.

"I didn't mean it," I say. "I did, but…"

Zaki leans over and kisses me. "I love you, too." His eyes seem to smile when tells me this. "I've been wanting to tell you that for a long time."

"So have I," I say. My heart pounds with a mix of fear, love, and hope.

Zaki pushes a strand of hair from my face. "But the world would not be kind to us, a Turk and an Armenian."

"I don't care," I say.

"My government will kill us both."

"Most of the British are kind people. Captain Wilson is a kind man; you've seen that for yourself.

"Captain Wilson is Australian," Zaki says.

"Even so, there are kind British people," I say, "the wounded soldiers, remember how they taught us English, and how we laughed and joked with them?"

"The dying will do anything to live," Zaki says. "We provided them with food and medicine."

"Yes, but…" I begin.

"The British," Zaki interrupts, in a disgusted voice, "they hate everyone. They want to rule the world."

I grab Zaki's hand, but he pulls away. "I'm ready, Father Eduard," he says.

I turn around just as Father Eduard steps inside the tent. He places his hands on Zaki's shoulders. "I tried," he says.

Zaki nods. "I know you did."

"Bring out the boy." The soldier with the scar steps inside the tent.

"I'll be fine," Zaki says.

"Write to me," I say.

"I will," Zaki says.

I quickly put my arms around him and kiss his cheek.

"Let's go," the soldier says.

We walk outside. The two soldiers hold Zaki at an elbow as they walk away.

I turn to Kazim. "Thank you for trying," I say.

"I'm sorry I couldn't do more."

I cry until my legs grow numb. I squeeze fistfuls of dirt, then stand up, wipe my eyes, and brush the dirt off my dress. I struggle to smile. I put my hands in my pockets. That is when I feel the handkerchief. I put a hand to my throat to constrict a sob. I tug at the handkerchief, clench my teeth, but say nothing.

Zaki smiles and is gone.

Chapter 21

The army moves forward and we move with them. Father Eduard and I travel for days in the back of a truck on a dusty road. The noise from hundreds of trucks and equipment rumble in my head. Like Father Eduard, I try to be optimistic. I think of Zaki. "How will he know where to send the letters?" I ask.

"The army will make sure the letters reach you," Father Eduard says. "Of course, you can write to him first, let him know where we are."

"I'll do that. But will they give him paper and pen?"

"I think so."

"What if they say he's a spy?"

"They'll read the letters before they send them."

I stare out the back of the truck. "Have you heard from Mr. Davis?"

"I should in a few days."

"They are expecting us in Meskene?"

"Yes, I wrote him that we are on our way, after Damascus. The courier took the letter yesterday."

"Good," I say.

The truck stops. "Riders approaching," a soldier says.

"Turks?"

"Arabs," the soldier says.

I recognize Kazim's voice. "Load these people on the trucks."

Father Eduard helps me down from the truck. "Kazim! Over here," I say.

A crowed of exhausted and ragged women and girls make their way slowly toward us.

"Spare some room?" Kazim asks.

"Certainly," Father Eduard says.

"Where did you find them?" I ask.

Kazim gestures to a clump of small hills in the distance and narrows his eyes. "The Turks had them stuffed in a cave." Smoke rises into the bright sky. "We couldn't save them all."

My eyes flash with grief. Anger no longer dwells in me as it once did. I have learned to accept this war, its casualties, the maimed and dead bodies lining the road, the smell of burning skin, and the screams. Or maybe I have grown immune to war. Either way, I am more grief stricken than angry. I suppose missing Zaki has much to do with my current feelings. "This way," I say, grabbing a girl's hand, helping her up into the truck. "Where is your family?"

"Gone," the girl says, shivering and clutching a doll to her chest.

A woman with two girls climb in. We help an old woman up and then another woman and more girls until we fill the truck.

"I'm Valia," I say. "What's your name?"

"Gayane."

"Does your doll have a name?"

"Zora."

"Such a pretty name."

"Where are they taking us?"

"These are good men," I say. I glance at Kazim. "We'll be safe with them."

"Damascus," Father Eduard says. He smiles and pats the girl on the head. "They're taking us to Damascus."

"But we just came from there," a woman says, her eyes welling up with panic.

"The Turks are in full retreat," Kazim says. "We'll capture the city easily."

"Then we go to Meskene," I say. "The Americans will help us when we arrive."

Relief cascades from the woman's drooping shoulders. "Thank God."

"Any other news of the war?" Father Eduard asks.

"We hear the Americans are rapidly pushing through France," Kazim says. "We think the war will be over soon."

"What of Russia?"

"They pulled out of the war. A group calling themselves the Bolsheviks are in charge now."

"What of the royal family?" I ask.

"What does a peasant girl know of the royal family?" a young woman with a husky voice asks.

"You're Russian," I say.

The woman, now staring at my feet, presses her proud lips together.

"I'm educated," I say. I straighten my tattered dress. "I haven't always lived this way." I put my arm around her. The woman's body jerks, but she does not pull away from me. "I'm Valia. Everything will be okay. You are safe now."

"Olga," the young woman says. "My father…"

"What is it?" I ask. "You can speak freely here."

"My father, he was Russian, my mother from Bitlis."

"Where are they now?"

The woman sweeps a tear away. "Dead, like the royal family." She points to the smoldering caves.

"We must say a prayer for them," Father Eduard says.

"Thank you, Father," Olga says.

"Where is Captain Wilson?" I ask.

"With General Allenby," Kazim says. "He and this Lawrence fellow we've heard so much about."

"He's helped your people a great deal," Father Eduard says.

"Yes," Kazim says. "I think we'll win our independence from the Turks because of him." He shifts his horse, adjusts the reigns. "I'll see you later," he says, and is gone.

I squeeze Olga's hand. "Captain Wilson is a great man," I say. "He will help you."

We ride the rest of the way in silence.

Chapter 22

We enter Damascus in October. It has been eight months since Zaki was taken. The cool air smells of snow. The locals cheer as we ride through Umayyad Square. Others stand there passively. Almost five years of war has clearly taken its toll.

A large crowd crosses a bridge. Our truck stops, and a soldier walks up to us and says, "Which one of you is Valia?"

"Me," I say. "What is it?"

"Kazim needs your help."

Gayane grips my hand. "Don't go."

"It's fine. It's the man I was speaking with earlier, remember?"

"I'll come with you."

"The girl needs to stay here," the soldier says.

I smile. "Father Eduard will watch over you."

"As will I," Olga says.

"See there," I say. "You have two new friends watching over you." I kiss her forehead. "You are a very special girl."

Gayane holds out her doll. "Take her with you."

I gently push the doll back. "Keep her close. I won't be long."

The soldier escorts me across the bridge. Kazim and Captain Wilson are standing outside a square stucco building. Plain rectangular windows catch the sun, holding on to the light like water in a glass. "Welcome to the Victoria Hotel, Valia," Captain Wilson says, "or what's left of it. "It's a pleasure to see you again."

Some of the upper windows have been blasted away. Fist-sized holes clutter the outside walls. "Pleasure to see you," I say.

"You've been practicing your English."

"Little," I say.

"Kazim told me about Zaki," Captain Wilson says. "I'm sorry, that was not supposed to happen."

"You promised you would help him," I say, crossing my arms.

"No harm will come to him, I assure you," Captain Wilson says, "but we have more pressing matters at the moment and I need your help."

"Really?" I ask. "You expect me to help you now?"

"Like I said, Zaki will be fine. I will personally look into it after you do this one thing for me."

"What is it?" My response drives icy thorns of anger into the warm air, stabbing the hustle and bustle of the city with silence. It is as if we are the only three people left on earth. The people of Damascus abandon my thoughts. Only Zaki's beautiful face remains. The strength of his hands, the force of his kiss, his whole body feels me with warmth.

"Please follow us into the hotel," Captain Wilson says.

Just then, an Arab man passes us and enters the hotel. A neatly trimmed dark beard gilds his stern and proper face, giving it the appearance of chiseled desert rock. Two guards follow close by.

I quickly cover my face with a scarf. "Who's that?"

"Prince Feisal," Captain Wilson says, "leader of the Arab revolt. Let's not keep him waiting."

"I cannot meet a man like that," I say.

"Why not?" Captain Wilson asks.

"It's just…it would be improper for me to go."

"It's okay this time," Kazim says. "Arrangements have been made."

"What purpose do I have here?"

"It might become very tense," Captain Wilson says. "I'm afraid General Allenby doesn't have good news for the prince. I think a woman's presence will help matters. It will mean a great deal to me if you join us."

"And to me," Kazim says.

Although I'm angry with them both, they did, after all, save my life, and I owe them for that, so I swallow hard the lump of shame in my throat and force myself to follow them inside the hotel.

"What do I say to him?" I ask. "I have no power over a prince."

"I think you might this time," Kazim says.

"I don't understand."

"You will."

A tall British man with a thick mustache and freshly polished boots stands when we enter the meeting room. Two soldiers stand beside him. Cheers from the crowd below rocket through the open windows. Plush curtains shift in the breeze.

Captain Wilson salutes and then shakes the large man's hand. "I hope your travel was pleasant, sir," he says.

"As to be expected Captain, in the midst of war," the large man says. He looks at me, then turns back to Captain Wilson, saying something in English I do not understand.

"Valia Stepanyan," Captain Wilson says.

"Hello, sir," I say.

"You speak English," the large man says.

"A little," I say, this time remembering that annoying part of speech. The letter A. How can one small letter cause so much confusion?

"Pleased to meet you, Valia. I'm General Allenby."

"Pleased, sir," I say.

General Allenby smiles. "Shall we begin?" He motions toward a coffee service.

Prince Feisal, looking disgruntled, remains seated, bolt upright, his back several inches from the chair. I bow to him. He takes a deep breath. His shoulders relax. The cracks around the corner of his eyes dwindle. A white man wearing traditional Arab garb stands beside him. Tucked in his belt is a silver handled knife.

Kazim leans close to my ear. "Major Lawrence," he whispers.

General Allenby and his men take their seats and I begin serving coffee, first to the prince and then to everyone else. Feisal takes his cup and readjusts himself in his chair. Then he leans back, takes a sip, closes his eyes, and inhales deeply. The stress in his face loosens even more. He opens his eyes, then looks around the room rather coolly. The crowd outside continues to cheer.

"Close the windows," General Allenby says.

A staff member jumps up, gently shuts the windows, and draws the curtains. Then the meeting begins, all the participants speaking English. I keep pace with them, happy to see how much I have learned from

Captain Wilson, Father Eduard, and the soldiers. My mouth curves with joy living such an experience.

"It seems that you drew a crowd, regardless of my wishes to avoid a ceremonial event," General Allenby says, grimacing.

"And I noticed none of your staff, other than Major Lawrence, understands how to address a prince," Feisal says. He glances at me. "Even this farmhand knows to bow and to serve a prince first."

I clinch my fist. "I am no farmhand, sir," I say, my tone firm, but humble.

Kazim holds his eyes on me.

I lower my head. "I didn't mean to speak out of turn, sir. Please forgive me."

"Nonsense," Feisal says, lifting his brow. "You are an educated girl?"

"Yes, sir."

Feisal turns to General Allenby and Captain Wilson. "Where did you find this one?"

"I'm a refugee, sir. My parents and brother were murdered by the Turks."

Prince Feisal grunts. "I see. You're Armenian."

"Yes, sir."

"Your people are great warriors. I will do what I can to help them." Then he turns to General Allenby and says, "Now, what of our plans?"

"I will be frank with you," Allenby says. "The French will be a protective power over Syria. And…"

Before he can continue, Feisal interrupts him. "I don't understand," he says. He grins awkwardly. "Maybe my English is getting…how you say… rusty."

The corners of Allenby's eyes frown. "Say it another way, Lawrence."

Lawrence turns to the prince. "What he's saying is that you will be the administrator of Syria, but with French guidance," he says in Arabic. Then he turns back to Allenby and translates. "Is that correct, sir?"

"That's exactly what I'm saying," Allenby says. "Lebanon will not be joined to Syria, nor will the Arabs be independent." He crosses his legs and readjusts his seat. "Also, Major Lawrence will no longer be your liaison officer. A French officer will be appointed instead."

Prince Feisal frowns. "What do you mean there will be no Arab independence? As for the French, I don't want their assistance. Lawrence has been most loyal to me. Furthermore, I want to be in control of a united Lebanon and Syria. What good is a country to me with no port?"

Allenby, his face flushed with surprise, turns to Lawrence. "Did you not inform him about any of this?"

Lawrence turns to the prince. "I'm sorry, sir, I was not informed about the French, or about my reassignment."

"But you were," Allenby says vehemently. "We discussed this."

Lawrence remains firm. "If we did, sir, my memory does not recall such a discussion."

Allenby quickly ends the meeting. "Prince Feisal, seeing that you are under my command, you will obey my orders." He stands up and straightens his uniform. Feisal follows suit. Without another word, he bows, first to Lawrence then to me. He salutes General Allenby, then walks out like a defeated old man.

"I will not work with the French," Lawrence says. "I'm due a leave and I see it fitting that I take it now and return to England."

"Yes! I think that's a splendid idea!" Allenby says.

Fuming, Lawrence salutes, then walks out, his fists clenching by his side.

"What is it?" Father Eduard asks when we return to the truck. "You were gone such a long time." He and Gayane are the only ones in the truck.

"Where is everyone else?" I ask. "Where is Olga?"

"Gone with the soldiers," Father Eduard says. "Gayane wanted to wait for you."

"What do you mean, gone with the soldiers?" I ask.

"Don't worry," Father Eduard says. "They're safe and will be well taken care of."

"But…"

Father Eduard tenderly grips my shoulder. "What is it, child?"

"It's just…she didn't wait to say goodbye."

"Where did you go?" Gayane asks. Her red puffy eyes force me to forget about Olga.

"In a meeting with some very powerful men," I say.

"Really?" Gayane asks, her face lighting up.

"Yes," I say, hugging her. "It was very…"

"Were you scared?" Gayane interrupts, holding out her doll. "See, you should have taken Zora with you."

I smile. "Yes, I believe you're right."

"General Allenby and Prince Feisal," Captain Wilson says to Father Eduard.

"I see," Father Eduard says. "And what transpired?"

"I'm afraid I failed you," I say to Captain Wilson.

"Nonsense," Captain Wilson says.

"I don't see how it was any better with me. I spoke rudely to Prince Feisel. I don't think he was at all pleased with me there."

"Nonsense," Captain Wilson says. He was impressed with your English skills. And he wants to help your people, you heard him say so himself."

"You really think so?" I ask. "He looked upset to me."

"I'm sure there is nothing to worry about," Father Eduard says.

"Indeed," Captain Wilson agrees.

"You did fine," Kazim says.

Captain Wilson grips his stomach. "Anyone hungry?"

"I believe I saw a café just over there, earlier this morning," Kazim says, pointing.

"An open café in all this mess?" Captain Wilson asks.

"One way to find out," Kazim says."

"Lead the way," Captain Wilson says. "My treat."

The café, a short walk away, has a patio with eight or more large broken tables and about the same number of umbrellas with metal ribs attached to tattered fabric. British officers take up most of the open seats.

"It looks dirty," Gayane says.

"Is it open?" I ask.

Someone waves us over.

"Looks like," Kazim says.

"A nice day to sit outside," Captain Wilson says.

"I agree," Father Eduard says.

Kazim and I nod our heads yes.

"Let's find a seat," I say, taking Gayane's hand in mine. We move around the broken tables, careful not to snag our clothes on any of the sharp corners. The officers continue to chat and eat, minding their own business. "Here's one," I say. "Looks like enough seats, too."

We all order a kebab and tea.

"How have you kept this place open?" Captain Wilson asks the server.

"My father is a wealthy man," the server says. "And an excellent negotiator."

"How do you mean?" Captain Wilson asks.

"I think what he means is that his father sacrificed a great deal to keep this place open," Kazim says.

"Precisely," the server says. "Even in war, people still have to eat."

"Especially officers from the liberating army," Father Eduard says.

"I suppose so, yes," the server says. He clears his throat. "Allow me to fetch your food," he says, and quickly walks away.

"What was that all about?" I ask.

"I think the owner made some kind of deal with the British," Captain Wilson says.

"I don't understand," I say.

"The café is probably running a spy network," Father Eduard says. A few heads turn in our direction.

"Let's focus on more pleasant conversation," Captain Wilson says, "shall we?" He reaches in his pocket and pulls out a coin. "Look over there," he says.

Our table is near a fountain.

Captain Wilson places the coin on the table next to Gayane. "Go try it out," he says.

"What do I do?" Gayane asks.

"It's our form of a Wising Tree, I suppose," Captain Wilson says. "Toss the coin in the water and make a wish."

"Seems wasteful," I say.

Captain Wilson smiles. "Go ahead, Gayane, run along, it's alright."

I nod, and Gayane dashes off to the well, dragging Zora along with her. We all watch as she drops the coin in the water.

"I'm sorry you had to see that" Captain Wilson says, "General Allenby's and the Prince's little spat," rekindling the conversation we had by the truck. He takes a bite of kebab, chewing vigorously. "Very unprofessional."

"I've seen worse," I say.

He wipes his mouth. "Of course, what I meant was it would have been worse had you not been there. Perhaps weapons would have been drawn."

"What of Prince Feisal?" Father Eduard asks.

"He'll still help us," Captain Wilson says. He holds up his Kebab. "I must say, these are tasty." Then he says, "I spoke to Major Lawrence just before we left the hotel." He turns to me. "The prince was pleased with you and because of that he will help. But there is one condition."

"What's the condition?" Kazim asks.

Captain Wilson sucks in his cheeks. Then he leans back in his chair as if a man with a full stomach. "He wants Major Lawrence to present another argument for Arab independence when he returns to London."

Kazim waves a fly from his plate. "Will your government listen?"

Captain Wilson leans over, places his elbows on the table, and folds his hands. "If they don't, then he'll write to the newspapers."

"What of your king?" Father Eduard asks.

Captain Wilson roars with laughter. "King George is as naïve as a child, sir. He's nothing but ceremony." He snaps his figures at the waiter. "There's talk that he wants to pin medals on everyone's chest. He has no idea how to run a country."

Just then, a soldier drives up and parks across the street, then walks over and exchanges salutes with Captain Wilson. "Good afternoon, sir," he says, a handsome young man with a chiseled face and dark brown eyes. "I am to notify you that Prince Feisal is on his way to Aleppo."

"So soon?" Father Eduard asks.

"Yes, sir. Major Lawrence is with him. They said that with the Turks in full retreat there is no time to lose."

"With support, I hope," Captain Wilson says.

"Yes, sir. The 5th Cavalry Division and an armored car division under General MacAndrew are supporting."

"Very well," Captain Wilson says, standing. "Then I must be on my way." Kazim and Father Eduard also stand.

"Please, gentlemen, finish your lunch," Captain Wilson says. "I'll meet up with you later."

"Godspeed," Father Eduard says. Kazim and Captain Wilson exchange salutes.

"Don't forget about Zaki," I say.

Captain Wilson smiles. "Certainly I won't. Oh, and before I forget, I reserved you all rooms at the Victoria Hotel." He smiles. "I suspect the accommodations are a little better than field tents."

"Thank you," we say.

"You are too kind," Father Eduard says.

"It's the least I can do," Captain Wilson says. "You all have been a great help to me, especially you Valia."

I blush, smiling.

The young soldier clears his throat, as if growing impatient.

"Well, we must be off," Captain Wilson says. The young soldier drives off, and the car disappears in a haze of dust.

"A most generous man," Kazim says. "If only all men of his kind were so liberal in their giving."

"Indeed," Father Eduard says. "Perhaps this war never would have happened with men like that in charge."

Then unexpectedly, the most beautiful voice I had ever heard decants from a loudspeaker.

"Allahu Akbar," the voice announces. "Ashadu an-la illaha ill Allah... Haya ala salah...Haya ala falah...La illaha ill Allah."

"It's time for prayer," Kazim says. "Will you accompany me to the mosque?"

"Certainly," Father Eduard says, "if we're allowed."

"I'll get you in."

"Come along, Gayane, it's time to go," I say.

We walk down the Street Called Straight, a very narrow street, walking on the right side to avoid British cavalry patrols. Gayane holds tight to my hand. We pass a building decorated in flowers, many now dry, and notice hosts of faded scarfs dangle from the balcony. It has been days since I have thought about the handkerchief Zaki gave me. I reach in my pocket to make sure it's still there and feel relieved when the fabric touches my fingers.

"Are you alright?" Father Eduard asks.

"Yes. Just remembering."

"About?"

"Are you sure Zaki will write to me?"

"Who's Zaki?" Gayane asks.

"A friend of mine." I smile. "Maybe you'll meet him one day."

"Is he nice?"

"Of course, he's nice. I think you'll like him very much."

"Is he your boyfriend?"

My cheeks warm, and I smile. Spending time with Zaki had touched something deep inside of me I had not fully realized until now. Something I had thought didn't exist anymore.; something that had been lost love. The kind of love that made me weak in the knees when I first woke up in the morning, hoping to see him chopping wood, our long walks through camp, or giggling at each other during English lessons. The kind of love that got me humming to myself while sewing a button on a uniform or cooking breakfast or kept me awake at night knowing he was only a few feet away. My love for Zaki, and I know this now, bleeds honey and warms my heart. It makes me feel like every day exists on the tip of a rainbow. "Yes, I suppose he is," I say.

Father Eduard nods at the building with the dried flowers and faded scarfs. "The place of St. Paul's conversion, where Ananias came to visit him." Then he smiles and says, "Only ask God and He'll give you what you wish."

"Maybe this world will experience its own conversion," I say.

"What is conversion?" Gayane asks.

Father Eduard and I smile. "A change of heart," he says.

Gayane hugs my arm. "Are you sad?"

I sigh. "I miss Zaki, is all."

"I think you've already experienced a conversion," Father Eduard says.

"How so?"

"You love Zaki very much. I can see it in your eyes."

"And?" I feel he's not telling me everything.

"And you've forgiven the Turks."

"I've forgiven one," I admit.

Farther Eduard smiles. "It's a beginning."

"Will I ever see Zaki again?" I ask.

He forces a smile. "If God wills it so."

The crowd grows larger as we approach the Mosque. We maneuver behind a man who seems to know his way around. He carries a silver-colored umbrella, making it easy for us to follow him. He turns onto Darwish Street, and enters a courtyard through an arched doorway. In the center of the courtyard stands a sixteen-sided fountain elaborately decorated with tile and polychrome stones. A line has gathered at the entrance of the prayer hall, forcing us to wait several minutes before entering.

"So many people," I say.

"Your church does not accommodate many?" Kasim asks.

"It does," I say, "it is just not as crowded."

"A pity," Kazim says.

"Indeed," Father Eduard says.

Then finally, it's our turn. We remove our shoes and then step inside. The sound of a man beating a wooden drum welcomes us to sit.

"Women to the left and men to the right," someone calls out.

I look up. The central dome, illustrated with inscriptions, exhibit sixteen arched windows. The sun slices magical colors of light through the colored glass.

"Follow those two," Kazim says, and points to two women.

Puzzlement stitches seams across Gayane's forehead. "I don't like it here."

"It's okay, Gayane," I say. "I'll be right here with you."

"It smells funny," Gayane says, and pitches her nose shut.

Kazim smiles. "It's the goat fat, it has an odd smell when it burns, especially if you're not used to it."

"Go on with Valia," Father Eduard says, "we won't be in here too long, isn't that right, Kazim?"

"A few minutes only," Kazim says, "just enough time to say our prayers."

"Come on, Gayane," I say, "lets pray for your family."

"And for your boyfriend," Gayane says.

It feels strange praying inside a mosque. My heart burns as I pray for my family. I pray Zaki will write me. I pray to be reunited with him and Artush soon. I pray to be reunited with Sister Gertrude and Mr. Davis.

Chapter 23

I help Gayane get cleaned up, then draw a bath for myself. Freedom tingles my skin as I peel off my dirty clothes. I feel the warm water crawl up my leg as I step into the porcelain tub. I stand there a moment looking at my reflection in the priceless water until the dirt from my legs turns the water brown. I grip the sides of the tub, gently slide in, and wash the war away.

There is a knock at the door the following morning.

"Who is it?" I ask.

"It's me, Father Eduard."

I open the door and step into the hall, quietly shutting the door behind me. "Gayane is still sleeping," I whisper. "Is everything okay?"

"Another letter from Mr. Davis."

I smile nervously, rub my chest. "What does it say?"

"He and Sister Gertrude were forced to leave Aleppo. He tells us not to worry, though. They're safe. The orphans under their care are safe. They are with a detachment of British and Arab soldiers."

"What of Meskene?"

"We'll remain there for the time being."

"We'll not see them?" I toy with the handkerchief Zaki had given me.

"We will," Father Eduard says, "once Aleppo is captured." He gently grips my arm. "Patience."

"Zaki should be here with us."

"I'm sure they'll let him go after the war."

"Does Mr. Davis say that in his letter?"

"No, but I'm sure he'll do everything he can to help Zaki." He folds the letter, then places it in his pocket. "Did you write Zaki?"

"Days ago," I say. "A soldier was kind enough to take the letter for me. He said he knew the location of the prison camps."

"I'll ask Captain Wilson the next time I see him."

Just then, Kazim steps from his room holding on to his rifle in one hand, and a bag in the other. He walks over to us. "Headed to the front." He looks at me and smiles. "I'll see you in Aleppo."

"Seems like capturing Aleppo may be more difficult than expected," Father Eduard says.

Kazim blinks confusion. "What do you mean?"

Father Eduard holds up the letter. "So says Mr. Davis. He's had to evacuate, along with the orphans. The British seem to have focused more on the evacuation of women and orphans than the capture of Aleppo."

"The Turks aren't going anywhere," Kazim says. "They bottled themselves inside, plenty of British and Arabs surrounding them, according to the reports that came in last night. We're going to push them into the sea."

"I'm sure you're right," Father Eduard says, nodding in confident agreement. "Mr. Davis doesn't seem too concerned about it, he just wanted us to be aware."

He turns to me. "Aleppo should be taken easily. Then we can see about finding Zaki."

Breaking the rules of public affection, especially between a Muslim and a Christian, I embrace him. "Thank you for everything you have done for me. I will never forget it."

Pressing a thumb to my cheek, he wipes away a tear. "Don't worry, Valia. I will keep him safe, if even it costs me my life."

"You would do that… for a Turk?"

"Let's just say this war has taught me that fighting doesn't solve anything." He swallows hard. "Accepting those different from you seems to be the first step toward peace. I see that now. The way you have accepted Zaki. You not only accept him but love him."

"Be safe," I say.

"We'll meet again," Kazim says. "I promise."

The door behind me opens. Gayane stands there rubbing her eyes.

"I'm sorry, did we wake you?" I ask. I lean down, and push the hair out of Gayane's face.

"The noise outside the window," Gayane says. "What's going on?"

"Let's go see," Father Eduard says.

Armored cars and trucks pass by. Officers shout orders. An Arab cavalry unit turns off the road, heading toward us.

"Time for me to go," Kazim says.

"I'll pray for you," I say.

"And I for you," Kazim says. He steps into the stairwell, gone.

"I'm hungry," Gayane says.

"We can arrange something," Father Eduard says. "What would you like?"

"Buttered bread."

Father Eduard clasps his hands together. "Let's head down to the dining room." He holds out his hand and Gayane takes it in hers. I follow them out into the hall, locking the door behind me.

British officers crowd the dining room. Cigarette smoke moves about like thunder clouds, producing an uneasy haze. My eyes and nose water, as if remembering the eerie sights and sounds of the battlefield.

We find a table in a corner.

"Is there a spy network here, too?" I ask.

"Don't concern yourself with such matters," Father Eduard says.

I am about to ask another question when the server arrives.

"What would you like?" a she asks.

"A coffee for me," Father Eduard says, "and some sweets."

I point to Gayane. "Bread and butter for her."

"And for you, dear?"

"Tea, thank you."

A man approaches us when the waitress leaves. Short in stature with a broad chest and muscular arms, he is wearing a double-breasted suit. "Are you Father Eduard?" the man asks in Turkish, his voice guttural. He possesses the sharp eyes of a politician.

"Yes," Father Eduard says. "Can I help you?"

"Mr. Davis sent me."

Father Eduard gestures to an empty seat. "Join us."

"Name's Kevin Batson."

"You're a Scotsman," Father Eduard says.

Mr. Batson looks around the room, then checks his watch. "I'm to escort you to Aleppo."

"We've heard it's dangerous," I say, "that we are to go to Meskene until its safe." I look at Father Eduard. "Show him the letter."

"You must be Valia. Mr. Davis has told me about you. He regrets that he could not help you that day at the market. He thinks about it often."

"I don't blame him," I say. "I hope he knows that."

"Certainly, he does." Batson smiles, then looks at Father Eduard and says, "Let me see the letter."

"Sure," Father Eduard says, handing over the letter.

"This was dated weeks ago," Batson says.

"I see," Father Eduard says, removing his eyeglasses, then begins cleaning them off. "Suppose I need some new ones."

Batson returns the letter. "We've taken Aleppo. The Turks are in full retreat. The war is close to over." He looks at me, folds his hands, resting them on the table. "There's no need to go to Meskene."

Father Eduard and I give each other a puzzled look. Before we can say anything, the waitress returns with our orders, then looks at Mr. Batson. "May I get you something?"

"No, thank you."

"Are we going home now?" Gayane asks. She smears butter on her bread. Steam rises like an apparition.

"This is Gayane," I say. "I'll won't leave without her."

"Of course," Mr. Batson says. "I'm to bring you all." He sniffs, raises his hand to the waitress. "Are there others?"

"They've been taken care of," Father Eduard says, "sent to orphanages or homes of sympathetic Turks. But…"

"I've changed my mind dear lady," Mr. Batson cuts Father Eduard off. "Would you be so kind as to bring me some tea?"

"Yes, sir," she says.

"My apologies," Mr. Batson says, "go on."

"There is one other who did not make it to an orphanage."

"A friend of yours?"

"Zaki," I say.

"Her boyfriend," Gayane says, giggling.

"I don't understand," Mr. Batson says.

"He's being held prisoner," I say.

"A Turkish soldier," Father Eduard explains.

"But he wanted nothing to do with the war," I add assertively.

Mr. Batson scratches at his beard. "I see."

The waitress brings Mr. Batson his tea. "Anything else?"

"Just the check," Father Eduard says. He takes a last sip of coffee, looks at Mr. Batson. "When do we leave?"

"Tomorrow."

"We must get word to Kazim," I say.

Mr. Batson raises his eyebrows.

"He's a soldier in the Arab army," Father Eduard says. "He recently left for the front. We planned to meet him in Aleppo." He clears his throat. "He's also looking for the boy."

"Kazim saved my life," I say.

"I'm sure he can take care of himself," Mr. Batson says. "As for the boy, a Turkish prisoner at that, it might be tricky, but I'll see what I can do about his release."

Papa's swollen eyes stare at me. Mama and Arsen, crying, stand beside him. Saabir's gun flashes in the sun.

I jump awake. It was only a dream. Sweat runs down my forehead. My body is sticky and cold. Gayane rests peacefully beside me. I uncurl myself from the blankets, walk over to the window, and breathe in the evening, quiet and clear. A soldier stands alone across the street. Cold air wafts from his mouth. He rubs his hands together, then blows into them. I wonder where his family is. He must miss them terribly.

"What's wrong?" Gayane asks, rubbing her eyes.

"Nothing. Go back to sleep."

"What are you looking at?"

"Thinking of home is all."

"I'm dreaming about home, too."

I smile. I sit on the edge of the bed and play with Gayane's hair. "I hope it was a good dream."

"It was only a dream," Gayane says, frowning. "I know I will never see it again." She wipes away a tear. "I don't want to see it again."

"I know it's hard," I say. "You don't have to." I kiss the top of her head. "Sister Gertrude will take good care of you until she finds you a new home."

"But I want to stay with you, like you said."

"Of course. But maybe she'll find your family."

"My family is dead, like yours."

"What about cousins? Certainly some of them survived." I glance at the window. "I have cousins in Europe."

Gayane picks up her doll. "This is all I have left."

"You don't know that for sure."

"You don't want me to live with you," Gayane says. She buries her head in the doll.

"There now, it's not that," I say, comforting her in my arms. "I just thought you'd like to find your family is all, like we discussed."

She lifts her head, her face now wet with tears. "There is no one."

"Are you…." Then I remember the caves, and the smoke rising out of them like black demons flexing their smoldering muscles. "We don't have to talk about it if you don't want, it's okay."

"So I can live with you?"

"Of course you can, if you really want to."

Chapter 24

November 1918. Aleppo is not the city I remember. Buildings turned to rubble. Busted wagons, dead horses. The waste of war litters the streets. Turkish and Arab soldiers lay together in a bitter union of death. Hollow and cloudy eyes stare at the sky with mouths agape. Souls rise toward the hands of God. I make the sign of the cross as I pass by them.

We walk down a narrow street. A cold morning. A light breeze blows trash down populated alleyways. An old man, squatting against the wall and smoking a water pipe, holds out his hand, gnarled by arthritis. He asks for money. Mr. Batson hands the old man a coin. The old man smiles, exposing a bottom row of rotten teeth. Mr. Batson and I reply with a smile. Father Eduard places his hand atop the old man's head, closes his eyes. His lips move, but no audible words come from them. Then we turn down the next street, wider than the last, and heaving with displaced women and children, their manner stiff and cold, and they pay us little attention.

Farther on, a priest calls out names, and hollers orders to form a line. Two British soldiers sit at a desk. One scribbles something on a piece of paper, the other one holds a stamp in his hand, and presses it against a man's forearm. "Step aside," the soldier says.

"What's going on?" I ask.

"Looks like they're being evacuated," Father Eduard says.

"Next!" the scribbler calls for the next person. "Don't shove. Everyone will have their turn."

"The orphanage is around the next corner," Mr. Batson says. "Anything look familiar?"

"No," I say. "Not really. I never made it to the orphanage, the town square only."

"Right," Mr. Batson says. "This way."

We pass a man boarding up the door of a large building.

"What are you doing?" Mr. Batson asks.

"What I'm told," the man says, his speech muddled because of the two nails in his mouth.

"What happened to the orphans?"

The man shrugs his shoulders. Then he places another board against the door, retrieves one of the nails, and hammers it into the wood.

Mr. Batson scratches his head. "They're supposed to be here."

"Wait here, I'll go ask the priest," Father Eduard says.

"Sure," Mr. Batson answers.

Gayane tucks her head inside her coat, presses her body against me.

"It'll be okay," I say. "We'll find them."

"Certainly we will," Mr. Batson says.

Father Eduard returns and says, "They're in the village of Imtan." He points. "That way."

"How far?" Mr. Batson asks.

"Half day's ride."

Mr. Batson studies the sky. "It'll be dark soon. Best go first thing in the morning."

I wake up to a gentle wind pelting rain against the tent walls. Gayane snuggles next to me, asleep and breathing peacefully. A spot of her dribble has discolored the sheets, and I gently flip her over on her back.

"Valia, are you awake?" Father Eduard's voice.

"Yes, Father, you can come in."

Gayane sits up, stretches, yawns. "Good morning, Father."

"Good morning, child," Father Eduard says. Then he turns to me. "It's a letter from Zaki."

My jaw drops as if unhinged. "What does it say?" I jump out of bed.

"Open it up and see," Father Eduard says. He smiles. "I told you to have patience."

I open the letter, blowing out a rejoicing breath. The letter reads:

5 November 1918

Dear Valia,

I hope this letter finds you well. I'm not allowed to tell you where we are, but I can tell you that we are close by, two days at most. The British soldiers speak to me in English, but I do not understand most of what they say. You were always a much brighter student than I. The other prisoners say they are teasing me, but I don't believe them, because the British give me plenty to eat and they do not beat me like they do some of the others. It goes without saying that many of my comrades are not so lucky. Executions occur daily. I thought, despite the kindness from the soldiers, I'd suffer the same fate. Tempers here change quickly. How surprised and thankful I was when your friend, Kazim, arrived a few days ago…

I look up from the letter. "Kazim is there with him! He found him."

"Praise God," Father Eduard says.

"I'll meet him soon," Gayane says, clapping her hands together, Zora caged between her chest and forearm.

My eyes begin to water as I continue reading.

I admire Kazim very much, something I didn't expect to say regarding an Arab. I suppose we could all easily live in peace if we tried hard enough. He is trying his best to have me released, but we are waiting for final word from Captain Wilson. I know that I am still alive because of them. How they found me and, most importantly, why my fate is so important to them, can only be credited to the mercy of Allah and, I'm sure, to you.

I miss you so very much, and my heart aches for the day I can kiss you again. Until that day, know that I love you. I always will.
Zaki

I fold the letter, then place it back in the envelope. "He's being treated well," I say. "He and Kazim are waiting to hear from Captain Wilson regarding his release." Worry lifts from my chest as I breathe a sigh of relief.

"That's great news," Father Eduard says.

I place Zaki's handkerchief against my nose, breathe in his secret smell, a smell that will soon be a part of me.

A car pulls up.

"That should be Mr. Batson," Father Eduard says. "Are you ready to go?"

"We need to get word to Zaki that we are moving again," I say.

"I'm sure Captain Wilson and Kazim are aware," Father Eduard says.

"Give us a few minutes," I say.

It has stopped raining by the time Gayane and I step from the tent. The wind slides away, replaced with warm crackles of fires, and soldiers talking and playing cards. The dark sky moves over Aleppo. The sun happily squeezes through the consenting clouds.

"Good morning," Mr. Batson says, holding the car door open for us. It is a shiny black car with a covered top with two official-looking flags attached on either side of the hood.

"Good morning," Gayane and I say, climbing into the car.

Mr. Batson shuts the door, walks around to the driver's side, climbs in. "I sent word to Mr. Davis last night. He's expecting us."

"Has he heard from Captain Wilson?" I ask. "Are Kazim and Zaki now with him?"

Mr. Batson cocks his head, puzzled. "He didn't say, but I wouldn't think so. They don't know to go to Imtan." He turns down a road going north. A flock of sheep hobble amongst long stems of brown grass. Their master follows behind them, his cane prepared to jerk a rebellious juvenile back in line.

"Someone needs to tell them before they reach Maskene," I say. "Zaki will be worried sick if I'm not there."

"I'm sure they've received word by now," Father Eduard reassures me. "Don't worry yourself."

"I must confess, though, I didn't find out the location of your friend, Zaki," Mr. Batson says. "I'm sorry. Had Mr. Davis found him, I'm sure he would have made me aware of it." He glances at me. "I'm sorry, but I doubt we'll ever find him."

"But I've heard from him," I say.

Mr. Batson raises his brow. "So you know where he is then."

"He's not allowed to say."

"Of course," Mr. Batson says, knocking the palm of his hand against his forehead. "In case the letter fell into the wrong hands."

"Zaki is no spy," I say.

"They don't know that," Mr. Batson says.

Perhaps Mr. Davis didn't tell you for the same reason," I suggest.

"Which is what?"

Father Eduard looks at me. "What I think she means is that Mr. Davis is a clever man, a secretive man. Should any of his correspondence fall into the wrong hands…"

"Of course," Mr. Batson says. He shakes his head, as if disappointed in himself. "I should've known. Mr. Davis is a very secretive man, paranoid if you will. I often don't know his plans until the very last moment. If Mr. Davis knows of Zaki's whereabouts, then I'm sure he's safe."

"Kazim is with Zaki," I say.

"Your Arab friend," Mr. Batson says, relief in his voice. "Good. That's even better."

The wind picks up outside the city. Patches of dead grass curl in the wind. We pass a British cavalry unit. Mr. Batson stops the car and speaks to them. "All clear?"

"Yes, sir," one of the mounted soldiers says. The other soldiers vigilantly watch the hills as the two men speak. Then the soldiers salute and we push forward.

Soon we crest a hill. The top of a building appears.

"Looks like a bell tower," Father Eduard says. "That must be it."

"That must be what?" I ask.

"The new orphanage," Father Eduard says.

"I don't see what else it could be," Mr. Batson says.

A British force controls Imtan Village. A rough group of young soldiers, many of them no older than me, have been here, we are told, for several weeks. It's clear to me these boys have seen enough of war. Weariness in their stares is a testament to that. With the end of the war in sight, relief overshadows all they have experienced. A glimmer of hope is etched across their young, handsome faces. They're drinking, all of them, and there is a bit of drunken chatter. Someone threatens to string up Kaiser Wilhelm II and burn Berlin to the ground. Another curses Ishmail Enver and suggests they strip him naked and drag him through the streets of Constantinople for what his men did to them at Gallipoli. They all quiet down out of respect when they notice Gayane and I. I grip her hand tight and gently smile at the soldiers. They drop their shoulders, lower their heads, not out of shame, but fatigue.

It looks as though the war will never end for Imtan Village. Many of the homes are in ill repair—collapsed roofs, crumbled walls— just as the Turks have left them. The smell of burnt wood reminds me of the day the Yeneze attacked Al-Kila, the fire so close it blistered my skin. They had massacred most of the inhabitants, abducted dozens of girls, and murdered Bashir, Esra, Emma, and Diana. The ghost of Narine's hand holds mine. Such memories make me feel sick with guilt. Who am I to survive when they were butchered like wild animals?

"What is it?" Father Eduard asks.

"Nothing," I say. "Just tired." Which is true. Four years is a long time without much sleep.

"Almost there," Mr. Batson says.

I pat Gayane's leg. "Ready?" I ask, hoping my weak voice doesn't startle her which, to my relief, it does not.

"I think so."

We discover a group of teenaged boys kicking a soccer ball around when we drive up to the orphanage. The boys immediately stop their game when our car pulls up. They run up to the windows and peek inside. One of the boys holds up the soccer ball. "Amerikatsi! Amerikatsi!" he yells. "Merci, Merci."

"Bloody hell," Mr. Batson says. "Do we look like Yanks?"

Gayane giggles. "What's a Yank?

"Another name for an American," he says, unhappily. He jumps out of the car, walks around to the other side, and opens the door for us. The boys follow him, tugging at his clothes, thanking him again for the soccer ball.

The front door of the orphanage opens. An old man appears with a scraggly gray beard the length of my forearm. He reprimands the boys in a gentle, yet disciplined countenance. The boys scatter like roguish mice, laughing and kicking the soccer ball as they make their escape. I listen and watch them until their little bodies disappear around a corner. A stone wall swallows their tittering echoes.

"Ah… Mr. Batson… come in," the old man says. "It is good to see you again. I'm sorry we could not get word to you about us moving. Mr. Davis thought it was too risky."

"I understand, Vahram." Mr. Batson says. "What's important now is that we found you." He smiles. "Allow me to introduce Father Eduard, Valia, and Gayane." Then he turns to us and says, "This is Vahram, the caretaker."

"Pleased to meet you," Vahram says. The old man's cheerful eyes conquer my uncertainty. He smiles, then gently pats Gayane on the arm. "A lovely doll you have there. Does she have a name?"

Gayane grins shyly. "Zora."

"I had a cat named Zora," Vahram says, "when I was a child. I remember her fondly."

"How many orphans do you have here?" Father Eduard asks.

"Fifty."

"Not very many," Mr. Batson says.

"All we could find," Vahram says.

Mr. Batson kicks at the dirt, thinking. "We should have done better."

Father Eduard places a hand on Mr. Batson's shoulder. "You've done all you can. For that, we are grateful."

Mr. Batson nods. "Has Mr. Davis arrived?

I tap Mr. Batson on the arm. "What about Sister Gertrude?"

"They'll both be here shortly," Vahram says. "A courier arrived this morning, said they'd arrive later today."

"Do you have news of Zaki?" I ask.

"Who?"

"A friend of hers," Mr. Batson says. "He is expected as well."

"Nothing regarding anyone by that name," Vahram says, thinking.

I shiver with concern. Father Eduard puts an arm around me, and rubs my shoulder.

Vahram holds up a hand. "Please, you must be exhausted from your trip. This way."

We follow him to the dining hall. A dozen or so tables align the middle of the room in perfect symmetry, every chair properly arranged. A young girl, no older than me when my parents were murdered, sweeps the floor and, another one, somewhat older, wipes a table. Their hair is neatly pulled back, and they wear clean dresses, and a new pair of shoes.

"We just finished breakfast," Vahram says. "Would you care for something?"

"A coffee," Mr. Batson says. "Thank you."

"I'll take a coffee, too… if it's not too much trouble," Father Eduard says.

"I'll bring plenty for everyone," Vahram says, "with chocolate candies."

Gayane smiles.

"Yes," I say, rubbing her back, "that sounds lovely."

"Fetch our guests some coffee," Vahram gently orders the girl sweeping the floor. She immediately props the broom against the wall and heads toward what I presume to be the kitchen.

Vahram smiles, then gestures to one of the tables. "Please, have a seat. Make yourselves at home."

The girl brings the coffee a few minutes later. She carefully places the small cups and saucers, and a small bowl of chocolate candy on the table, bows, then returns to her chores. She never speaks, not once, even to Gayane and I.

Mr. Vahram must have seen me watching the girl, because he says, "The Turks cut out her tongue. She was half dead when we found her."

No one says anything. I don't know what to say. I painfully narrow my eyes. Father Eduard clenches his fist, then reaches for a piece of chocolate, not eating it, but angrily twirling the foil between his thumb and index finger.

"What about the other one?" Mr. Batson asks, nodding at the girl wiping a table. "What's her story?"

"She's just shy," Vahram explains.

I scan the room and try to block the horrors of my first experience of war. Mother's eyes stare at me, her mouth open in fear and disbelief. Sound spills from her mouth, but her words are smothered by the screams and confusion of war. Father's body, curled up beside her, lies motionless, as if asleep. Arsen's eyes, open to the sky, seem to look into a darkness as any evil I had imagined then or since.

I take a bite of chocolate, its sweet taste like home; heavy on my tongue. My thoughts transition to me sitting by the fire reading a book. Mother is knitting a pair of socks on the sofa. Father is tinkering with a watch. His pipe is snug between his pursed lips. Arsen is playing with a wooden spin top, his eyes entranced with the zipping sound of the pointed end tapping against the wood floor.

"The orphanage is very clean," I say.

"I have good help," Vahram says.

"Mr. Davis is a good man," Father Eduard says. "He has done a great deal for the Armenians."

"Indeed," Vahram says. "If not for him," he gestures to the girls, "they would have been killed long ago."

"Why do the Americans care so much about us?" Father Eduard asks. "What's in it for them?"

"Don't rightly know," Vahram says.

An hour or so passes. "Where is Mr. Davis now?" I ask. "He's on his way, isn't he? We were expecting him to be here by now."

"Ah, yes, of course, that's what I forgot to tell you," Vahram begins, scratching his head. "He had a meeting at the consulate. Sister Gertrude is with him, that's the other thing I was to supposed to tell you." He smiles. "They'll be here but may be a little late. My apologies. My memory isn't so good anymore."

"It's quite alright," I say, although my voice is clearly impatient.

"I'm sure they'll be here in minute," Vahram says, rubbing his hands thoughtfully. He curls his pinkie finger, picks at his teeth, then says to me, "In the meantime, do you like to read?"

"Yes, why?"

"Sister Gertrude said you're intelligent. I thought maybe you'd like to visit our library."

My lips pucker inquisitively.

"She can sense things about people, a gift of hers," Vahram says.

"I want to see it," Gayane says.

"It'll help pass the time," Vahram suggests.

"Thank you," I say. "We would love to."

"Shall we all go?" Vahram asks.

Mr. Batson and Father Eduard nod.

Vahram points the way. "Follow me, then."

The library is quiet and empty. A half dozen bookcases line the walls of the small room. The books lie neatly on the shelves. "Why is no one in here?" I ask.

"We bring the children here every morning for an hour or so before they begin their chores," Vahram says.

"May I?" I ask.

"Of course," Vahram says, "that's why I brought you here."

I run my fingers along the spine of each book, scanning for a particular theme, finally finding what I want. "A book on Egypt," I say, pulling it from the shelf. "My little brother's favorite topic."

"Well," Vahram says, "I must attend to chores." He opens the door. The sound of children's feet ricochet off the hallway floor. Little voices whisper around corners. "Stay as long as you like. I'll let you know when Mr. Davis arrives."

"He's a very nice man," Father Eduard says when Vahram leaves.

"He's been with Mr. Davis since the beginning," Mr. Batson says.

I take a seat at one of the four small tables and open the book on Egypt. Its spine cracks to life, happy to be opened after such a long time. I run my fingers along the pages, sniff the ink, the smell of immortality on text. Wafts of dust tickle my nose.

"What are those?" Gayane asks.

"Pyramids," I say. "It's where the Egyptian Pharaohs are buried."

"What's a Pharaoh?"

"A king. They lived long ago." I flip to a world map. "See, this is Egypt. And here is where we are."

"Are we going to live in Egypt?"

"No," I say, fighting back tears. "My little brother, Arsen, he wanted to be an explorer when he grew up. He was fascinated with the Egyptians."

Father Eduard sits next to me and places a hand on my forearm. "Are you okay?"

"I feel guilty."

"You do not need to feel guilty."

My heart is wretched with pain. "Why was I allowed to live while so many others were not?"

"You fear for Zaki."

"Yes, of course."

"I'm certain God has a plan for you both."

"I want to see my house."

"Perhaps it will be possible," Mr. Batson says. "We'll see what Mr. Davis says." He squints his eyes. "But I thought Great Britain was your destination."

"Yes, I would like to go there…but…I prefer home if it's safe to return."

He nods. "I see. I'm sure Mr. Davis will do whatever he can to help."

My unsteady hand, full of nerves, flips to another page in the book.

"Who's that?" Gayane asks, pointing to a shirtless man with a square-shaped beard, and wearing a stripped headdress. He holds a staff in his right hand, a symbol of leadership and power.

"He's a Pharaoh," I say. "This one's name was Ramesses II."

"Who was he?"

"The one from the Bible. Moses convinced him to free Jewish slaves."

Gayane looks up at Father Eduard, disbelief sketched on her face.

"Let's see," Father Eduard says, leaning over my shoulder. "Yes, that's him alright."

"How do you know?"

Father Eduard places his finger on the text. "Say's it right here." He smiles. He must have noticed the memories of my brother have caused my eyes to grow puffy with grief, so he turns to Gayane and says, "How about something to eat?"

"Yes," Gayane says.

"We'll be back in a few minutes, then," Father Eduard says.

"Take your time," I say.

As I read, light thrashing the back window catches my attention. I return the book to its proper shelf, then press my face against the window, looking out into the valley, thinking of the day I left Adana. I see Father's face again, Mother's face, my brother's face, all of them down in the dirt, their bodies wilting like dry desert flowers.

Then my thoughts focus on Lori and Hakob, Mr. and Mrs. Badalian, Artush, Bashir and Esra, Narine, Emma, and Diana, even Yasmin. Everyone I've ever known now gone, either by death or separation, and it pains me to the point of tears. I wipe tears away and try to forget— the way I always try and forget—but find it impossible. Images like that never leave you.

A knock at the door jars me from my memories. I jump up, put my hand to my mouth, and yelp.

Father Eduard barges in. "Are you alright?"

"The knock startled me, that's all."

"Mr. Davis and Sister Gertrude are here." His eyes tremble with joyous relief. "They have a surprise for you. Come on."

I clasp my hands together. "Zaki?"

Father Eduard reaches out a hand. "Just come."

We gather in the dining hall. I find myself speechless, only to gradually accept their faces. A long and painful two years have passed since I last saw them. Uncertainty silences my instinctual reaction to run and hug them. Mr. Davis has aged, his face hardened by war, a few extra streaks of grey in his hair, but he still possesses a strong, stately disposition.

Sister Gertrude looks as young and beautiful as the day we met, her piercing green eyes still hopeful, confident, and resilient.

Davis speaks first. "Hello Valia. It is so wonderful to see you again…safe and sound."

"Hello," I say, my voice cracking.

Gayane nervously grips my hand.

"I prayed for you every day," Sister Gertrude says. "I can't believe it's been so long." Then she kneels beside Gayane. "Who might this lovely girl be?"

Gayane shyly tucks her head against my chest.

"This is Gayane," I say.

"That's a pretty doll you have there, Gayane. What's her name?"

Gayane unearths her face from my chest, smiles timidly. "Zora."

"I see," Sister Gertrude says. "Well, I'm happy that all three of you are safe."

"Shall we take a seat?" Vahram asks. "I'll have coffee prepared." He snaps his fingers. "Coffee," he says, and the girl with no tongue dashes off toward the kitchen.

"I apologize for my candidness," I say, "but Vahram said you had a surprise for me."

"On its way shortly," Mr. Davis says, "thanks to Sister Gertrude."

The coffee arrives and a small plate of cookies and chocolate. Sister Gertrude takes a sip of coffee, and smiles. "Delicious," she says. "Armenians make the best coffee." Then she turns to me. "I never stopped looking for you, Valia, I want you to know that."

"I know you didn't," I say. "I always knew…hoped you'd find me again."

"What of Saabir?" Mr. Davis asks. "How did you manage to escape from him?"

"Yes," Sister Gertrude says, "such a wicked man."

"He was killed by the Yeneze," I say.

"I see," Mr. Davis says. He blows on his coffee, takes a delicate sip, then sets the cup down. "Then an Arab…" he rubs his chin for a moment… "Kazim…rescued you."

"Mr. Davis," Sister Gertrude says, "that was part of the surprise."

"So you found him," I say, gripping the arms of the chair, trying to contain my composure. "He and Captain Wilson both...and Zaki, please tell me you found Zaki..."

"That's the biggest surprise of them all," Mr. Davis says. "We didn't find him, or shall I say, we are not the full reason why Zaki was released into our custody."

"I don't understand," I say, my heart pounding in panic.

"Every culture has its brutes and heroes," Mr. Davis says, "but sometimes it's difficult to tell them apart. Sometimes..."

"What Mr. Davis means to say is that we found someone in the Turkish government to help us, a very influential man—Berkant Hasim," Sister Gertrude says. "In fact, he's from your home town. Perhaps you know him?"

"Look who's spoiling the surprise now," Mr. Davis says, clutching his belly, laughing.

I sit there in shock, not believing my ears. I mean, Mr. Davis had mentioned him in his letter, but it had been just as surprising then as it is now.

"I know his daughter, if it's the same man," I say.

Sister Gertrude smiles, embraces me, then kisses my check. "This has been one of the happiest days of my life." She studies the floor for a moment, then looks up. "We lost so many," she continues. "A good outcome is rare in this part of the world."

Memories flood my mind like a dam breaking: the gold coin Yasmin gave me, the note from Belma, letters from Mr. Davis, our planned journey to Meskene cancelled, only to arrive here at Imtan. Is it possible an army of people had been searching for me all this time?

"Tell us more about Zaki," Mr. Davis says. "I haven't had the pleasure meeting him yet."

"Are you saying everyone is coming here?" I ask.

"What do you mean?" Mr. Davis asks.

"Sorry," I say, "perhaps my English isn't as good as I had hoped."

"The question is clear," Mr. Davis says, "but who are you referring to?"

"There was this woman in Meskene, Belma, and..."

"I see," Mr. Davis interrupts. "No, not everyone, just Mr. Hasim as far as I know."

"And Zaki," Sister Getrude says.

"Yes, of course, Zaki," Mr. Davis says. He pauses a moment. "But this Belma that you speak of, she has done a lot for us. She's already safely in Europe somewhere." He pops a piece of chocolate in his mouth. "Now tell me, Zaki is a special young man, yes?"

"That he is," Father Eduard says.

"He's been unjustly caught up in this horrible war," I say.

"Aren't we all," Mr. Batson says, after being silent for so long. "Caught up in this horrible war, that is."

Mr. Davis smiles, then scans the room as if counting chairs. "There are a lot more orphans than when we were here last, especially boys. We saw some of them playing soccer when we arrived. I haven't seen Armenian boys for months."

"It's a miracle they're here," Vahram says, brushing a tear away. "Mr. Hasim's people found them hiding in the woods."

"He has done great work here," Mr. Davis says, "and at the risk of his own life and the lives of his family."

"Where will they go?" I ask.

"Different places," Mr. Batson says.

"We've taught the girls needlepoint and rug weaving," Sister Gertrude says. They'll find jobs in Lebanon or Jordon."

"But many will return to their homes," Mr. Davis says. "They are in the process of rebuilding some of the villages and towns as we speak."

"But how?" Father Eduard asks, "with the war still raging."

"The war is all but over," Mr. Davis says. "Only a matter of time before the Germans raise the white flag. The Ottoman Empire will easily collapse after that."

"What about the boys?" I ask.

"They are to return home more than likely," Mr. Davis says. "Question is, what does a smart young lady such as yourself want to do?" He smiles. "You look like a teacher to me."

"You will do quite well for yourself with your English skills," Sister Gertrude says.

"I have Captain Wilson," I glance at Father Eduard, "and Father Eduard to thank for that, as well as many soldiers."

"Oh, yes, Captain Wilson," Mr. Davis says. "I never thought I'd say it, but the Australians produce some fine officers."

"Amen to that," Mr. Batson says.

"I want to be a professor," I say.

"A noble profession," Mr. Davis says. "Where?"

"I'm not sure. I'd rather return home, but..."

"It's because of Zaki," Father Eduard says."

Mr. Davis smiles. "He is your fiancé I take it?"

"Not exactly," I say, "but..."

"But you want to be with him."

"Yes, I suppose I do."

"I can see how that may be a problem," Mr. Davis says, snapping open a napkin, and wiping the corners of his mouth with it.

"They won't understand back home," I say.

"Even so," Father Eduard says, "is it even safe to go back there?"

"Adana, yes?" Mr. Davis asks, eyeing at Mr. Batson.

"Yes," I say.

Mr. Batson gives me a sympathetic look, his Scottish drawl more evident than it has been, as if reminding us of the land from where he originates. "Adana is slowly coming to order, but still far too dangerous."

"Yes, I suppose the cities would be more difficult to control," Mr. Davis acknowledges. "But if you wish to return to Adana, I suggest..." he rubs his chin... "it's going to take a lot more time before Adana or any other major city is back to normal, more so than the villages."

"How long?" I ask.

"There are so many displaced people it's hard to keep count," Vahram says.

"And there is no guarantee that Armenians will receive equal treatment or reimbursement of lost property once the war is over," Mr. Batson adds.

"You say that like you expect the war to end tomorrow," Father Eduard says.

"Should be any day now," Mr. Batson says. "I assure you."

"In the meantime," Vahram says, "I will have rooms made up. Is everyone staying?"

"Sister Gertrude and I need to get back to the city," Mr. Davis says, standing. He looks at Mr. Batson. "What about you? Need a ride?"

"Yes, sir, if it's not too much trouble."

"No trouble at all."

"But what about Zaki?" I ask. "Won't he be here soon?"

"Oh, yes," Mr. Davis says, "I will have to check on that…" he pauses, "but I assure you, he's on his way. And, as far as we know, Kazim is still with him."

"Thank you," I say. "Thank you for all you have done for us, for me."

"Thank Mr. Hasim when he arrives," Mr. Davis says. "He has saved hundreds, maybe thousands, of lives.""

"We shall," Father Eduard says.

"We'll be back in a week," Mr. Davis says, "maybe sooner."

Chapter 25

Cheers startle us awake. We arrived at Imtan Village two weeks ago. I scan the room. My eyes adjust to the surging light.

"What's happening?" Gayane asks.

"Let's go see," I say, stretching out my hand.

We follow a line of children down the hall and gather around a large window.

"What's going on?" I ask a child in front of me.

"The Americans are back," she says, looking out the window with great interest.

"I can't see," Gayane says.

"Come here," I say, lifting her up. Her legs wrap tightly around my waist. Her arms cling to my neck.

Father Eduard emerges from the hallway, rubbing his beard, puffy gray bags hanging below his eyes like rain clouds. "What's all the noise?"

"Mr. Batson is here," I say.

"He must have news," Father Eduard says. He peers out the window. Mr. Batson is surrounded by a group of soldiers. He's talking and waving his arms around like a child at Christmas time. "Let's go see," Father Eduard adds.

We follow Father Eduard outside. The cheers grow louder.

"The war is over," Mr. Batson says, waving a telegram in his hand.

The soldiers shoot their guns in the air, run around and screech like a troupe of wild animals.

"You're sure?" Father Eduard asks.

"Says so right here," Mr. Batson says, handing over the telegram.

"Thank God," Father Eduard says.

"Mr. Davis will be here soon," Mr. Batson says, looking at me, "bringing more good news."

"Zaki," I say. I squeeze Gayane tight against my chest. We press our noses together, bobble our heads like two playful kittens.

"I'm afraid not," Mr. Batson says, shaking his head uneasily.

My eyes burn with worry. "But Mr. Davis promised."

Father Eduard places his arm around me. "I'm sure no harm has come to him. Let's wait and see what Kazim says." He smiles. "Perhaps he escorted him home."

"Not exactly," Mr. Batson says. "He…"

"I don't understand," I say, interrupting. "Where is he?"

Mr. Batson clears his throat. "If you would allow me to explain, I'll tell you."

"Yes, sorry," I say.

"He's on a ship to Greece," Mr. Batson says. "That's all I know. Mr. Davis will fill you in with the rest."

"Why such a change of plan?" Father Eduard asks.

"I don't rightly know," Mr. Batson says.

"What about Kazim?" I ask.

"Still with him as far as I know."

"I want to see them."

Father Eduard places a hand on my shoulder and squeezes it gently. "Valia, they are doing the best they can. Let's continue to pray for their safety."

"Arrangements will be made," Mr. Batson says.

"How long?" I ask.

"I'm guessing in a few weeks," Mr. Batson says. "In the meantime, we wait for Mr. Davis. "He'll be here in a matter of hours."

Two government cars arrive a few hours later. Mr. Davis steps out of one of them. He's wearing a crisp new suit with a double-knotted tie. His black leather shoes welcome the sunlight, so much so I can barely look at them. Sister Gertrude follows, her habit just as fresh as the day I met her. No one emerges from the second car.

Snow clouds roll across the distant mountains, heading our way.

"So good to see you again, Valia," Mr. Davis says.

Sister Gertrude gives both me and Gayane a hug. "So good to see you are both well." She smiles. "Zora, too."

"Shall we head inside?" Mr. Davis asks. "The storm looks to be getting closer."

We head to the dining hall and gather around a small table. Vahram serves us coffee. The playful noise of children can be heard outside. Soldiers are singing. Someone is playing a harmonica. "It's good to see them so happy," Vahram says.

"Yes, we're grateful for all the hard work you have done to keep them safe," Sister Gertrude says.

My hands sweat with impatience. "Please, what about Zaki?"

"Have you found them new homes?" Vahram asks, clearly not hearing my question. Not only his memory, but his hearing seems to be fading as well.

"For most of them, yes," Mr. Davis says. He looks at me. "I assume Mr. Batson has informed you about Zaki," he adds.

"Just that he's headed to Greece," I say.

"What does that mean for us?" Father Eduard asks.

"And what exactly is the good news you have for us?" I ask. "I was promised Zaki would be here, now he's not. There is nothing I want more."

Mr. Davis eyes Mr. Batson with a curious look.

"I assumed you wanted to tell her yourself, sir," Mr. Batson says.

"Tell me what?" I ask, my fists a ball of nerves. "Has something happened to Zaki? What?" It begins to snow now. Flakes stick to the windows like little white bugs. The singing and the shouts of playful children die down. Many of them return to the warming arms of the orphanage. Happy feet clack down the hall.

Mr. Davis looks at me like a proud father. "He's fine. But there is one other thing I must tell you." Then he turns to Mr. Batson. "Go get them."

"Yes, sir," Mr. Batson says.

I'm unsuccessful in reading Mr. Davis' face. What on earth could it be? I look to Sister Gertrude for answers, but she only smiles, the corners of her mouth giving away nothing. Her eyes are as balanced as the planets, unblinking, her secret tucked away like a coveted treasure.

My jaw drops to the floor when they enter the room. They study me as though I'm an illusion standing here before them. Then Artush pulls me toward her, her embrace almost violent in its strength. "I can't believe it's you," she says.

"Neither can I," I say.

"We heard stories," Yasmin says. "We thought you were dead." She glances at her father, Berkant Hasim. "We thought you were all dead."

"Did others make it?" Mr. Hasim asks. "Your parents and brother? I tried so hard to…" He reaches to touch my shoulder, but I pull away, my body not fully caught up to my mind. His large, meaty hand reminds me of Saabir's hands—I will never forget them—forcing me to the ground, pinning my arms behind my back, holding me there until he completes his carnal and sinful deed.

A Turk saving hundreds of Armenians from being murdered still baffles me. The only Turk I trust is Zaki. He's different. He never believed in the war, he never raised his rifle against anyone or anything but the sky. In a sense, he is like me, forced into a frightful situation, enslaved to the wills and appetites of greedy and corrupted men.

"It's just me," I choke.

"I'm sorry to hear that, Valia," Mr. Hasim says. "I knew your father from my many times visiting his shop." He wipes an eye, catching a tear. "He was a good man." He sniffs, then continues. "He spoke about you often, about you and Arsen. He was a very proud father."

I nod, then return my attention to Artush. "How are *your* parents?"

"Father died last year. Mother is ill but doing okay." She looks down at the shy girl curled against me. "And who are you, child?"

"Gayane," she says, then buries her face behind me.

"And your husband," I say, "he's treating you well?"

"Oh, yes. We have two children, a boy and a girl. Selim is a good man. You'd like him."

"I'm sure I would."

"I'm glad you're safe," Yasmin says, so quickly it startles me. She tries to make her voice less forceful as she adds, "I mean, I assume the gold coin I gave you helped in some way."

"Yes, it did, thank you."

She steps closer. "And I'm sorry about how I treated you, but there really wasn't a choice. The police soldiers watched us all the time, we had to..." she paused "...put on a show for them. Our neighbor was executed for hiding Armenians in his home." She covers her mouth, trying to compose herself, then says, "They made us watch. They..."

"I understand," I say.

"Hello, I'm Father Eduard." He steps forward, shaking Mr. Hasim's hand. "On behalf of the Armenian Apostolic Church, I want to say how grateful I am of your service to our people and your sacrifice."

"Thank you," Mr. Hasim says. "I wish I could have done more."

"You've done more than you know," Father Eduard says.

"Indeed," Mr. Davis says. He looks at me. "This is the man responsible for Zaki's passage to Greece."

"It's her friend, Kazim, who should be thanked," Mr. Hasim says. "It was he who had to bring him to the port...under dangerous circumstances, I might add."

"Are they alright?" I ask.

"Quite alright," Mr. Hasim says. "Don't worry. It's just...some feel all prisoners should be executed. Rest assured, Kazim never left Zaki's side, and they made it safely to the ship." He glances at his watch. "They should have arrived in Greece by now."

"When can I see them?" I ask. I turn to Sister Gertrude. "You will go with us?"

"Of course," Sister Gertrude says.

"Soon, now that the war is over, I'd say in a week or two," Hasim says.

Father Eduard kisses the top of my head, his strong hand steady on my shoulder. "Of course, child."

"I have something for you," Yasmin says to me.

"What is it?"

"I found this hanging on the olive tree at your house, thought you'd like to have it." She smiles. "It's a little faded, but I know such symbols are important to you and..."

I don't know what comes over me, but I leap into her arms, holding her as tight as I can, my eyes wet with bittersweet tears. "I don't know what to say."

"Don't say anything," Yasmin says. "Let's take it outside."

"What's the significance?" Mr. Davis asks.

"It was my mother's," I say. "Father and I tied it to a tree in the back yard before we were deported." I sniff the handkerchief, searching for the scent of home, but it has faded. "The house is still there?" I ask.

"Yes," Mr. Hasim says. "I purchased it. We have been saving it for you."

I narrow my eyes. "So it's safe to go back there?"

"We hope so one day," Mr. Hasim says. "It's best that you are reunited with Zaki first, live in Europe a few years, and then, if you want to return, I'll do my best to help you."

"I don't know what to say, sir. Thank you."

"Come on," Yasmin says.

We step out into the cold. The snow continues to fall. We find a small apricot tree, its branches wickedly shaped with expressions of guilt and sadness. This tree has seen so much. If only it could talk.

But it does talk. It stands there defiantly, a piece of cloth still hanging from one of its many branches, a prayer spoken many years ago.

I reach into my pocket. "This handkerchief belongs to Zaki," I say. I grab hold of Yasmin's and Artush's hands and we quietly approach the tree. Everyone else stands back, watching in silence.

"You will tie them both to the tree?" Artush asks.

"Yes," I say, "I think Zaki would like that."

I tie Zaki's handkerchief first, then the one Mother had given me. I stand there several minutes, then return my hands to Artush's and Yasmin's hands. "I want to remember my family's life," I say, "not their death."

"And your friend, Zaki?" Yasmin asks.

"I pray I will see him again." I pause a moment, glance back at Mr. Davis and Mr. Hasim, and smile. "In fact, I *know* I will."

"I'm so happy we found you," Yasmin says. "I hope you'll find it in your heart to forgive me."

"You did what had to be done," I say. "I see that now." I squeeze her hand. "I hope you can forgive me…for calling you stupid."

"It's okay," Yasmin says, "I know you didn't mean it."

It stops snowing. The sun slowly battles its way out of the clouds. With the last drops of precipitation, a full rainbow stretches its colorful arms across the sky, and arches over the village. A wish fulfilled.

Epilogue

Yerevan, Armenia - April 10, 1965

The Armenian Genocide Memorial sits on top of a hill in Tsitsernakaberd Park. Zaki holds my hand tight as we walk across the large stone walkway leading to the sculpture dedicated eight years ago.

Zaki and I have been married for almost sixty years. We have three grown children and six grandchildren. We are all here together. Our children and grandchildren follow close behind and Zaki and I slowly move toward the two stone structures. One of the structures gives the impression of a blooming flower. It's twelve slabs are bent in mourning for the thousands of men, women, and children murdered by the Turkish government. The other one is arrow shaped. It symbolizes the violent struggle of the Armenian people and our universal bond to overcome oppression.

It happened sixty years ago to this day. I can still hear the eerie voice of the town crier: *You must be ready to leave in two weeks.* I see him clearly through the open window as if it happened yesterday. The harshness of his voice finds its way inside my head as it found its way inside the house so many years ago. I rub my arms as we inch our way closer to a set of stairs leading to the belly of the flower-shaped monument. As we step inside the monument, the intruding sounds of the town crier's voice push goosebumps across my neck. My feet are unsteady. A cold shiver runs up my back.

"Do you want to go back?" Zaki asks. He places his hand at the small of my back and cups my elbow with his other hand, steadying me.

"I'm fine," I say.

I watch the town crier turn off the main road. He fades from memory.

In the center of the memorial burns the eternal flame. It honors all of the victims. Around the flame are hundreds of flowers. I brought I white tulip. It represents forgiveness. I place it on top of the wall of flowers. A tear digs a deep trench down my cheek. Those who saved my life are no longer with us, having passed from this world to the next many years ago.

I am especially indebted to Kazim, a dear friend of mine until his death in 1955.

Our next leg of our journey is Adana. I have not been back there since the day we were deported. Artush and Yasmin will be waiting for us with their extended families. They are doing well and are at peace. Artush says the house is still there and the tree in the backyard continues to grow. Most of the Turkish people refuse to recognize the genocide. Many, like Yasmin, do. I am grateful to her and her family. Without them I would not be alive today. Shnorhakalut'yun (Thank you) my dear friend. Astvats orhni ke'z (May God bless you).

Acknowledgements

Writing is often seen as a private exercise. I disagree. This book would have never been written without the patient dedication of a legion of people. Unfortunately, I cannot name them all here, but I would like to mention a few of them. My deepest debt of gratitude must first go to my mother, who read to me many marvelous books as a child and encouraged me not to give up my dream to become a writer. Next, to my wife, Romekka, who left me undisturbed in my office while, along with a full time job, managed household chores, grocery shopping, and cooking fabulous meals. I love you more than words can express. To my mentors and colleagues in the Fairfield University MFA Program, especially Baron Wormser, Michael White, Bill Patrick, Deb Henry, and Tina DiMarco, whose first readings and critiques of this book helped me chisel away unnecessary words, and to build strong and lasting characters. Finally, to everyone at Winter Goose Publishing, especially Jessica Kristie, for recognizing the importance of this book. I am forever in your debt.

About the Author

Matthew Hamilton holds an MFA from Fairfield University and a MSLIS from St. John's University. He is a 6-time Pushcart Prize nominee. His chapbook, The Land of the Four Rivers, published by Cervena Barva Press, won the 2013 Best Poetry Book from Peace Corps Writers. He and his wife live in Richmond, VA.

Made in the USA
Middletown, DE
18 September 2020